THE FIRST MAGE

Book One

Exec Tails

ISBN: 979-8-88993-030-3

Written by Exec Tails
Edited by Jyorin

Published 2024 by MoonQuill
www.moonquill.com

Table of Contents

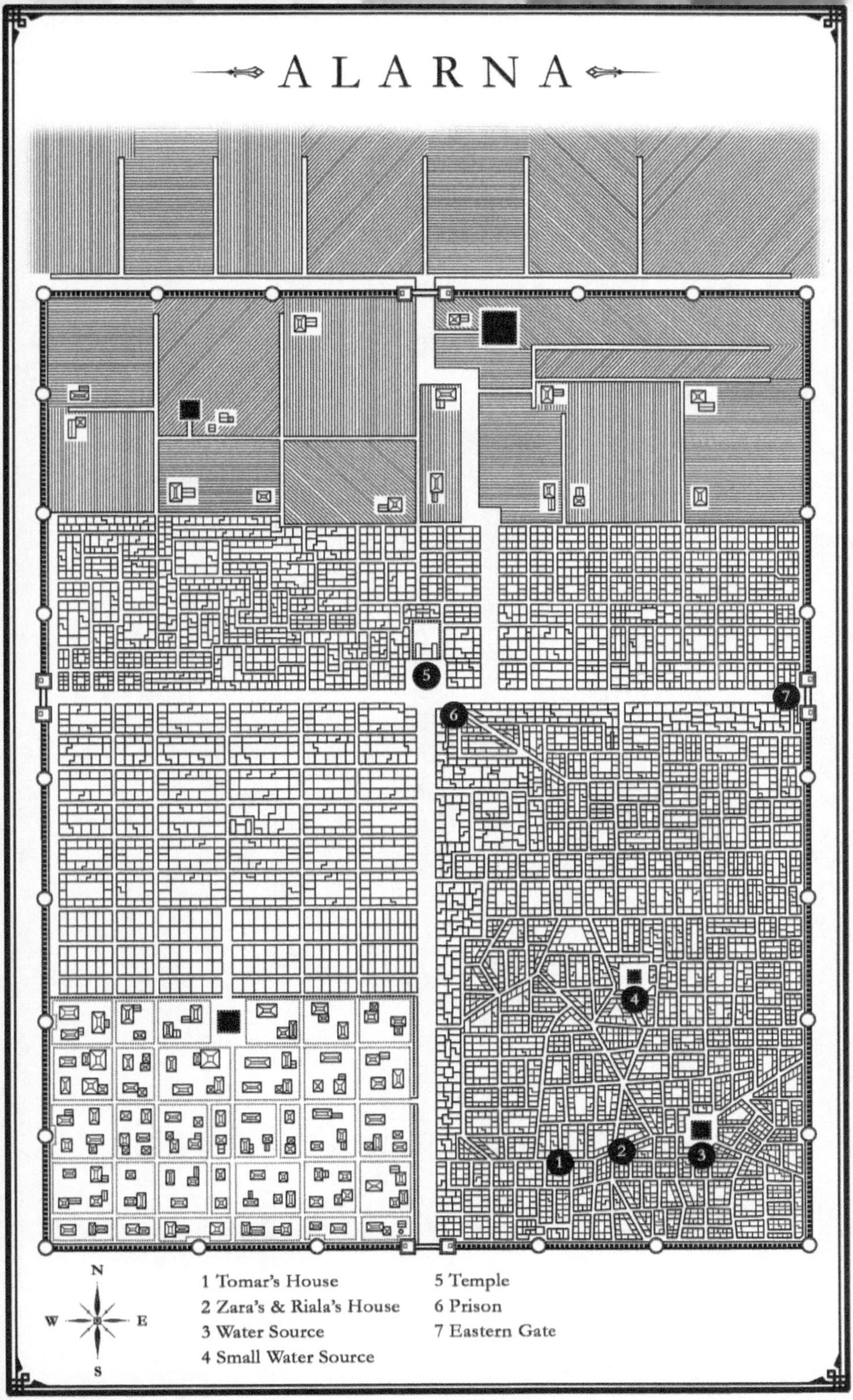
ALARNA
1 Tomar's House
2 Zara's & Riala's House
3 Water Source
4 Small Water Source
5 Temple
6 Prison
7 Eastern Gate
N
W
E
S

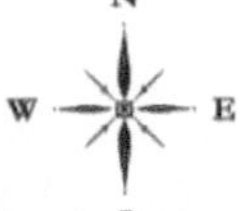

CHAPTER 1

DESTINY GONE AWRY

Fifteen years of age—that's when you receive your Calling. Your destiny, "Bestowed upon you by the grace of the gods," as the priests would say. There are a variety of Callings, but most common people have equally common destinies, like Fighters and Handiworkers. The former usually end up as soldiers or guards, and the latter as carpenters or seamstresses. Though, other exciting possibilities exist as well.

Everyone knows the stories of commoners becoming aristocrats or even monarchs. Most kids I know had dreamed of that at some point in their lives. However, most of them eventually realized that it was exceedingly rare to get a Calling different from those of your parents. As the son of two Handiworkers, I was certain this would be my destiny as well. And it was. Just not in a way I could've ever anticipated.

* * *

I was standing in front of the temple: a large, stark-white building at the center of town that was visible from the southern gates. It took me a while to get here from our house on the outskirts of Alarna, but as far as I was concerned, this was preferable to living near the center. Nobody I knew could ever afford more than a small flat there.

I had been lucky enough to live in a single-family home, with an entire room to myself. Before my father had been killed by a beast, he worked as a carpenter for the aristocracy, making good money. My mother vowed to never remarry, and with only her income to rely on, we barely scraped by, but I was hoping to change that. With my Calling being bestowed upon me, I would finally be able to contribute properly. With this thought, I entered the temple through large double doors that were almost twice my height.

I walked into the reception area, a room with archways on either side leading deeper into the temple. The floor, walls, ceiling, and even most furniture were the same white as the temple's exterior, which had always felt wrong to me. Everything blended together, and it didn't help that the plain robes most priests wore lacked color as well.

A middle-aged man stood behind the reception desk, expectantly waiting for me to come closer.

"Good morning, young man. Ritual?"

"Yes," I replied.

"To your right. We don't have many candidates this year, so the wait won't be long."

"Thank you."

Entering the other room, I saw about thirty people already waiting, some seated, some standing together in groups. The rituals were to start at noon, and I had been the last one to arrive.

I recognized a few of the faces; some neighbors I had played with when I was younger, and others I met in class years ago. There were also some considerably well-dressed men and women who didn't seem all too pleased sharing a room with commoners.

I greeted those that I knew and then waited, staring at the door to the ritual chamber on the far side of the room. A pair of guards were stationed nearby, scanning for would-be troublemakers.

Since the school was here, I had visited the temple in the past, but the only time anyone was permitted inside that room was during the Calling ritual. After a short while, a priest appeared from inside and started calling people in. The door closed behind them, and a minute later they came back out, with the brightest smiles I had ever seen.

I knew that the first couple of minutes after a ritual were supposed to be quite overwhelming, but I hadn't been prepared for the strange recountings I was overhearing.

"There was a blue light that came from the ceiling. I swear I saw a goddess within it! When she touched my forehead, all my fears washed away, and I felt like I had been a soldier forever!"

"Yeah? Well, when I got *my* Calling, the light was green, and a god *showed* me how great I would be."

When asked what the ritual was like, some would describe it as a rush of feelings, power, knowledge, and purpose flowing into you, even for the most mundane of Callings. My mother had described it slightly differently. She said she had felt like another person's memories had entered her mind. From one moment to the next, she knew things she had never heard of before and could do things she had never done. She also felt as if she had been alive longer than she really had. That last part, she said, was why you truly came of age at this point. You felt differently, acted differently. You became an adult.

"Tomar Remor."

A priest called my name. This was it.

I made my way through the small crowd and arrived at the door to the ritual chamber. The priest motioned me inside, and the lack of decorations immediately surprised me. Given the gravitas of this event, it was rather underwhelming.

Unmoving guards stood on either side of the doorframe, mirroring their colleagues outside. An altar stood prominently at the wall across from the door, laden with several stacks of loose papers and files, writing utensils, and a bowl that held white stones. A bookshelf to my left also caught my eye, but the focal point was a shallow, circular platform in the center of the space. The blue scripture sigils painted on its surface gave the environment a much-needed splash of color. As I walked closer to the platform and altar, I saw my name on a piece of paper from the Registration Agency, which recorded every citizen and their Callings.

"Please wait a moment," the priest instructed, closing the door behind me.

He walked around the platform, stopping in front of the altar as he turned to face me.

"Good morning, Tomar. I'm Father Firela, and I'll administer your ritual. There's no need to be nervous or scared. I promise you, the process is simple and painless," he said tonelessly. "Please step into the marked area and stand still."

It was apparent that he was in a hurry. At least a dozen candidates had come before me, and he still had more to go through. My eyes wandered from him to the platform. A white stone had already been placed on it, and after stepping up, I waited as instructed. I didn't see or feel anything at first, until, for a split second, there was a sharp pain in my head.

«Huh?»

My eyes widened. *Is this...*

«What's going on?» a voice said.

Oh no... No, no, no, no!

With a smidge of panic in my eyes, I looked at the priest, who had assumed the ritual was over, as he stepped closer.

"I didn't notice any signs indicating which Calling you've received, but the shard has disappeared, and the look on your face tells me the ritual is over. Please tell me the Calling the gods saw fit to bestow upon you."

I didn't know what to do. If I told him what had just happened, I would be in trouble. But there hadn't been a sign. There were no known Callings without one. *Wait... There was no sign at all?*

«Hello?»

First and foremost, I had to get out of this room. I looked at Father Firela and did my best to act confused.

"I don't feel any different. W-Was the ritual really a success?" I said, stumbling over my words.

The priest furrowed his brows, looking me up and down. This was not supposed to happen. As far as I knew, this had *never* happened. I didn't know what he would do about a "failed" ritual, but it couldn't be worse than the alternative.

"You don't feel anything at all? I find that hard to believe," he said. "Your Calling becomes a part of you, like finding true purpose for the first time in your life. It was a revelation to anyone I've ever administered this ritual to. As was it for myself."

It was to be expected that he wouldn't just believe me, but his reaction was still friendly enough—more curious than inquisitive. I might have a chance.

"I've read a bit about the ritual. The books said there would be a divine sign indicating my Calling, but I saw nothing. Is that normal, Father?" I asked. Switching from confusion to worry, I took a small step forward. "Did I not receive a Calling? Will I not be able to help my mother now?"

At this dejected display, his stern expression softened, and he placed a comforting hand on my shoulder.

"Please don't worry. There is not a person in the world without a Calling, and you will receive one as well. Say, are you certain you are of age?"

Am I certain of my age? Of course I—wait... A mistake, I thought. *Is that the conclusion he's come to? He thinks I'm too young!*

"My last birthday was in spring, Father. It was supposed to have been my fifteenth. Do you think my parents made a mistake?"

"That would appear to be the case, otherwise the ritual would not have failed. Unfortunately, this means you will not yet receive your Calling. I would advise you to speak with your parents. They need to visit the registration office to correct your birth data immediately, as it's illegal to provide incorrect information."

I lowered my head and nodded. "Thank you, Father."

«What the fuck...?»

As he walked over to the door, I turned around and stepped off the platform, ignoring the nagging pain in my head.

"Have a good day. I'll see you again once you are of age," he said, opening the door for me.

I walked past the guards and the other candidates and left the temple as fast as I could.

* * *

My mind was racing. I had received my Calling, except it was the one truly problematic Calling in the world. *What do I do now?*

The priest had believed my excuse, but this wouldn't hold up to scrutiny. He didn't know me, but others did. And a lot of them knew my true age, having known me since birth.

Providing incorrect information to the authorities wasn't just frowned upon, it was illegal. Harsh punishments were handed out if such deception was done intentionally, and they might see people who knew about such lies as accomplices. I would get reported as soon as anyone found out.

Venturing across the main square, I made my way home. However, I didn't make it far before I ducked into an alleyway and sank to the ground, leaning against a wall.

«Hey! Can anyone hear me?»

There's the headache again.

Clutching my head in pain, I buried my face in my knees. I was supposed to receive my Calling and start my life as an adult today. Instead, I received a death sentence.

After a few minutes of sitting there, I got to my feet, dusted myself off, and hastily left the alley. *I have to tell Mother.* She was waiting at home, and I hoped that she would have some idea about how to save me.

I trudged down the main street, eventually turning down a winding side street leading to our house in the southeastern part of town. With my leaden-footed pace, it took me twice as long as usual to arrive at the small wooden house my late father had built for our family. After taking a deep breath, I opened the front door and stepped inside.

"I'm back..." I timidly called out, wishing this was all a dream.

"Tomar!"

My mother came out of the kitchen with quick steps and a bright smile on her face. She had been even more curious than me about what Calling I would receive, but when she saw the look on my face, her own expression changed to one of worry.

"Tomar? What's wrong?" she asked, drying her hands on her apron.

I wanted to say something, but the words crashed into one another, creating a tightness in my throat.

"What happened? Please talk to me."

"I... I received the Mad Calling, Mom."

Silence.

My mother stood there, wide eyed and mouth agape. She lowered her head and stared at the floor as she attempted to collect her thoughts. When she looked up again, a glaze of confusion replaced the motherly gaze she once gave me.

"H-How are you still alive?"

Heart pounding in my chest, I took a moment to organize my thoughts. "There was no visible sign during the ritual. The priest thought there had been a mistake. That I had been too young, and that the ritual had failed because of that. I just... left."

My mother mulled over my words. The Mad Calling had been something I feared as a kid, but she had always assured me I wouldn't receive it. The fact that there hadn't been a Mad One in our town for hundreds of years had been reassurance enough. But unlikely didn't mean impossible, and in the back of my mind, I knew it. She knew it. And so did everyone else.

"No sign?" she finally said. "But if you received *that* Calling, you would've gone mad! *That* would've been the sign! Maybe you didn't actually—"

"Mom... I'm hearing a voice."

Just as she became quiet again, pain shot through my head once more.

«You can hear me? Please, talk to me! What is going on here?» the voice hysterically called out.

"I don't know why I'm not going crazy right now, but I'm sure."

The telltale signs of the Mad Calling were strong headaches and strange voices that nobody else could hear. These voices were said to drive one mad in a matter of seconds, making them lash out against anything and everything in sight in an attempt to make the voices stop. It was a futile effort, of course; none of the previous Mad Ones had ever recovered.

"What is the voice saying?" my mother asked.

"He seems confused. He's asking what's going on."

«Damn right I'm confused! Why are you ignoring me?!»

My mother came closer, cupped my face in her labor-calloused hands, and looked me in the eye, searching for something.

"Are you still my Tomar?"

Her question stunned me for a moment. My head was pounding and there was an unknown voice demanding answers, but I wasn't going crazy. In fact, I hadn't changed at all. Based on everything I knew about Callings, I should've changed somehow.

"I think I am. I feel like myself. I'm just—"

«Talk to me!»

"—hearing that voice. And every time it speaks, I feel a sharp pain in my head. Mom, what am I to do now?"

It appeared that the initial shock of me not being dead after receiving this Calling had started to fade, and the question of "What now?" had entered her mind. This was evident in my mother's constant pacing—something she would do when she needed to think something through.

"The temple will report your failed ritual to the authorities," she said. "Once that happens, they will come to us for confirmation. We can't fake your age. Our neighbors know how old you are. You played with their children when you were young."

I figured we would have time to come up with some plan, but it had never crossed my mind that the priest would report this.

"The authorities will come here?" I asked, crestfallen.

What if the books are wrong and it isn't an instant transition but a slow descent into madness over a few hours or days? What if the authorities did some kind of test to find out? Would they simply kill me on the spot once they knew?

Would they lock me away for experimentation? Various scenarios ran through my mind until my mother broke my train of thought with an expression of curiosity creeping onto her face.

"The voice," she started.

"Hmm?"

"Have you tried talking to it?"

I hadn't. The thought had never even occurred to me. *Would talking to it be safe?*

"You think I should talk to it? But what if that's what drives people insane?"

My mother had always had a curious streak, while my father had been laid back and cared little about anything outside of work. I, on the other hand, was the shy and cautious type. Mother would embrace anything new with an open mind and encourage me to do so as well. But this seemed like an unnecessary risk.

"You hear it, you understand it, and you acknowledge it. If it was going to drive you insane, would it not have happened by now?"

She usually turned out to be right when she started asking me questions like that. But the thought of something bad happening still terrified me.

"Can the voice hear me?" she asked.

«Yes! I can!»

"It... It says yes."

"Would you let me ask it something?"

Nothing had happened thus far. She was right; I was already acknowledging the voice. And just now, I had essentially interacted with it by forwarding what it had said to my mother. *It should be fine... right?*

"Okay," I said, hesitantly.

CHAPTER 2

MOM AND THE VOICE

I didn't know how my mother could think about talking with the voice while I was scared for my life, but I trusted her. *She wouldn't do this for no reason, I think.*

"Hello, Voice."

«Hello!»

"It says, 'Hello.'"

"Do you have a name?"

"'My name is Miles! What's going on here?'" I relayed.

"It has a name," my mother said, amazed. "Do you know what you are?"

"'I'm—,'" the voice began, but then stopped for a moment before continuing. "'What do you mean *what* I am?'"

"You're a Calling. The Mad Calling."

"'I don't know what that means.'"

"A Calling is a gift, granted by the gods to people after they come of age. At least that's how it's supposed to work. You're my son's Calling."

"'A gift? I'm a human being! Why would I be inside some kid?'" he bellowed.

My mother and I stared at each other, wide-eyed. This voice was either delusional or something we couldn't begin to comprehend. I didn't know what to think, but I started to believe that communicating with it wouldn't cause me any harm. My mother looked at me encouragingly.

"Voice," I began, "earlier, I attended my Calling ritual. It's supposed to reveal one's purpose in the world and grant the necessary tools to fulfill that purpose. But I received the Mad Calling—you. Based on the stories I've read, this was supposed to drive me insane. They say I should've lashed out at others, that I would be dangerous, and that Mad Ones would be killed on sight."

Miles grew silent for a moment, possibly digesting the new information. If it was truly a human being, how could he end up in someone's head? And why was I still sane?

"'Is it possible to remove this *Calling*? Can I get out of here?'" he finally asked.

My mother and I weren't sure how to respond. You don't remove Callings. They were irreversible blessings by the gods. The idea seemed absurd, but the question would make sense from the viewpoint of a sapient being stuck inside someone else.

"Miles, right?" my mother said. "A Calling isn't something that can be removed. It's like your ability to think or laugh. It's just... there."

"'You can't be serious. What am I supposed to do? Ride shotgun in this boy for the rest of my life? For the rest of *his* life? Wait. You said this isn't normal! A Calling isn't supposed to be a human. Maybe you can get me out of here! You said this Calling is a problem, just get me out and you're good!'"

Miles wasn't wrong. If there was a way to remove a Calling, wouldn't that solve everything? Granted, the ritual wasn't supposed to fail, but if I could remove my Calling and get a new one at the temple, a normal one, I would be in the clear.

"But I don't even know where to start," I said. "I've never read anything about a Calling removal ritual. We would have to go back to the temple and talk to the priests, but that's way too risky."

«Because you think they will just kill you? Come on, you're obviously fine! Why would they hurt you? Just explain the situation!»

"And what if that doesn't work out? Then I'm dead!" I said, stomping my foot in frustration.

«And if you do nothing, I'll be stuck in here! This can't be my life!»

"I'm not thrilled about it either, but what am I supposed to do?"

"Tomar," my mother interjected, "what is he saying?"

"He wants me to kill myself!"

«I just want to get out of here! If talking to the priest is the only way, that's what we'll do!»

"I won't just walk into the temple and tell them I have the Mad Calling!"

"Boys, please calm down," my mother said. "Miles, there might be answers at the temple, but it is too risky. We don't know what they'll do when they hear about this. As fascinating as I find you and this situation, the Mad Calling is typically a death sentence. Of that, I can assure you. Best-case scenario, Tomar would be imprisoned. But in the worst case, they'll execute him immediately. And that most certainly wouldn't be in your best interest either."

"'I might die. Huh.'"

My mother scrunched her face and nodded.

"'Well, fuck me... What's the plan then?'"

"I'm sorry, but getting you out will have to wait. We have a more urgent problem. The excuse that Tomar isn't of age won't hold up with the authorities. We'll need a better one before they arrive. Unfortunately, talking to you didn't bring us any new insights, so I'm not sure what our options are."

Of course! She wanted to gather more information, I thought, understanding why talking to Miles had been a priority. *I'm so glad she's the one still with me. Sorry, Dad.*

My mother motioned me into the kitchen, and we sat down at the dinner table. I didn't know how much time we had, but we would have to do something soon. To the best of my knowledge, there had never been anyone without a Calling. Nobody would skip their ritual. That would make absolutely no sense. You need it to get a job, which every citizen of age is required to have, as declared by the authorities. But I actually didn't know what would happen if you tried to a*void* receiving your Calling. *You can't not have one, right?*

Regardless, I had gone to the temple and attended the ritual. There was no changing that. But how would I explain myself to the officials from the Registration Agency?

«Hey.»

I was startled by the sudden pain interrupting my thoughts. *This will take some getting used to.*

«Can't you just skip town?»

"I'm trying to *not* die here, Miles!"

I noticed my mother's gaze at my sudden outburst.

"He's saying I should leave town."

My mother's curiosity flared up once again, apparent by a sparkle in her eyes. "Perhaps he doesn't know about the beasts, Tomar."

* * *

Miles seemed to know nothing about the world. He asked question after question but was reluctant to answer any himself. He didn't know about the beasts that roamed the Wildlands, and that nobody would be crazy enough to leave town without guards—especially at night. He didn't know that the nearest town was three days away. He definitely didn't know where we were, or *when* we were. Even the fact that noon was at eight o'clock appeared to confuse him somehow. As we explained to him the most common knowledge, he and my mother seemed to be getting along well, while I was mostly sitting there, parroting everything he was saying in my head.

"'So he can't go to the temple, because they would kill him. He can't leave town, because monsters would kill him. And he can't stay here, because they will come for him, and *then* kill him.

"'But why is this Calling such a problem? I understand they don't want people going berserk, but Tomar is fine, right? It should be obvious that they don't need to kill him. At least not before they're sure he's a threat.'"

"People don't like talking about the Mad Calling," Mother responded, shifting in her seat. "It's said that those who receive it are not only confused, they are also much stronger than your average guard. If they're not put down with force, or if they escape—gods forbid—they'll kill everyone in sight. One story speaks of a Mad One destroying an entire town.

"Normal people would believe you're joking if you told them you had this Calling, but the authorities would be scared for themselves and the citizens. And I worry they would be even more fearful of someone who wasn't acting crazy. If one deranged person can destroy a town, what could a sane person do with the same power?"

"'Okay. How about faking a different Calling? The priest didn't see a sign or whatever, so let's say he hadn't paid attention.'"

"Tomar would have to prove he received the fake Calling in that case. There is no Calling you can fake easily. The gods grant you more knowledge about your destined profession than you could ever hope to learn until you come of age. That's why most people don't learn much until they have their ritual, aside from reading, writing, and everyday skills. You receive all the knowledge you need during the ritual."

"'Hmm.'"

Miles began to think about what my mother had said. I wished he didn't have to give me a headache for a simple "Hmm," but he didn't seem to care much when I told him so.

"'Do you know what a computer is?'" he asked.

"No, I don't," my mother said.

This was the first time he had said a word I didn't know. I hadn't received a real Calling, so I was limited to everything I had seen, heard, and read during my life, but my mother was very knowledgeable. It was rare for her not to know something. I had always assumed that she had received a powerful Calling, even if she was *just* a Handiworker.

"'Right. Didn't think so.'"

"What is it? Can it help me?" I asked.

"'It could if you knew what it was, but based on what I've seen of this place through your eyes, that probably won't work.'"

I didn't think he could see things through me as well. I wonder what it feels like to not have a body.

He was clearly trying to come up with a solution, while I was mostly busy speaking for him. The more Miles learned, the more pointed his questions became. I felt like he was thinking similarly to my mother, and I was hoping the two of them would come up with an idea.

"'Do you have a merchant Calling or something? One for bankers or architects? Anything heavy in math?'"

"There are some options," my mother mused. "Can you handle it?"

"'It depends. I would have to know what the test would look like, what the exact requirements are.'"

Test? Was I missing something here? During my parroting, I must've stopped paying attention to what they were saying, because I wasn't sure where exactly these two were going with this.

Mother stood up and walked over to the cabinet where she stored her writing utensils. She returned with a quill, an inkwell, and a piece of paper. After placing them on the table, she began jotting down numbers. After a few lines, she pushed the paper across the table for me to look at.

I stared blankly at the sheet. My mother knew I didn't know this kind of math, and Miles only knew what we taught him. Even if he turned out to be intelligent, he wouldn't suddenly—

"'I think we can work with this.'"

"You understand that?" I asked, bewildered.

My mother beamed at me. Or maybe at Miles?

"'Somewhat. I recognize the formulas, but I don't know these numbers. Could you write down all the base numbers?'"

"What's a *base* number?" I asked.

My question received no answer. Instead, my mother contemplated what she had been asked before realizing what Miles was referring to. She pushed the ink and the quill across the table.

"Tomar, write down the numbers zero to seven."

I could do that much, and I did as instructed. After I was done, I looked back at my mother, only to be admonished by Miles.

«Keep looking at the paper!»

Grumbling, I lowered my head and started pondering. If he could understand this, would we be able to fake a Calling that incorporated a lot of math? Even then, would that be enough? After a few moments, and for the first time, I heard Miles laughing in my head. Weirdly enough, the pain was much more bearable than before.

"'Hahaha, octal? This is amazing. Tomar, write down what I say.'"

Once more, I did as instructed. I added a few lines under what my mother and I had written before. He was dictating calculations to me that I had never seen before. When I pushed the paper over to my mother at Miles' request, she looked over it and smiled.

"I don't recognize some of these formulas. You know more than me!" she cheered.

"'Alright. What can we do with this?'"

"I have an idea," she said. "One of our neighbors, Gean, is a statistician for the authorities. Apparently, he does nothing but solve equations at work. His wife always complains that it's all he ever talks about. Do you think you can handle this?"

"'It would be good if I had a few hours to get used to this number system, and I need some more information. After that, yes.'"

"Gean should be home in about an hour," my mother said. "I will talk to him and try to pry him for information. I will reveal that something went wrong with Tomar's ritual, but that he came home with an unusual amount of knowledge about math. If he's willing to show me some of his work, I believe we'll know what they will test you for if we claim Tomar to be a statistician."

«Statisticians. In this place. Seriously?» Miles mumbled.

"What's a statistician?"

CHAPTER 3
Non-Decimal

Gean's family lived a few houses up the road and Mother had left to meet him as soon as we solidified our plan. In the meantime, I was still sitting at the table, staring at several pieces of paper that were now covered with numbers, tables, and calculations. Miles had said he needed to get used to this number system, but I wasn't entirely sure what that meant. As I started to relax ever so slightly, I finally decided to ask him. "Miles, what is octal?"

«Non-decimal,» he responded curtly, before returning to whatever he was doing in my head. Occasionally he would mumble something, or repeat number sequences like a mantra.

«11467... 11470... 61... 4012...»

"Will this really work?" I asked.

Miles let out an exasperated sigh. «Listen, I'm not used to calculating in octal. I can do it if you let me practice—and your mother is optimistic that it will be enough—but I need some time.»

I stayed quiet and let him continue until I heard the front door swing open a few minutes later, and my mother came walking into the kitchen with Gean in tow.

"Hello, Tomar! It's good to see you," he said in a jolly voice.

With how Gean was acting, I had figured he wanted to see me for himself. Maybe hoping to have found a kindred spirit.

«Too early. This wasn't the plan,» Miles hissed.

My mother looked at me with an apologetic face, accompanied by a hint of worry in her eyes. Miles had mentioned needing several hours for preparation, but only eighty minutes had passed.

Gean sat down on the chair to my left and looked at me. "Another statistician. You wouldn't believe how long I've waited for this day, Tomar. Do you know I've been the only one in this town for the past twenty years?"

"No, sir," I said. Gean and his wife didn't have any kids, so I hadn't interacted with him outside of greeting him in passing.

"Alright, let's get down to business!" His expression shifted, and he had a sharp glint in his eyes. "What's 42,776 divided by 32?"

«Something isn't right,» Miles said, sounding alarmed.

My eyes shifted from Gean to the papers on the table. *Am I supposed to—*

«No, look him straight in the eyes. Don't waver, act normal.»

I didn't understand what was going on. Miles was worried about something, and I couldn't see my mother behind me, but she was squeezing my shoulders with her hands.

«Say 1261.»

Gean's brow twitched at my response, barely noticeable. "Accuracy is important. Another try?"

«Oh, come on! Stupid little... Okay, 1261.11. No, wait! 1261.12, go.»

I repeated the last number and Gean gave me a nod. "Acceptable." He then took a sheet from the pile and added several formulas similar to the ones that were already there. When he finished, he put the paper down in front of me and waited.

The answers appeared to come relatively easily to Miles, and I wrote them down one after the other. Gean took the sheet back and looked it over. Satisfied, he grabbed the quill once more and wrote a formula that included characters I had never seen before.

"Please solve this for me and you pass."

«Is this the test?» Miles asked in surprise.

I stared at the formula and waited for him to tell me what to do. It took me a moment to realize that these characters weren't entirely unfamiliar. *Huh? The scripture? What does this have to do with math?*

Involuntarily furrowing my brows, I sat in silence for several seconds before Miles spoke up again.

«Tell him you don't know how to solve it.»

My eyes widened. *What? Gean said I have to solve this to pass.* Unable to ask Miles if he was serious, I kept staring at the paper without moving a muscle.

«Tell him, Tomar.»

"I… I don't know how to solve this," I said, feeling my heart drop. I didn't dare look at Gean until my mother let go of my shoulders and I felt another hand slap me on the back. I glanced up at Gean's face to see a toothy grin.

"Very good, boy," Gean proclaimed. He stood up and looked down at me. "You will make a fine statistician. I'm looking forward to working with you. Phiona, make sure Tomar comes to the office next week." He gave my mother a paper slip, said his goodbyes, and left our home as quickly as he had entered it.

I got up and turned to my mother, who enveloped me in a hug. "Mom, Miles. What just happened?"

* * *

Mother and I were standing in front of an office building close to the temple. After Gean had left the house, my mother had hurried me to the Registration Agency to update my citizen information. My new Calling had been added, and I was now officially a Researcher.

My mom hadn't known this, but apparently Gean was not only a statistician, but also the town's Determiner: the person responsible for resolving any issues with the records, particularly issues related to Callings, rare as these might be.

When she told him about the supposed failed ritual and her suspicion that I had become a statistician, she had effectively expedited the test that would've otherwise come in a day or two.

As we made our way across the main square, my mother spoke up with sadness in her voice. "I'm sorry, Tomar," she said, followed by a hushed, "You too, Miles."

She must've been just as scared as I had been, and she jumped at the first chance that presented itself to find a solution. She had done her best to help me. I could hardly blame her for that.

"It's fine, Mom. I'm just glad it worked out."

The slip Gean had given my mother was a written confirmation of our claims, and with this done, I would be fine for the moment. Citizens were expected to start work within two weeks of receiving their Calling, and Gean had invited me to work with him, but I could finally breathe a sigh of relief.

It was getting late by this point, and my mother stopped to look toward the market west of the main square.

"I will buy a few things for dinner. You go on ahead and relax," she said. "We have a few days to decide our next steps."

I nodded and watched her walk off before making my way to the main street, once again heading back home. There were many people bustling around at this time of day. Closing up shops, going home from work, or heading out for night shifts.

"Hey, Miles," I said under my breath, careful not to be heard by anyone. "Where did you learn all that?"

«Let's just say I have a Researcher Calling myself.»

"My Calling has a Calling?"

«Heh, something like that.»

Sauntering down the street, I finally had the peace of mind to ask Miles about the test. I had learned some basic math, and sometimes I saw Mother calculate things, but that last formula looked weird. I was admittedly curious about how these symbols related to mathematics.

"What was that last formula Gean gave me? Why were there scripture sigils in it?"

«What? You know what that was?»

"Well, kind of. Did you truly not know how to solve it?"

Miles was silent for a moment. It appeared that I hadn't been supposed to solve it, but I assumed Miles would've been able to.

«That's not it. I could've solved it, but—» He paused before continuing. «Shit, we got lucky there. How do you know these "sigils?"»

"They're on the water sources. Oh, and the ritual platform. Those are the only places I've ever seen them."

«Water source? Like a well?»

"No, a water source."

We became quiet for a moment, both of us confused about the other one not understanding what we were trying to say.

«Can you show me?»

"Can't I go home for now? I'm really tired. I have to get water in the morning, anyway. I'll show you then, okay?"

«Hmm. Alright.»

Miles seemed displeased, but I was truly exhausted. I had gotten up at the break of dawn, did most of my chores, and hurried to receive my Calling, just to end up fearing for my life. Mixed with being tense and hungry, I couldn't find it in me to walk further than necessary.

Still, I was looking forward to tomorrow morning. Miles clearly knew something about the sigils. Everyone knew of them, but I had never assumed that they meant anything. That's also what my mother had said. They looked like glorified scribblings to me. *Do they actually have a meaning?*

* * *

A priest in white robes was standing in front of a desk inside an office on the highest floor of the temple. Across from him sat a man in his early fifties, clad in white robes embroidered with gold thread. His cold eyes and soured expression were unwavering as he updated files of citizens after the day's Calling rituals. After a moment, the man paused and put down his quill.

"There was no sign at all?"

"No, sir. I am certain," the priest said, gripping the hem of his robes.

"Hmm..." The man furrowed his brows as he looked down at one document in particular.

> **Name:** *Tomar Remor*
> **Parents:** *Leander and Phiona Remor*
> **Birth:** *Spring 3006*
> **Calling:** *Researcher (Determined)*

"Was I m-mistaken, sir?" the priest carefully asked.

"It appears so." The man picked up his quill and scribbled more notes about the failed ritual to the record. "But the matter has been resolved. There won't be any repercussions."

The priest let out a breath and his grip loosened on his clothes. "Thank you, sir." He bowed and scurried out of the office. As he closed the door behind him, he was able to make out a barely audible "Interesting..." coming from inside the office.

CHAPTER 4
Otherworldly Letters

Morning arrived, bringing with it the worst migraine of my entire life. Groaning, I rolled over and sat up on the edge of my bed as I massaged my temples.

"Ugh…"

«Morning,» Miles greeted, displeasure in his voice.

"Ow… Could you please not talk right now? My head hurts."

«Hmph.»

Leaving my room, I made my way into the kitchen. Leftovers from last night's dinner were standing on the table, as well as a bowl of fresh water. I took a few sips, washed my face, and sat down to eat the soup my mother had made. *I hope she wasn't disappointed that I fell asleep right away.*

The night prior, I had had a weird dream that I was wandering around the house, looking into every room and out every window, searching for something. I rarely dreamed, and if I did, it wasn't this vivid. In the end, I wound up back in my room and laid down on my bed, where I eventually woke up. I kind of wished I could go back to sleep. I didn't have a headache in my dream.

I shoved the last spoonful of food into my mouth and washed the dishes. With my other chores waiting for me, I walked out the back door, grabbing a tub filled with clothes on the way. The headache was letting up slightly by this point, and I started talking to Miles.

"I'll go to the water source now. You want to see it, right?"

«May I talk now, o' master?» he said sarcastically.

"Sorry. It was really painful after waking up."

«Yeah, yeah.»

I set out down the path behind our house, deeper into the southeastern part of town. Weaving through a myriad of narrow roads and beaten tracks, I soon saw the water source square in the distance. To my dismay, a long line had formed, though this wasn't surprising, given how late I already was. Getting in line as well, I set down the clothes, and watched people wash their laundry.

«For the record, last night sucked,» Miles said. «Apparently I don't need to sleep, so I was bored out of my mind.»

"Were you talking to yourself all night? That might explain the headache," I jokingly said in a hushed voice.

«Smartass.»

Twenty minutes later, I made my way to the front of the line. Before me was a smooth, black obsidian cube, about one and a half meters on all sides. In the middle of the front face was a hole, and above it were light-blue scripture sigils painted onto it.

"Here we go," I said, stepping closer to the water source Miles had wanted to see. Positioning the tub of clothes on the ground beneath the hole, I grabbed the blue stone that was nestled between the clothes and placed it on top of the cube. In a matter of seconds, the stone dissolved and water started streaming out of the opening and into the container.

"See, Miles, this is the water source," I whispered.

His response was delayed, surprising me when he suddenly cried out, «What is this?!»

For how smart he acted, this seemed like a rather dumb question. Confused, I explained, "Uh... It's where you get water."

He made a sound as if that much was obvious and a pain shot through my skull. In hindsight, I'm sure that was Miles' way of smacking me. «I mean the Omega script! Are those the sigils you were talking about? Look again!»

Taking my eyes off the laundry, I glanced back up at the sigils. It didn't take long for someone to clear their throat behind me in annoyance. I realized I had been crouching in front of the water source for several seconds, staring at it like an idiot, while others were waiting their turn.

As I picked up the tub and hurried out of the way, Miles spoke up again. «Stay close! Somewhere you can still see the script!»

I carried the tub a few meters before plonking it down, getting ready to wash the laundry inside. Occasionally, I'd eye the water source so Miles could observe the others gathering water.

«What's with the stones? Are they payment?» he asked, fascinated.

"Um, I guess? You need it for water to come out."

«So it's a well with a paywall?»

"It's not a well. The water isn't coming out of the ground."

He wasn't easily convinced that the water didn't come from below the cube. It wasn't until I told him about another water source that was the size of a bucket and could be picked up and looked at from all sides that he came around. Though, the authorities put it on a chain to prevent people from stealing it.

I scrubbed a few shirts in silence for a moment but grew curious about what Miles was thinking. Hesitant to ruin the sweet, painless silence, I probed Miles for information. "What are the scripture sigils? You know them, right?"

A few people gave me confused looks in passing.

«Where did you get that name from? 'Scripture sigils.'»

Whispering to Miles, I explained that the priests always preached a little during class. They would go on and on about the grace of the gods, and how the water sources were gifts. After all, they allowed us to go about our day in peace, without having to travel out of town in search of wild water.

Everyone who had ever attended any class had heard the term "scripture sigils" from the priests. They described them as the visual representation of the voice of the gods.

«Can anyone read the sigils?»

"I don't think so," I said. "The priests say it's 'not for mortals to understand.' I always thought they were just decorative."

«'Decorative,' huh?» Miles laughed, and once again, the pain subsided. *Note: Happy Miles equals less pain. Will I have to tell him jokes all day?*

* * *

«I know it as Omega,» Miles explained on our way home. «It's a kind of language.»

He was excited. I didn't realize it at first, but as I was listening to him, his voice in my head became less and less painful. He still wouldn't answer many of my questions directly, but by now I had guessed that it was because he assumed I wouldn't know what he was talking about. Or maybe he didn't have all the answers either.

«Programming languages affect things,» Miles went on. «You can make things happen by writing sigils; they're basically just characters. Anyway, you said the water source is not a well. And then there are those stones and the script...»

Having arrived home, I hung the clothes up to dry in the backyard, while listening to Miles ramble on. Though, I admittedly started tuning out here and there.

«Have you ever tested it?» he suddenly asked.

"Tested what?"

«Using Omega! The sigils. Whatever.»

"Like creating a new water source?"

«Yes!»

"That doesn't work. Nothing happens if you paint the sigils on random things. The priests also don't like when kids talk about trying it."

«Maybe there's more to it.» Miles got quiet before piping up again. «Let's do some tests.»

First you tortured me for hours with math, and now you want me to paint sigils?

I let out a sigh. "You think you can create water sources?"

«If I'm right, that will be the beginning of what we can achieve,» he said with confidence.

* * *

An hour later, sigils were scrawled on paper, wood, stones, and bricks. I had painted one on a metal pot and even on my arm. I had tried ink, chalk, and paint I had borrowed from a neighbor.

Initially, it had taken minutes to get every sigil right, as Miles kept hounding me to correct my mistakes, but now I was able to draw everything in seconds. Right now, I was behind the house, drawing the sigils into the dirt with a stick. When I put one of our blue stones on the finished product, nothing happened, and I hurriedly removed the drawing so no passersby would see it.

"Told you," I said, a little disappointed.

«Hmm... I have to think about this.»

Miles had explained his theory to me. He believed the sigils were responsible for turning blue stones into water. If the water source was not a well drawing the water from the earth, it had to come from somewhere else, and to his understanding, the sigils converted the stones into water somehow. Though I found it hard to believe that a stone half the size of a thumb could create several liters of water. The gods sending the water sounded more plausible.

His unwavering certainty persuaded me to go along with his trials, but I was glad he wanted to think for a bit, because I was getting tired of this.

After cleaning up all the failed experiments and spending some time tidying up the house, I started preparing dinner. Mother would come home from work soon. I used the remaining ingredients from yesterday's market visit and made a vegetable soup. It wasn't long after I was done when I heard the front door open.

"Tomar! How are you feeling?" she immediately said after seeing me.

"I'm okay, Mom. I had a headache this morning, but it's all better now."

"And how is Miles?"

He didn't say anything. *Lost in thought?*

"He's okay as well," I said.

We sat down at the table and ate. She listened with curiosity as I told her about the experiments. She had tried drawing sigils herself when she was younger, as did most kids I knew in the past. This was usually done around the time they'd first attended classes at the temple at seven or eight years old. Many believed that the sigils had a meaning, but my mother concluded for herself that they didn't, and I trusted her wholeheartedly. That's why I had never tried it myself, and after today, I was even more certain that they were useless.

"But if it *were* possible, we could have our own water source in the backyard," she said, half-jokingly.

«Or the kitchen. And the toilet,» Miles said absentmindedly.

"The toilet?" I said, unsure of what he meant. But he went silent again right after.

My mother looked at me questioningly.

"Oh, nothing. Miles is saying random things," I said.

During dinner, we talked about what we would do about my job situation. Gean had declared me to be fit to be a statistician, but I wasn't entirely sure what that would entail. And while Miles said it would be fine, and my mother was mostly just glad that I was alive, I didn't want to get my hopes up too much yet. I couldn't fathom that solving a few equations was enough to qualify for a job. *If that trick question was a special test, will it be safe to work with Gean?*

Mother suggested that we explore what other options were available with the Researcher Calling. Since it was too far removed from the Handiworker Calling that we assumed I would get, neither my mother nor I knew too much about it. This could wait until tomorrow, however.

I enjoyed the silence in my head while talking to my mother about this and that. We played cards for a while, and eventually I went to my room to read. As I dozed off, I wondered if I would have another weird dream.

CHAPTER 5

A Job

Another morning, another headache.

"Seriously, Miles. What are you doing up there at night?" I asked.

He didn't respond.

Bucket in hand, I was on my way to the water source before the sun had cleared the horizon. I would usually gather water for the day even before my mother got up.

"About getting you out of my head; we didn't talk about it yesterday, but—"

«Working on it,» Miles cut in.

Ever since yesterday afternoon, his responses were curt, assuming he would respond at all. It seemed like he was quite busy up there, though I couldn't comprehend how, given that he was simply existing in my brain.

"Okay... But I want to know what happens *after* that. Say we find a way to get you out of my head, I would be without a Calling." *And if I lose my Calling after taking on a job...*

«We'll figure it out when we get there. Don't worry too much. I'll make sure you guys will be okay.»

It was the longest response I had gotten all day. It would have been easy to go with the flow and trust him, but a concrete plan was more important. Miles always sounded sure of himself, and was confident his plans would work out, but two days ago, he hadn't even known what a water source was. I was unsure about how much I should indulge him, but I could sympathize with his wish to escape this situation soon, and his theories were admittedly intriguing.

I arrived at the mostly empty square and was able to go right up to the water source. I placed a stone on the cube and looked at the sigils while I waited for the bucket to fill. Curiously, one of them was scratched up. I had never noticed this before.

"Hey, Miles. That sigil on the right—was it scratched up like that yesterday?"

«Yep.»

Even after the bucket was full, I stared at the script for another minute or two. We had copied it one-to-one onto various surfaces—albeit without the scratches. I wondered if it needed to be different to work somewhere else.

To figure that out, you would need to understand it—which Miles does—but he hadn't instructed me to make any modifications yesterday. Let's suppose this cube turns blue stones into water, and the sigils control that somehow. Omega... Language... Instructions... Miles' words from yesterday floated through my mind.

"Declare CTR... Set empty vector for REL... IN... Define DIR as an upward vector... CONV MNA—" I mumbled, staring at the sigils.

«What?» he exclaimed, breaking my train of thought.

"Huh?"

What was that? Did I just read the sigils?

I was still staring at them, but all I saw was the same old scribbling.

«You understand it?»

"No," I said hesitantly, trying to recall the moment. "I don't know what happened."

«Fascinating,» Miles said, going silent again.

I looked around the square. Nobody had seen or heard me, and that was probably for the best. I bent over to pick up the water bucket and made my way back home.

* * *

Mother was already making breakfast when I entered the kitchen through the back door. "Good Morning," she said, smiling at me.

I replied in kind, and placed the bucket down to help her. I was still confused about what had happened at the water source, but for some reason, I didn't feel like telling my mother about it.

"Are you going to the job agency later?" she asked as we sat down to eat.

"I am. I don't think I want to work for Gean. I'd rather find something else."

Of course, I'd have to talk it over with the currently mute voice in my head.

"What does Miles say?" she asked.

"Honestly, he's been pretty quiet. I don't know what he's up to, but I won't take any risks."

Before she left for work, we talked a bit longer. Usually I would only see her in the mornings and the evenings; sometimes only one of the two. I knew she worked a lot, and I wanted to get a job as soon as possible to lighten her load.

"Miles, I need to talk to you."

«I know,» came his immediate response.

"So you *are* listening."

«Occasionally.»

I asked him if he'd be able to get me into another job. After the Calling ritual, you were supposed to already have a sense for what kind of job you would be most suited for. More often than not, that job would then be what people did for the rest of their lives.

As far as I knew, Researcher Calling jobs involved being in an office all day. I had also heard that Researchers could be an odd bunch. Intelligent, but not necessarily sociable. That description sounded eerily familiar.

«Based on what your mother has told me, and the test Gean gave us, I'm fairly certain we should be fine. These job tests don't actually test whether you're a master in a given profession. They basically just test the theory, which is good for us.»

Mom had described what her own test had been like. She had felt the seamstress in her, and after just a few questions at the Job Agency, and a quick practical assessment, she was given a job at a tailor in the market district.

"Mother had a practical test, though."

«Yes, but she's a Handiworker.»

Oh.

I understood. Researchers didn't typically work with their hands, it was presumably all numbers and theory for them. That's why Gean had only given me math questions—that's the knowledge I would've needed for doing his job. Miles wouldn't be able to help me become a soldier or a carpenter, nor would I have the muscle memory that came with these Callings. But theory Miles could handle.

"You really *do* have the Researcher Calling, don't you?"

«Not exactly. I've learned everything I know without a ritual.»

"Really? How?"

«By reading a few books here and there.»

It wasn't unheard of for people to learn things outside of their job. I enjoyed reading books myself, and I knew that a considerable amount of knowledge could be absorbed this way. Mother had even told me about an old man she once knew, who had spent four decades learning enough to switch jobs into an entirely different Calling. But even then, he would've had at least *some* base knowledge to work with that he received during his ritual.

"How old are you, exactly?"

«How old?» Miles paused for a moment. «Going by your calendar, I would be about one hundred and twenty.»

I stared blankly at our kitchen wall. "Excuse me?"

«Speaking of time. The sixteen-hour days here are kind of irritating.»

* * *

I was on my way to the main square. That last comment from Miles had come without any pain whatsoever. He had stopped responding to my questions again, but I could practically feel his amusement over my confusion.

One hundred and twenty, I thought. There were no people that old. As far as I knew, the oldest person in town was ninety-something. The man gained a degree of fame because of his age. *I have an old geezer in my head... Assuming he isn't making it up.*

"Keep your secrets then," I whispered, giving up.

Exiting a narrow alleyway, I left the web of roads that was the southeastern part of Alarna, and stepped foot on the well maintained main street. Unlike the district I lived in, the rest of town was neatly divided into pre-planned rectangles where homes and shops had been erected. The main street was over one kilometer long, running up from the south gate until it met the main square at the heart of town.

I made a beeline for the eastern street leading into the office district, where I eventually found the Job Agency. This part of town wasn't nearly as busy as the rest, since most people had no need for the agency past their job assignments.

The Job Agency was a surprisingly small building compared to the others in the area. I walked through its oak doors and found myself in an open office space with several desks strewn around. Save for one, each was occupied with an office worker assisting a younger person with their first job assignment. Packed like this, the air inside was stifling.

The woman sitting at the unoccupied desk waved me over. As I made my way toward her, I glanced at the other desks where job interviews were held or tests taken. The tests all seemed to boil down to answering questions on a sheet, and most of the young adults didn't look like they were having trouble.

"Good morning. Your name, please?" the woman said after I took a seat.

"Tomar Remor," I responded.

She skipped through the files lying on her desk, but appeared to come up empty. Getting to her feet, she motioned for me to wait while she walked over to a shelf at the wall to skim through more folders, returning a moment later with two pieces of paper.

"Tomar Remor, Researcher." She plopped down in her chair. "We don't have a lot of you this year. Do you have a specific job in mind?"

I pondered for a moment before responding. "I'm supposed to be a statistician, but I'd like to know what other options there are."

"Alright," she said without any qualms. "It's not unusual for Researchers to choose a different field."

She looked through her files again and pulled one out before skipping through the pages in it. "Though it is unfortunate, statisticians are quite uncommon."

"I've heard," came my response. There had apparently been only one for the past twenty years.

She picked out one piece of paper and laid it down on the desk in front of me. "This is a list of Researcher jobs we have available. You know best what knowledge your Calling has granted you, so please pick something out. I'll be right back."

As I started browsing through the listings, she left to talk to one of her colleagues. The first listing said "Statistician!" in bold letters. *Gean really is desperate.*

I went through everything, line by line, until Miles spoke up.

«Wait, back up. What was the fifth from the bottom?»

I scrolled back up and looked at the entry he had pointed out.

"Stoner?"

«Haha. Now that's a marvelous job.»

I didn't know what a stoner did, nor what Miles found so funny about it, so I read the description.

Stoner

*Management of shard acquisition and
distribution networks, statistical
analysis of water source usage,
research of water distribution,
monitoring of population growth and
its effects on resources.*

Available: 2

Miles stopped laughing abruptly. «Tomar, what are shards?»

I looked around carefully to see if anyone could hear me before answering him in a hushed voice. "Stones. Like the blue ones. I thought only the priests called them shards."

He went silent for a moment. «Are there other colors as well?»

I was about to answer him, but I noticed the office worker had returned. Looking at the listings, I nodded to let Miles know that there were stones in other colors. Most families used the blue ones daily, and the white ones I had only ever seen during the ritual.

"Have you decided?" the office worker asked.

«Take that one!»

Once again, I felt left out. *Why does Miles want me to choose that job?* Pointing at the listing, I told her I wanted to become a stoner, which elicited another hearty laugh from Miles.

"Very well," she said, shuffling through papers again. She pulled out a two-page test and handed me a quill. "This is the stoner test. Twenty questions, thirty-two minutes. If you get everything right, we'll make it official." After a glance at the clock, she said, "You may begin."

* * *

Miles had breezed through the questions as if he had known every single one beforehand. It took him all of fifteen minutes, and I'm sure he could've gone even faster had I been able to match his pace in writing. My job title became official, and they gave me a slip of paper that detailed where I was to go next week. The whole thing was almost anticlimactic, but I was glad it was over. I left the building and headed toward the main square, my spot quickly being taken by a girl that had just arrived.

I was walking back toward the main square when Miles offhandedly commented, «See? Easy.»

He certainly made it look easy, but it couldn't be that simple.

"How long would you have to study to pass this test without a Calling?"

«Hmm... The coverage was pretty broad, I admit. Maybe eleven years?»

Eleven years to pass the test. I was fifteen, so I would've needed to start at four just to prove that I had the necessary knowledge. There would be more to it once the job actually started. What I had been told all my life held true: you couldn't gain enough knowledge to work before you came of age. Not without a Calling, and definitely not if you had other responsibilities as well.

"Good job," I said.

«Mm-hmm.»

We walked in silence for a bit, and just as I stepped into the main square, a hand grabbed my shoulder.

"Morning, Tomar. I must say, I'm a little disappointed you didn't want to work with me."

I turned to see a grinning Gean look down at me. Even with me standing upright, he was two heads taller than me. He had an imposing presence, especially in his freshly pressed, black suit.

I was a little startled by the surprise attack, but managed to calm myself. "Sorry, sir. The job didn't seem quite right for me."

"Too bad. Too bad," he said. "A stoner though? Not the most exciting choice, is it?"

It hadn't even been ten minutes since I left the Job Agency.

Great. He's monitoring me.

«Great. He's monitoring us.»

He must've wanted me to know. It was blatantly obvious with the way he approached me. *Should I play along?*

"I think it's an interesting field, and I will be directly involved with getting vital resources for all citizens. It seemed like a noble profession," I said, parroting what Miles said in my head.

Gean rubbed his chin. "I suppose so. A good boy, aren't you? I'll let you be on your way then. But I'd still like for us to sit down at some point. I'm sure there's plenty we could talk about yet."

With that, he waddled off toward the Registration Agency as I stared at the back of his flapping coat.

"Am I still okay?" I asked Miles, after a time.

«What do you think?»

"I think he's suspicious about something. But as long as I don't make any mistakes, it should be fine."

«There you go.»

In hindsight, it would've been nice to know what exactly would constitute a mistake.

CHAPTER 6

SUIT UP

«We need a tree.»

"We already tried wood," I responded, shielding my eyes from the rising sun.

Miles had gotten just a tad more talkative when he saw that we were heading to the water source. He had come up with new theories for me to test.

«We tried it with deadwood, I want a live tree.»

"Where am I supposed to get a *live* tree from?" I said in exasperation.

«Go to where there's a tree?»

Here we go again with the suicide plans. I thought we had left those behind us.

"We can't go outside the walls! *That* would definitely be a mistake!"

«What? I didn't say anything about—wait. There are no trees in town? None at all?»

It seemed obvious to me. We had told him about the beasts and how they roamed the woods outside town. There also hadn't been a tree in sight while I kept walking around town with him in tow.

«Well, that sucks,» he said, accompanied with a tinge of pain flaring back up in my head.

I had been thinking about the sigils as well—the "Omega Script." Even if I didn't fully believe in what Miles was trying to do yet, I was curious. Even more so with how excited he got while talking about his theories. We had tried scripting on almost anything we could find, using all the painting solutions we had available. His newest theory was that the surface needed to be "alive."

"The water source is a stone, and we *did* try painting on my body," I said, unsure where this theory fit in.

«Actually, I think the stone might be alive.»

"Oh, sure. Let's ask the stone how it works, then."

If Miles found my joke funny, he didn't say. However, his silence wasn't accompanied by pain this time. Shrugging off the thought, I arrived at the square where a girl and a young woman were already doing laundry a few meters away from the water-giving cube. It was unusually early in the morning for it, but some people had to take care of such chores before going to work. I briefly waved at the younger of the two, who returned my greeting happily before going back to her task. Meanwhile, her sister gave me the cold shoulder as usual.

As I went up to the water source, Miles said something weird. «Put an ear to the water source, close your eyes, and concentrate.»

I glanced over at the girls. They weren't paying attention to me.

"Why?" I whispered.

«Just do it.»

Hesitantly, I did as instructed. A moment passed. Then several moments. It must've been almost a minute before—

BADUM.

There was... something. My eyes shot open, but I quickly closed them again and kept listening. This time it took an entire two minutes before I heard it again.

BADUM.

I backed away, incredulously staring at the water source. I was in a daze until I noticed a little girl beside me.

"What are you doing, Tomar?" she asked, having scurried over after seeing my strange behavior.

I snapped back to reality and waved her off. "It's nothing, Riala. Go help Zara finish the laundry."

Being unsatisfied with my answer, she tilted her head and inspected me. She eventually did as asked, but only after her sister called her over. As Riala trotted back, I could make out Zara uttering the word "Weirdo," but I ignored her taunting.

«See what I mean?»

"What *was* that?" I whispered, turning away from the sisters.

«Sounds like a heartbeat to me,» Miles said, matter-of-factly.

A stone with a heart? I thought, looking at the water source again. As my eyes fell on the script, they focused on one sigil in particular. "ITL..." I mumbled.

«That's right,» Miles said in a suspicious tone. «Stands for internal, I presume.»

Stepping closer to the cube once more, I touched it and traced the sigils with my fingertips. "You don't know exactly what every single one of these means," I said, before snapping out of my trance.

With no reply, I picked up my bucket in a hurry, and made my way out of the square.

* * *

Mother had already left for work when I got back. Pacing around the kitchen restlessly, I tried to make sense of what had happened.

"Miles, are you doing something to me?" I asked, carefully.

He stayed silent.

"Miles!"

«Huh?»

He hadn't been listening. "Tell me what's happening to me!" I demanded.

«Beats me.»

It hadn't been a fluke, nor my imagination—I had read the sigils. To some degree, I even seemed to understand what they were referring to. How or why this came to be I didn't know. And Miles either didn't know or he didn't want to tell me.

"I'm scared..." I said in a low voice, letting myself sink to the ground against a cabinet.

At this prompt, Miles tried to appear understanding. «I don't know what is happening exactly. But it's not a bad thing. You're learning something new, that's good, isn't it?»

"I'm not learning, though. It's just there. You have a theory, don't you? You always have a theory."

More silence.

This was really irritating me, and that anger pushed away the fear. Unexpectedly, Miles responded with a question a few seconds later.

«What does a Calling do?»

Realization dawned on me. A Calling gives you knowledge. Things you didn't know before, abilities you didn't have. Miles was my Calling, and he knew Omega, so—

"I know Omega as well?"

«I don't know if it's quite that straightforward, but you asked for a theory.»

It makes sense, I thought, but that was as far as he was willing to indulge me. I was entirely unsure if I even *wanted* to understand the script. The priests say it's not for humans to know, as it's coming from the gods. What if knowing it would be dangerous? With worry in my mind, I forced myself back to my feet and took the money Mother had left me on the kitchen table. I certainly wasn't in the mood for it, but I had to visit the market district to see a well-respected tailor that specialized in suits for men. I would need some new clothes before starting my job next week.

* * *

The market district was off-limits to those not of age, and this was actually the first time I had been here. The reason for that was the Charmer Calling, which typically produced entertainers, merchants, and prostitutes. It's said that they can be immensely persuasive with sales and requests, but my mother assured me that I'd be fine if I were careful.

The streets looked ordinary enough, with shops and market stalls lined on both sides and a mass of people browsing the wares in front of them. I didn't have to go too far before I saw the tailor a few buildings down.

On a corner between me and my destination, a scantily clad man and woman were appraisingly observing the passersby, only leaving their positions when a potential customer grew near. Hurrying past them, I made my way to the tailor's, and ducked into the shop, letting out a sigh of relief.

Taking in my new surroundings, my vision was drowned in all l sorts of fine outer coats and crisp dress shirts hung from racks and mannequins in neat rows. In the middle of the store stood a fitting platform occupied with a tailor measuring an older gentleman.

"Good morning, sir!" said a voice from behind a counter to my left.

"Good morning," I replied, approaching him. "I'd like to get a suit for my new job."

"Certainly! Do you have the requirements on hand?"

I put the note with the information about my job's attire on the counter. Until this point, I had always worn shirts and pants made of simple cotton. Generally, you weren't looked down upon for that as long as you were well groomed, and your clothes spotless. But at work, that wouldn't fly.

The clerk behind the counter took a quick glance at the information, nodded, and walked around the counter. "Please, follow me."

We made our way over to his colleague, who was finishing up with the previous client. The tailor was an older man with graying wisps of hair that stuck out every which way. A tape measure was draped over his shoulders like a makeshift scarf and he held three pin needles between his teeth. "Another simple fit," I heard him say to the desk attendant. It was a wonder he could talk without swallowing the pins, and I found myself staring.

"I'll ring it up right away," the clerk said before turning to me. "Aran here will take your measurements. Please come back over once you're done." He handed his colleague the note and walked back to the counter with the other customer in tow.

"Step on the platform," Aran said, wagging one end of the measurement tape at me.

I quickly did as asked, and before I could properly get my footing, the tailor spun me around a few times before facing me forward again. While he was taking my measurements, we made small talk. He asked me about my new job, but I kept my answers vague, not knowing what I'd be doing exactly. It was a little awkward.

Ten minutes later, I walked back to the counter. Aran, who I guessed to be the owner, nodded with the clerk and he turned to me. "Preparation of your suit will take three days. Will that be acceptable?"

It would be ready two days before I was to start my job. They were probably quite busy this time of year. The store would also be closed one of the two remaining days, so I had to get here on the appointed date.

"That's fine," I said, handing them the requested payment.

"Thank you, sir! Do come again!"

I left the shop with a copy of the order and a receipt. After a quick glance at the now vacant corner where the provocatively dressed pair had been, I heaved a silent sigh of relief. Not wanting to find out when they would return, I hurried back toward the main square. My footfalls had landed on the solidly set cobblestones when Miles broke his silence.

«Fruits! Vegetables!»

"What?" I blurted out, garnering me weird looks from the surrounding people. *The awkwardness continues...*

«Get a tomato or something. Not exactly what I had in mind, but I guess it's technically still alive.»

With the leftover funds I had from purchasing my suit, I did as he asked. Approaching merchants was less nerve-wracking than I imagined, and I wondered what all the rumors were about. Maybe you wouldn't be swindled left and right, but there had to be *some* basis for the bad reputation of Charmers.

With a plump tomato in hand, I was finally able to go home.

* * *

«Careful,» Miles said admonishingly.

"I know."

«You also said on the second try, and yet—»

"I could just stop right here."

«Sorry. Just... you know.»

Hunched over our kitchen table, I adjusted my grip on the tomato, doing my best not to poke another hole in it with the quill. Writing on its thin skin had turned out to be challenging, but getting an entire script on its surface without damaging it seemed almost impossible.

"Hey, this looks correct, right?" I said, breathing a sigh of relief as I finished the last sigil and put down the quill.

«It does. Good job! Now put the blue stone on it.»

With anticipation rising inside me, I carefully balanced the stone on top of the tomato. It had taken a while to get to this point, but if this worked, the trouble would've been worth it.

A second passed without anything happening. Then another, and another, until the only conclusion I could come to was that we had failed yet again. Still staring at our art project, I leaned back in my chair in disappointment.

"That's too bad."

«That's quite an understatement,» Miles grumbled.

"We can still try paint." I stood up to get some from a sideboard. "The sigils on the water source are painted as well, so it would make sense, right?"

«I suppose,» he said, not sounding hopeful.

I turned to the last free side of the tomato and went to work. Having gotten only a relatively big brush from our neighbor, this fourth attempt wasn't much easier than the previous, but at least I wasn't running the risk of stabbing the poor vegetable. Surprisingly, I finished this one with more ease, and proceeded to unceremoniously plop a blue stone on the tomato. I didn't say it, but I did share Miles' sentiment that we were most likely done here.

The result proved us right. Our efforts were in vain, and all we had to show for it was a mangled tomato. With the failed test looming over our heads, Miles became increasingly cranky.

"At least it's still editable." I said, taking a bite of the freshly washed tomato. "And there's almost no aftertaste." The ensuing stinging in my brain spoke volumes about Miles' nonexistent amusement.

«What else can we try…»

I figured that I might be able to at least contribute to developing new theories, and I brought up something I had been wondering about. The current running hypothesis was that the blue stones weren't actually converted into water, but that the water came from inside the cube somehow. Nevertheless, I didn't know what their purpose was in that case.

"What if the stones are an offering to the gods?" I suggested. "Even if the script does something, maybe they can only accept offerings placed on the cubes, thus activating the script."

Miles snorted. «I don't believe in gods.»

That one took me by surprise. "What do you mean you don't *believe* in gods?"

One could hardly deny their existence. Granted, I hadn't seen a god in a while, but it wasn't like you'd go out of your way to meet them. When I told Miles this, I felt as though he had frozen in place.

«You have *seen* gods?» he asked.

"Of course. Haven't you?"

My last time had been a few years ago, when one of them had appeared in the main square to bless their followers. The god was human-like, but had no defining features, and their body glowed a blinding white. My family wasn't following any gods, because doing so didn't appear to have any real benefits, but some people believed their blessings would bring good fortune. And then there were the priests, of course, who truly worshiped the gods.

«Can you show me one?»

"I'd really rather not."

It was an unpleasant experience. They had an oppressive, suffocating air about them. Even from across the main square, I had felt like my head was about to burst open. Their appearances were also kind of random. Supposedly, the priests would try to summon them sometimes, but I had been told even that didn't produce reliable results.

My description convinced Miles that I had seen *something* powerful, but he was still hesitant to call it a "god" and said he'd wait to see it for himself. Having given him new things to think about, I continued on with my day in relative peace... until Mother came home.

"You paid *how much* for a tomato?!" she shouted while we were eating dinner.

I had known how much she usually paid for produce, yet the price hadn't seemed unusual. *Charmers must not be underestimated under any circumstances.*

CHAPTER 7

HOPES

The moon sat high above a torch-lit town wall. Well past curfew, a guard made his rounds between the towers, scouting for beasts and wrongdoers. Eastward across the fields, he spotted a small shadow scuttling around just outside a dense forest, when another, much larger shadow launched from the trees' shadow and killed the critter in a single bite. A shiver ran down the guard's spine as the beast's faintly glowing, red eyes vaguely looked toward the walls before it carried its prey into the darkness.

This wasn't an unusual occurrence. Such scenes were regularly visible from atop the walls, particularly at night. Yet, it always unnerved the guards. From time to time, the beasts would approach the walls, looking for a way in, and those moments were when the guards were scared for their lives. The walls were believed to be impenetrable, but not impassable. With a height of over ten meters, nothing would get over them easily, though it would happen. And when it did, a single guard would rarely stand a chance.

While still surveying the forest, the guard was startled by a noise. Shockingly, it hadn't come from outside the walls. He looked around and saw a shadow zigzag through the small pathways between residences.

Running back to his tower, the guard quickly reported the incident to his superior, but the team that was sent to investigate the sighting came up empty—the shadow was gone.

* * *

Mother hadn't stayed mad for long. While I had paid almost ten times the normal price for a tomato, it *was* just one tomato. It was a good opportunity to learn, and she used it to drill the lesson into my head. To my surprise, she was more mad at Miles than me.

Everyone was susceptible to being influenced by Charmers, but adults were expected to be more resistant to them. The sense of life experience gained from receiving a Calling should have protected me, but my mother hadn't fully considered the consequences of the failed ritual. She figured that Miles would have kept me from doing something ill advised, but that hadn't quite worked out.

«How was I supposed to know the price of a tomato?» he responded to my mother's questioning. She couldn't argue against that. Miles still knew little about this world, and certainly nothing about the market prices of fruits and vegetables. I wasn't sure he really would've cared either way, seeing how fixated he was on getting a hold of another test subject. Anything to further his theories and hypotheses.

With a defeated sigh, Mother gave us a rundown of what we could expect everyday items to cost and what kinds of tricks merchants typically tried to pull. She was thorough, and Miles promised he would pay attention from then on. Regardless, I decided to stay away from that part of town.

Per my usual routine, I was currently on my way to the water source. But unlike most mornings, a little girl was hopping along beside me, her medium-length, dark-brown hair swaying as she did. Riala was a sweet girl who would strike up a conversation with anyone. I had barely known her when she approached me a few months ago, shortly after her father's passing, and straight up asked if I would help her with their family's laundry when her sister had to work early. With her adorable smile, I couldn't imagine anyone ever saying no to her.

Unfortunately, she wasn't one to easily forget about weird occurrences after they piqued her interest. "Tomar, why did you cuddle with the water source?" she asked on the way. "Sis called you a weirdo."

That's hard to explain, I thought.

"'What do you think?'" Miles and I said, hoping she might come up with an explanation on her own.

Riala tilted her head this way and that, thinking it over. "Dunno," she said with a slight frown.

I knew I would have to be careful about what information I shared, but I was suddenly overcome with curiosity about what her reaction to the truth would be. What would *I* think if someone told me they were looking into working with the scripture sigils?

"Can you keep a secret?" I asked.

"Of course!" She perked back up.

«Uh, Tomar?»

I ignored Miles' interjection.

I told Riala that I was researching the water sources to figure out how they worked. Saying such a thing wasn't risky in itself. They were a vital resource, and tampering with them was illegal, but nothing severe would happen unless they were damaged and large portions of the town lost access to fresh water.

Her eyes shone as she listened to me talk about the scripture sigils. She was at that age where she would soon attend classes at the school, meet other kids, hear more about the gods and the sigils, and then maybe attempt to draw them herself. To my surprise, she had already done that.

"I drew it on the wall at our house, but nothing happened! I hate getting up early to do laundry," she complained.

She was a bit young to do all the housework on her own, but with both her parents already gone, and her older sister being the sole breadwinner, Riala had no choice but to step up, regardless of how much she hated doing chores.

"Can you make us a water source?" she asked with hopeful eyes.

"Not yet," I said, "but maybe soon."

"Yay!" She threw her hands up as her cheeks flushed.

I sounded more confident than I really was, and I revealed something to her that would have better stayed a secret for the moment. *Wait. Why did I just tell her all that?*

"Um, Riala?"

"Hmm?" She fiddled with the edge of her shirt.

"Don't tell anyone, okay?"

"Of course not. Promise!"

She's just a little girl, I thought, trying to convince myself that it would be fine.

On our way to the water source, Riala kept gushing about the possibilities. Washing clothes in the backyard, having a bathtub at home... She had thought about the potential in even more detail than I initially had. But true to her word, she stopped talking about it when we reached the square and were surrounded by townspeople.

* * *

«You think that was a good idea?» Miles asked after I had accompanied Riala back to her house.

"I don't."

«You did it though.»

"You think I didn't notice?"

I was disgruntled with my slip-up, but Riala's reaction stuck with me. An hour later, a knock on the front door broke the silence in the house while I was sweeping the floor. On the other side was a guard in dark light armor and silver chain mail, with a spear in hand. The bags under his eyes were an obvious sign that he had been on duty for too long—a fairly common predicament among the limited number of guards in town.

"Morning," he said curtly. "There was an incident last night and we're questioning the citizens to ensure everyone is okay. We would appreciate any information you may have."

"What happened?" I asked.

"There was a suspicious sighting. That is all we can confirm at this time."

I hadn't noticed anything, nor had Mother or Riala, or they would have surely mentioned it. My response made the guard sigh. If he was questioning everyone in this part of town, he had probably been at it for a while already, and he had a way to go yet.

"Alright," he said. "Have a good day. If you do see or remember anything, please report it at the nearest guard station."

"Of course," I said. I wished him a good day in return and closed the door. "Hey, Miles. You're awake at night, right? Did you hear anything?"

«There were noises last night, but it sounded like guards.»

That was probably when they had initially looked into the incident. All I could hope was that this sighting hadn't been a beast. Though according to the stories, beasts typically went straight for the first human in sight. They didn't try to hide.

Through the front window, I saw the guard walk to our neighbors' house, and I resumed my chores.

"If I had gotten a Fighter Calling, I could protect people," I mused to no one in particular.

«Unsatisfied, are we?»

"I didn't mean it like that. But—"

«Yeah, yeah. I know what you mean. Would that have been so great, though? Honorable, maybe, but you'd be putting your life on the line every day.»

He was correct about the job being dangerous, but the town could always use more Fighters. Had more patrols been on duty that fateful night, my father and Riala's mother might not have fallen victim to those monsters.

Later that day, I saw the guard make his way toward the main street, having finished his rounds. I struck up a conversation with him, but he hadn't learned anything new. The incident would most likely be declared resolved for the moment. Since there had been no signs of beast activity, it must have been a person. Being outside in the middle of the night wouldn't go unpunished if you were caught, but it was primarily about protecting the citizens. If you were to surprise a guard, they might mistake you for a beast and accidentally injure or even kill you. Worse, you might actually encounter a beast should one make it into town.

News of the incident had already traveled through the town by the time my mother came home. She had heard all about it from customers and friends, and under the circumstances, she made me promise not to leave the house at night.

"I won't, Mom," I assured her.

That evening, I had trouble concentrating on my book, *The History of Alarna*. It wasn't exactly a page-turner, but I found it interesting, nonetheless. The first settlers had come here in search of a new water source, when the source in their previous village had stopped working. What they found was not one, but several water sources in close proximity to one another. That had made this area ideal for a settlement that could keep growing.

Another discovery that had excited them was the ritual platform, the second "divine instrument" in recorded history, after the water sources. Its function was quickly discovered after people tried placing stones on it, and it essentially became the basis for our society.

Instead of this history, which might be of actual use to me, I was thinking about Omega. Our failed tests and the various things we had tried so far swam around in my head until I had an idea. With sleepiness taking over my thoughts, my eyelids grew heavy, and I fell asleep.

CHAPTER 8

A STEP FORWARD

The next morning, I deviated from my usual routine and took a sharp turn down a secluded path leading north. It was a cooler morning than most, and I found myself wishing I had waited until the sun was higher in the sky.

«Where are we going?» Miles asked.

"We've tried scripting on small leaves and flower petals, but how about a larger plant?"

I had remembered a particular house in our neighborhood that hadn't been occupied or tended to in months. Reasoning that the plants there must have grown wilder and larger than usual, I realized this might give us a decent chance to find something new to script on. Arriving at the plot, my eyes scanned the wild growth.

"That one," I said, looking at a plant with a thick stalk and leaves twice the size of my hands, fanning out in every direction.

Due to the upkeep, most people didn't maintain elaborate gardens, and the authorities usually kept them regulated. When Alarna had only been a dinky, fortified camp, the first inhabitants gradually removed all nearby trees, because they believed they attracted—and even produced—beasts. For that same reason, people became wary of forest-like gardens. Whether this was nonsensical superstition or not, I didn't know.

«This might work!» Miles said eagerly.

Careful not to get spotted, I hopped the fence and crept through the garden toward our target. With the plant's impressive size, scripting on it wasn't an issue, and the thick leaves even agreed with the chalk I used. After drawing the appropriate symbols, I balanced a blue stone on it and waited. I honestly didn't expect anything in particular to happen. At this point, I was mostly doing these little experiments for fun. It was interesting to come up with things to test, to develop theories and hypotheses. Not to mention that the headaches would go away when Miles was happily theorizing.

As with all the other attempts, no stream of water appeared. I picked the stone back up after a moment, a tinge of pain rising up in my head as I did so. But just as I was about to leave, I noticed a few droplets of water forming on the leaf.

Dubiously, I stared back and forth between the stone and the plant. "Did I just…"

«Test it again,» Miles urged.

Placing the stone on the leaf again did nothing. Neither did scripting on another leaf. On a different plant, however, droplets of water *did* form, just like they had on the first one.

"I'm not imagining this, am I?"

«Nope…»

"'We did it!'"

Following the initial successes, I tested the script on various plants. As I did, the stone I was using appeared to shrink slightly, even on the plants that didn't have a visible reaction. Only some plants produced water, and apparently only once they had reached a certain size. It also wouldn't work on a leaf that had been detached from the main plant.

The amount of water we could produce this way was pathetic. This method would require hundreds of plants to fill a bucket, but a part of the theory had been proven: some living things would react to Omega scripts.

* * *

Having left the garden, I rounded a corner to get back on track toward the water source. "What do we do now?" I asked, squeezing the stone in my pocket.

«We need to replicate the results. First, establish a baseline and determine the requirements. Then, you modify.»

I wasn't sure where to go from there, but I knew we needed something else to get us better results. "Modify? What is there to modify?"

«The water source.»

"Wait, what? You want me to change its script? What if I break it?"

«The chance of that happening is negligible. You saw the plants, that proves the script works. Even if something goes awry, we can just fix it,» he said with conviction.

To Miles' dismay, this was a line I wasn't willing to cross. Too many people relied on this water source on a daily basis; I didn't even want to think about what would happen if anyone found out who was responsible for damaging it.

«I'm certain it'll be fine!»

"No."

We argued all morning, going back and forth over our options. Certain that they might produce an actual stream of water, Miles brought up trees again. However, without access to them, I had no choice but to repeatedly shoot down that idea as well.

«Hypothetically, how would one get outside the walls?»

"One wouldn't," I responded. "The only people that go outside are miners and woodcutters. Even then, they're accompanied by at least one squad of guards. It's too dangerous to let just anyone stroll around the Wildlands."

Sometimes there would also be caravans coming or going from the nearest town, three days away. But these were large-scale affairs that required a permit and a good reason for wanting to accompany them. Merchants specializing in imports and exports were a prime example.

«What about stones?» Miles asked out of nowhere.

"What do you mean?"

«Are they being imported?»

Stones were sold directly by merchants working for the authorities, but I didn't know where they came from. I had watched Workers return from outside the walls before, yet I had never noticed them transporting blue stones. My ultimate conclusion was that they must come from somewhere else, and I told him as much.

Didn't my job description say something about shard acquisition?

«Maybe that will be an opportunity.»

Miles revealed that he had chosen my job specifically because it was the only one directly related to the water sources and the stones. He had seen the potential even when I had first shown him the water source, and he wanted to learn as much as possible about them.

I didn't know if I would be permitted to travel out of town as a stoner, but the prospect was exciting—and terrifying. Should this come to pass, he would expect me to walk right up to a forest and doodle on the trees there. It would also have to be done at night, when the caravan stopped to rest, and beasts were most active.

My response was not a definitive "no," but I didn't plan to put my life on the line for this. As I made my way back home, I started getting a little giddy about telling Mother what we had discovered. With her natural curiosity, she would love this.

* * *

From his house to the abandoned garden, from the garden to the water source, and all the way back home, Tomar hadn't noticed that someone was following him, peeking at him from behind corners and fences. He had gotten careless this early in the morning, when most people were still asleep. As a result, parts of his conversation could be made out from a distance. The parts that were spoken out loud by him, at least.

After Tomar had arrived back home, the individual made their way back to the abandoned house, but proof of the experiments had been cleaned up. With a slight pout on their face, they left.

* * *

"Mom, we did it!" I cheered as soon as I caught sight of her.

Over breakfast, I told her a bit about what Miles and I had been doing. About the theories, the frustrations, and today's success. She listened intently, her expression a mix of fascination and disbelief, until she asked a question I should have seen coming.

"And you think it's possible to modify the sigils on the water source?"

Not you too, Mom...

"Miles thinks so," I said with trepidation, "but I don't want to risk it."

My mother contemplated my words. I was worried she would urge me on as well, but she understood my worries.

"You're right," she said. "If anything went wrong, that would be a real problem."

Go, Mom!

"However," she continued, "you *could* alter the water sources that are used less often than ours."

Speechless, I listened to her explaining that it wouldn't be nearly as tragic if a smaller water source stopped working, like the one on a chain. The amount of water it could produce was barely enough for people in that area to get water for the day anyway.

Her second argument made for an even more convincing one. If we were to accomplish something here, we would not only make history and change people's lives, but it could also be very lucrative. It was a calculated risk, and she was delighted at the mere idea.

"My son, the Water Source...erer," she said, laughing softly.

«That's the plan,» Miles said ominously.

CHAPTER 9
BLUE AND RED

My mother and Miles had convinced me that running tests on a water source would be worth it, though I was a little concerned about how exactly we would approach making our discoveries public. The temple would be adamant that the scripts must never be touched, because of religious reasons, and the authorities might be worried about their bottom line, as the sole suppliers of blue stones. Ultimately, we decided that such concerns could wait until we'd get to that point, however.

There were also no guarantees we'd ever be able to use Omega on anything but water sources, but even then, there was a chance they could be improved. To make them more convenient, more powerful, or more versatile.

Over the past few days Miles had apparently analyzed the water source script over and over. Omega was not a simple language, and how it operated depended on the environment it was executed in, but he had identified several potential improvements already. One of them was reducing the size and amount of blue stones required. Another could possibly increase water output. Neither would be good for blue stone sellers, but knowing that my new job would have me directly involved in this was quite entertaining.

Even though the chained water source was not very popular, any experiments would have to wait until the next morning, due to the day and evening foot traffic. To pass the time, we kept talking about the script, Miles being more forthcoming with ideas and theories than he had ever been.

«If we could control mana somehow...»

"MNA?" I asked.

Every day, my understanding of the language deepened, but I was still missing a lot of context. Just being able to read something doesn't necessarily mean you understand it, and some of the concepts that were used in the script were entirely foreign to me.

«Yes. The script takes MNA, presumably from inside the object, and converts it. I'm assuming it stands for "mana," which would typically be a kind of energy.»

He was thinking about transferring mana to other objects, at which point they could hopefully be scripted on too. That would be our greatest goal. If this were possible, we might be able to create water sources as we saw fit.

We spent a good portion of the day writing out modified scripts, so I would be able to write them quickly once we were at the water source. Miles came up with dozens of things he wanted to test, but one script in particular caught my eye.

"On this one, you only changed a single number. What does FRC do?"

«That's a random test to figure out just that. Some of these variables you can guess by context, but that one could be anything.» Continuing, he mumbled, «Could be a fun one though.»

* * *

The southwestern area of Alarna was mostly populated by the ruling class. Here, the aristocrats lived in extravagant mansions, with the largest and most awe-inspiring one situated in the center of the district, housing the current ruler of Alarna, King Hertar.

Sitting at an ornate desk, the king furiously scribbled on some paper. The jacket of his neatly cut, black suit lay discarded by his side, his sleeves rolled up. Across from him sat a patient, young man holding a letter from the Registration Agency.

"You may begin, Lait," King Hertar instructed his subordinate, slowing down his writing.

"Your Majesty, we have received a report from the Registration Agency about a failed ritual."

"Oh?" King Hertar said with curiosity, keeping his attention on the papers in front of him. "What happened?"

"Apparently, the ritual ended without a divine sign. The performing priest came to the conclusion that the candidate was underage; though, Determiner Maila corrected the assessment that same day."

"And the result?"

"The boy was reassessed to be a Researcher."

At this, Hertar halted his work and glanced up at Lait, raising an eyebrow. "The priest missed the divine sign for a *Researcher*?"

Most signs were impressive displays of light and particles flying through the room, entering the candidate's body. There was even one that looked like human shapes merging with people. The sign for Researchers was on another level, with onlookers calling it the most spectacular thing they've ever seen. It was impossible to miss it unless you were asleep on the job.

"This came from the Registration Agency?" the king asked.

"Yes, Your Majesty."

"Nothing from the temple?"

"I'm afraid not," Lait said apologetically.

The king acted as the ruler of the town and was in control of its military, but there were other powers at play as well. One was the authorities, which handled most of the day-to-day business. They were composed of the town's agencies and would act on behalf of the king. However, as an integral part of every aspect of their citizens' lives, they could be a danger to the ruling class, should there ever be any dissatisfaction.

The other major player was the temple, with the acting High Priest at its top. While not directly involved in any parts of the government, they had a large amount of sway over the religious population. As the administrators of the Calling rituals and providers of educational classes, the temple also fulfilled important services and was seen as one of the most crucial institutions in town.

A careful balance had been established between the three most prominent powers, but every one of them was looking for advantages over the others.

"Did the High Priest try to hide this information?" the king asked.

"My apologies, Your Majesty. It has not yet been made clear."

It might have been an honest mistake by the supervising priest, but it seemed unlikely, and the High Priest would know that. If King Hertar was right, there were two possible explanations for what had happened. Neither of which would be desirable.

"Have an agent look into this incident," the king said. "We must determine the actual result of the ritual. Who is the citizen?"

"His name is Tomar Remor," Lait said. "I will launch an investigation immediately."

* * *

When the next morning finally came, my mother and I made our way to the chained water source. She had been adamant about not missing this potentially historical event. We had gotten up before dawn to arrive at the water source before anyone else.

Knife in hand, I knelt in front of a small, black cube very similar to the one I'd visit on a daily basis. Turning my head around, I met my mother's gaze, who nodded at me encouragingly.

My hands were shaking as I put the knife to the cube, scratching away part of the paint that made up the Omega script. Mom looked on in fascination, while also keeping a lookout for other people.

«Alright,» Miles said, «now replace DST with a declaration for SFC with a vector of 0, 1, 0.»

I did as instructed, scratching away more of the script and replacing the previous sigils using chalk. Looking over my work, I took a deep breath. This was the moment we had waited for—the experiment that would determine whether our theories had legs to stand on. All that was left was the blue stone, which I carefully placed on the cube's top surface.

Focused on the hole below the script, we didn't immediately realize when the water source had started producing water, due to it flowing out of the top.

«Heh. I figured the hole didn't actually do anything.»

My mother and I stared blankly at the display, watching closely as the water slowly washed away the chalk until the water stopped.

«Success,» Miles said matter-of-factly. «Let's continue with test number two.»

Still processing what we had just witnessed, his words didn't quite register in my head.

«Tomar?»

"I... I can't believe it actually worked," I said.

We had talked about it and theorized for days, but this was different. It was mind breaking, and I realized I hadn't actually been convinced that this would go as planned. Still in a daze, I turned to my mother again, who looked between me and the water source with a sparkle in her eyes.

"I was right," she said, her smile widening. "My friends made fun of my obsession with the scripture sigils, but it is possible to change them, and you two proved it."

She crouched down and embraced me from behind. I had never known how much this meant to her, and her reaction increased my own happiness about this successful experiment tenfold.

"We're not done yet. Right, Miles?"

«I'm just waiting for you guys...»

After releasing my mother's grip on me, I dried the cube a little and moved on to the second test. The same part of the script was replaced, but slightly adjusted. The result was that the water didn't appear *on* the cube, but in the air above it. Once again, I was slack-jawed as I watched the water stream down. This time I managed to recover more quickly, and moved on to the next test in a hurry, excited for whatever would come next.

I increased the value of FRC a hundredfold, while keeping the other parameters the same. With this script, the water shot into the sky before raining down on us. Mother and I were drenched, but this hardly mattered as we were quietly laughing. As far as I knew, we were the first people to have ever altered a script. I knew Miles was excited as well, but he was far more composed than we were, having expected that his theories would play out like this.

«The next one probably won't be as exciting,» he said with a chuckle.

I adjusted the script once more, returning it to its original version for the most part. Instead of replacing things, I mostly omitted several sigils. The result was no water appearing at all, but the small blue stone had still dissolved.

"You're right, that wasn't exciting," I said, laughing. "What was it?"

A second after my question, I felt something. I couldn't say what it was, but the air seemed thicker than before. Moving my arm around, I felt a resistance, and the closer it got to the hole, the harder it became to move it toward the cube.

«I believe that's mana,» Miles said.

He had made me remove the conversion part. What was flowing out of the cube now was not water, but raw mana. As I waved my hand through the air in fascination, I heard my mother say my name in a whisper as she crouched down beside me.

"Tomar, don't move."

The expression I saw on her face as I glanced at her was not one I had ever seen before; it was one of panic and fear. I slowly followed her eyes to see some kind of animal almost as big as I was. It had four legs, a tail, pointed ears, wild, black fur, and red eyes. It stared for several seconds before it started walking toward us.

My mother carefully put herself between me and the beast as she took the knife out of my hand. At this, the beast halted and growled.

"When I call for help, run north to the next guard station. Do you understand?" my mother said.

I didn't reply.

"Tomar!"

Her panicked, raised voice snapped me out of my daze. My eyes locked onto hers and I saw her determination. I nodded.

"I love you," she said. A moment later, she yelled at the top of her lungs. "Beast! Help!"

After struggling to my feet, I started running, but after a few meters, I stumbled and fell to the ground. Looking back at my mother, I saw the beast pounce. She drove the knife into its body, but it didn't even flinch before digging its sharp teeth into her neck.

Crack.

My mother's body went limp, and the beast relaxed its jaws. Her body fell to the ground and blood dripped from the beast's teeth.

"Mom!"

CHAPTER 10

Aftermath

It was a little after three in the morning when the warning bells on the east side of Alarna rang, warning the citizens that a beast had appeared within the town walls.

The captain of the eastern guard had immediately armed himself before rushing out of his home. When he arrived at the scene, the captain was disappointed to see that the situation was already under control. Sprawled on the ground was the beast, a battered water source on a chain, and a dead woman who appeared to be approximately thirty years of age.

"Captain Lera," a guard greeted with a salute; he had been the first one on the scene.

Lera nodded, and his eyes fell on the beast. "A category three? That's what I got out of bed for?" he said with a sigh.

While any random beast posed a threat to the citizens, the guards could easily handle them, thanks to their Callings. A category three wouldn't require more than two or three guards to put it down, and the captain could have easily done the same by himself. After decades in this line of work, little fazed him anymore, and anything below a category four wasn't worth his effort.

"One casualty?"

"Yes, sir. And one survivor. We assume he's the woman's son, but he's in shock. Hasn't spoken a word since we got here."

The captain examined the scene. "You were close enough to rescue someone? Good work, Jara," he said nonchalantly.

"Actually, sir..." the guard started, "the response time was below average because no patrol was in range. When we arrived at the scene, the beast was already on the verge of death. All we did was put it out of its misery."

Captain Lera stopped and looked at his subordinate before shifting his eyes back to the beast. "How old is the son?"

"Fifteen. A neighbor identified him as Tomar Remor. He's just had his ritual."

"A Fighter then? Impressive," Lera mused.

Any freshly baked Fighter that could injure a category three to such a degree was one to keep an eye on. They would inevitably become one of the greats—given enough time and dedication.

"No, sir... Apparently he's a Researcher."

"Ha! That's a good one, Jara."

"I didn't mean to jest, sir. It hasn't been confirmed, but word is that he is indeed a Researcher."

Lera furrowed his brows and thumbed the pommel of his sword. Researchers were typically the weakest of the weak physically. It simply made no sense that one could have survived this encounter.

Kneeling to examine the beast up close, the captain noticed a small hole in its chest. Something had pierced through the matted padding of fur, and bored a hole clean through to the other side. The wound did not look like it had been caused by a sword or a spear. There was also a small knife sticking out of the creature's throat, but that wouldn't have done any serious damage.

"What happened to you?" Lera asked the dead beast in a low voice. "Let's see what our witness has to say. Get this thing over to the market district. Pay good attention so they don't destroy evidence before stripping it for what it's worth."

"Yes, sir!" Jara responded with a crisp salute.

Captain Lera stood up to begin his journey to the eastern guard station, where the boy was being held. As he passed the water source, he noticed the sigils were scraped up. *This needs fixing,* he thought, halting briefly to call back to his subordinate. "Inform the temple about the damage done here as well."

* * *

At the station, Lera saw Tomar sitting in a chair, stock-still. His hands and clothes were stained crimson from when he had held the woman in his arms.

"Are you Tomar?"

The boy blankly stared down at the floor.

"I'm Captain Lera. Can you tell me what happened?"

Again, there was no answer.

"The woman we found, was she your mother?"

Tomar twitched slightly, but didn't react otherwise. Just like Jara had said, the boy was in shock, and further digging would be fruitless. Lera made his way over to another guard and instructed them to examine the woman's body and send the boy home with her belongings. There would be time for questioning once everything had calmed down.

An hour passed before a guard escorted Tomar home. A look of disdain was plastered on Captain Lera's face as he fumed over the lack of information they had received from the morning's event. Despite all of that, he was excited. For the first time in years, something in this quiet town had piqued his interest. By all appearances, it looked like this boy had crippled a category three beast by himself—a logically impossible feat. He was looking forward to investigating the incident further, as he watched Tomar's silhouette grow smaller in the distance.

* * *

"Your Holiness, the eastern guard station has informed us that a water source was damaged during the incident with a beast," a priest reported.

"What?" the High Priest growled. "What did those inept guards do?"

"All we know is that half of the scripture sigils are missing. Someone tried to fix them with chalk, but they have been partially obscured by blood, and some of them were washed away."

"Chalk? That surely didn't happen during the fight, did it?"

"That is unclear."

"Whatever the case, get over there and restore the water source," the High Priest instructed, exasperated.

"Of course, Your Holiness." The priest bowed and exited the office, immediately leaving to gather the required materials to restore the sigils.

Upon arrival, he saw that a few people were already attempting to use the water source.

"Stupid thing!" a woman said, kicking the broken source lightly before heading for the other square further south.

"Good morning," the priest said as he approached the cube. "May I have some space?"

With a collective groan, the remaining citizens gathered their things and went to another water source. Once they had all dispersed, the priest donned his spectacles and pulled a dry cloth from his satchel of materials.

Upon examination, he noticed that about three-fourths of the sigils had been scratched away entirely, and half of those had been redrawn with chalk. The remaining fourth seemed to have been erased accidentally during this morning's incident.

"Quite a remarkable job. Had they used blue signmaker's paint, we'd have been none the wiser."

Opening his satchel once more, the priest pulled out his tools to restore the scripture. As he cleaned remnants of blood off the cube, his eyes lit up.

"What's this?" he mumbled, adjusting his glasses. "This sigil doesn't look like any sigil in practice. I wonder…" Overcome with curiosity, he restored all the missing parts, keeping the mysterious sigil as it was. With a steady hand, he placed a blue stone on top of the cube, but nothing happened.

A short-lived chortle escaped his lips, and the light in his eyes faded.

Silly me. I should have known better than to think that a commoner might have found an unknown sigil.

Quickly wiping it away, the priest restored the scripture properly, and made his way back to the temple.

* * *

A boy knelt in front of a laundry tub, vigorously scrubbing a soiled dress stained with haunting hues of blood, his efforts seemingly futile. The compassionate looks and words of condolences of the passersby at the water source didn't reach him, until a pair of girls approached him from behind. The younger hesitated for a moment before embracing him in a tight hug, resting her cheek on his back.

"Tomar, why are you washing that?" the older girl asked.

"It's dirty," came his response in a whisper.

Zara looked down at him, her face scrunched ever so slightly before softening, as she noticed the beige dress having worn thin where he had scrubbed it the most. She knelt down beside her sister and him, gently placing her hand on his arm. Her warm touch seemed to radiate through his body, reminding him of what he had lost, and his incessant scrubbing slowly came to a stop as he clenched the dress in the red-tinted water. The three sat like this for a moment before the young woman spoke again. "Come with us," Zara said, getting to her feet and picking up the tub.

He looked up at her with a blank expression and nodded, prompting Riala to release him and grab his pruned hand instead. Together, they walked to the girls' home in silence.

When they arrived, Zara set the tub down in the kitchen while Riala escorted Tomar to her room and instructed him to rest, per her sister's orders. She joined them shortly after, choosing to stand in the hallway, monitoring Riala's attempts to get Tomar to drink a glass of water.

A deep breath escaped Zara's lips. The need to keep her feelings under control was at the forefront of her mind, but she struggled at the view of this helpless boy, the sensation of losing your last parent all too familiar to her. Nibbling at her thumb, she considered the ramifications of inviting him of all people into her home. Could she trust him? Was this the right choice? What would her sister have thought of her if she had ignored her friend?

Lying still on the bed, Tomar's breathing gradually grew more ragged until he finally began weeping and buried his face in a pillow. Riala did all she could to calm him, but it was for naught. At a loss of what to do, she looked at her sister in a panic. But Zara knew nothing would help him in this situation. With a frown, she shook her head, signaling as much to her sister.

Riala approached her, close to tears herself. "Will he be okay?"

"He will," Zara responded encouragingly. "But it will take some time."

He was just a forlorn young man, almost still a child. He didn't have to go through this alone. *I can do that much for him*, Zara thought as she gathered her courage and stepped into the room, closing the door behind her.

* * *

"Your Grace, I have an update on Mr. Remor," Lait informed.

"That's sooner than I had anticipated," King Hertar said with light astonishment.

It had been just yesterday that he had instructed his subordinate to start an investigation on the boy and his ritual. He knew his men were capable, but it still came as a pleasant surprise. The king leaned back in his chair and straightened his suit, organizing his thoughts.

"Do we know more about his Calling?"

"Not yet, sire. My apologies. However, he was involved in the beast incident yesterday morning. The detailed report from the guard station just came in."

The king had received a preliminary report right after the incident, but all it said was that a beast had breached the walls, and there was only one casualty. They even had a survivor. A good outcome, all things considered.

"There was more to it?"

"According to the newest report, the beast appeared near a water source and a middle-aged woman was killed. She was later identified as Phiona Remor. Her son, Tomar, was also present, but survived the attack." Lait paused and straightened his posture. "Curiously, this report states that the guards weren't the ones who defeated the beast. They simply put a spear through its skull to finish it off. Nobody knows exactly what happened before that, nor do they know what injured the beast."

King Hertar sat up in his chair. "*Nobody*? Not even the boy?"

"Mr. Remor was questioned, but he didn't comment on the incident. The guards escorted him home after his mother was processed."

The king fell into thought. Everything about the boy was suspicious, yet there had been no signs of him being a Mad One. On the contrary, the guard captain believed him to be the one who brought the beast to the brink of death, saving lives instead of endangering them.

"Any word from High Priest Orthur about why he didn't inform us of the failed ritual personally?"

"Yes, sire. He believed the situation had been resolved with the redetermination and didn't see a need to report it."

"The nerve," King Hertar said under his breath. "We need to monitor Mr. Remor and keep up the investigation."

"As you wish, Your Grace."

CHAPTER 11
STEP BY STEP

I woke up to the muffled sounds of a lute playing somewhere beyond the wooden wall in front of me. My lips contorted in annoyance upon hearing the beautiful melody, perhaps by a new Charmer in the neighborhood practicing their skills. I scowled until my mind started to clear, and I noticed the surface I was staring at seemed wholly unfamiliar.

Propping myself up, I scanned my surroundings. The floor of the bedroom I was in was littered with papers bearing both childlike drawings and foreboding symbols. The identity of the artist quickly became apparent once I saw Riala. She sat across the room, hard at work on her next masterpiece.

"Riala?" I said sleepily.

Her head shot up and around, her eyes sparkling with joy as they met mine. "Tomar!" She jumped to her feet and sprinted over to the bed, tackling me into a hug.

"What am I doing here?" I asked, looking around the room in confusion.

Riala let go of me and explained that they had found me at the water source. They had brought me here because of the state I was in, worrying that I wouldn't be able to take care of myself properly.

"You didn't say anything, and you looked sad," she said with worry.

Whatever had happened was still foggy to me. I remembered that the beast had attacked us, mother had protected me, and then...

"She's dead. Mom is..." Everything after that was a blur. "Hey, Miles—" I started, but quickly realized my slip.

The girl cocked her head and looked at me curiously. "Miles?"

"Riala, I mean. How long have I been here?"

She looked into the air, deep in thought. "Six days."

She proceeded to tell me that I had been unresponsive, but that I did what I was asked to do. I had even carried the washing tub to the water square for her once, as usual. This morning was the first time I had said anything, which was the reason for her happiness.

Looking down at myself, I saw that I was wearing fresh clothes. *They must have gone to our house to get me these.*

"Thank you, Riala," I said in a quiet voice, garnering me a bright smile from her.

She led me to the kitchen and sat me down for breakfast. I felt a little guilty at how familiar she was with the routine.

As she prepared to put a spoon in my hand, I took it and smiled at her. "I got it."

She sat down beside me as I ate, watching like a hawk.

I wasn't sure what to do at this point. Mother was dead, and after six days, her body would've already been cremated. Was I supposed to just continue my life, parentless and alone?

I sat and tried to think, but I couldn't concentrate with the tiny girl hovering around me. Quickly finishing my breakfast, I thanked Riala again and told her I wanted to go home, but she was having none of it.

Determination in her eyes, she proclaimed, "Sis told me to watch you!"

Defeated, I stayed, helping her with chores until Zara came home for lunch. She was happy to see me up and about as well.

"You can stay a little longer, if you want," she said. "Riala enjoys having someone around."

She emitted a warmth uncharacteristic of her. I had never had the impression that Zara was a big fan of me, but after having lost both parents herself, she must've understood what was going on inside me. Still, I couldn't stay here forever and I said my goodbyes to them after dinner before I headed home.

«Welcome back,» Miles said on the short walk back home.

"Hey," I responded. "I don't remember what happened."

«Maybe that's for the better. You were in a bad place.»

My mind was evidently thinking the same thing, though I was surprised by how sharp it seemed. Never would I have believed myself to be able to calmly consider my next steps in this situation. That mother's death wouldn't break me. But this feeling and the question of what had come over me didn't last long. I came to a sudden stop and swallowed hard when our home came into view. Or rather, *my* home. Mother wouldn't be there. Never again. I was all alone now.

"I think I'm still in a bad place," I said quietly, my stomach churning.

Entering the house, there was the door to my room on the right, and the door to my parents' bedroom on the left. I went straight into my room and shut the door behind me. As I looked around, I noticed that the suit I had ordered was here, hanging over a chair.

"Did Zara get it?" I asked, puzzled.

«No, you did.»

"Really?"

«Yeah, before the girls found you. You were unresponsive, walking around like a zombie.»

"What's a zombie?"

«Doesn't matter. Just know that it's good to talk to you again.»

I started cleaning up the house a little, avoiding even a glance at the door to my mother's room, when there was a knock on the front door. On the other side stood a guard who seemed surprised to see me.

"Oh, Mr. Remor. We've been looking for you," he said. "My condolences on the death of your mother. I'm sorry to come to you at such a time, but do you have a moment? We have some follow-up questions about what happened that morning."

We sat down and the guard asked me several questions. I pretended that Mother and I had just been on a walk when the beast attacked us. Regarding anything that happened after, I told him the truth. It was all a blur; I didn't remember any details.

The guard had probably not given his speech for the first time and he appeared to sympathize with my situation. After a few minutes, he departed with hardly any new information. As he left, the sight of his back called forth a memory—little more than a glimpse.

"Miles. I don't want to know all the details, but did we kill the beast?"

«We crippled it, the guards did the rest. You did good,» Miles said with compassion and encouragement.

"Okay..." I said and continued on with my day. I would have to go to the office and clear up my job situation. After putting on my new suit for the first time, I looked at myself in the mirror. It felt weird, but not uncomfortable. *I wonder what Mother would've said...*

«You look good, Tomar.»

That... probably...

* * *

"Captain Lera," a guard said, spotting his superior across the hall.

"Jara! Any news?"

"Yes, sir," Jara said, giving a salute. "I finally encountered Mr. Remor at his residence. Apparently he spent the last few days recovering at a neighbor's house."

The boy had been unresponsive and appeared mentally broken when the guards had found him that morning. It was no surprise that he had needed a few days. Though the captain had still been surprised that they failed to locate him.

"Did he have anything to add?"

"Unfortunately not, sir."

The guard repeated what Tomar had told him, but the more Lera thought about it, the less likely the story seemed. An autopsy on the beast revealed that something had pierced several internal organs and its spine. It had been paralyzed and would've died in time, even if the guards hadn't arrived when they did. No weapon known to him would cause this kind of damage, and the beast certainly hadn't committed suicide. The only eyewitness not remembering anything was too convenient.

Lera dismissed the guard and went back to his desk, composing a report for the king. The two of them had been friends since childhood and he knew that King Hertar was also investigating the boy. The information that Tomar was back home would be of interest to him, even if they still didn't know what exactly had happened.

* * *

"You're starting right now," a middle-aged man told me shortly after I had arrived at the Stoner Agency, an office on the second floor of a building on the eastern side of town.

"Right now? But—"

"I know. I've heard what happened. My condolences. But you've had your grieving period, and we're in dire need of more hands."

Behind the man was a girl furiously working on some papers, a stressed expression on her face. I was a few days late, and even though there were more than three desks here, this was apparently the entire team.

"Let's get started. I'm Borus, that's Mirya," he said, pointing at the girl. "Mirya, Tomar. Tomar, Mirya."

I lightly waved my hand at her. She opened her mouth to say something, but was immediately cut off by Borus. "Now that we all know each other, get acquainted with your new job."

He ushered me to a desk, sat me down, and pointed at a tower of files on it. "You have until the end of the day to familiarize yourself with everything. Tomorrow you start for real."

"O-okay," I stammered.

Borus rushed off while I was still trying to process what was happening.

"He's been stressed all week, but he's actually nice. I think," Mirya said, her meek voice quivering. "Nice to meet you."

"Nice to meet you as well," I responded, though Mirya had already gone back to work.

I glanced around the office before my eyes fell back on the pile of papers on my desk. The first file I skimmed through was full of diagrams and statistics, none of which I understood. Looking at the next one, I saw more things I had never seen before, but Miles kept pointing out what I was looking at.

«Bill of delivery, order form, profit-and-loss account...»

I had heard that the first week at a new job could be a little overwhelming. Bosses would expect one to be an expert in their chosen field. All that remained was getting acquainted with the new work environment as quickly as possible. Borus appeared especially expectant about quick results. However, this assumed that the worker actually knew what they were doing. I, on the other hand, was entirely clueless.

Slowly working my way through the pile, I looked at every paper, diagram, and form, so Miles could get an overview. He often commented with a "mm-hmm" or "okay," but was otherwise silent. This had taken two whole hours, while Mirya was still working furiously and Borus was nowhere to be seen.

"Are we good?" I asked Miles quietly, so Mirya wouldn't hear.

«It's about what I expected,» he said. «Full honesty, I've never actually done this kind of work myself, but I know the theory. We should be fine.»

I blankly stared at the desk. This was the first time Miles had mentioned never having done a job like this. The entire time, I assumed he knew exactly what he was doing, but if that wasn't the case, we might not have been fine at all.

"Are you sure you can do this job?" I asked, while looking at the papers again.

«Let's give it a try. The worst that can happen is that they see you as inept,» Miles said.

"The worst that can happen is that they kill me when they realize I don't have an actual Calling!" I snapped at him while keeping my voice low. I thought Mirya might've heard, but she was focused entirely on the work before her.

«We won't do *that* badly. Ask her what she's doing.»

From that moment forward, I acted as Miles' puppet, saying what he asked me to say and doing what he asked me to do. He coordinated with Mirya about what she was currently working on and what needed to be done before going to work himself.

About an hour after we had started, Borus finally came back. He looked surprised when he saw me working on something instead of acquainting myself with the assigned documents. He came over to my desk and took some papers to look them over.

"Not bad," he said, nodding. "If you got this much done on your first day, I'm truly looking forward to working with you."

With a pleased expression, he walked over to an empty desk and resumed working. "They finally sent me two decent workers," he murmured.

* * *

It was already early evening when Borus announced that we would stop for the day. "Good job, Mirya, Tomar. Tomorrow will be another long day of catching up. After that, you will work from five till ten."

He talked to us about his plans for a few more minutes before finally letting us go home. I was happy to hear that my schedule would be relatively moderate. We were only three people, but Borus repeatedly pointed out that just because you got a Calling, and you knew what you're doing, didn't mean you were good at doing it efficiently. He had sent people back to the Job Agency more than once, because they didn't meet his standards. As far as I knew, that was rather unusual. After seeing Borus today, however, I believed it.

Mirya and I walked across the main square when she pointed at a house to the southwest. "I live over there. See you tomorrow."

"See you," I said, and we parted ways.

I walked down the main street for a few minutes, and my head started to clear. For the past four hours, I had been so busy that I didn't really think about anything. *If work is going to be like that every day, the moderate work times won't help much*, I thought with a smile on my face. But at least it was a distraction.

CHAPTER 12

NORMALCY

When I opened my eyes the next morning, a young girl's face was intently staring at me. "Good morning, Tomar!"

"Wuah! Riala?"

She was smiling at me, as if standing there—in front of my bed, in my room, in my house—was the most ordinary thing in the world.

"What are you doing here?" I asked after I had recovered from the shock.

"We made you breakfast!" she replied.

"We?" I looked out into the hallway, where Zara was waving at me.

"I couldn't convince her that you didn't need us to bring you breakfast anymore," Zara said with a reluctant smile.

"We also got you water!" her younger sister followed up.

It was nice of them to still worry about me, but after accepting the food and water, I sat down with Riala and reassured her that I would be fine, that she didn't have to worry anymore.

"Do you promise that you're better?" she asked.

"I promise."

She looked at me with suspicion, but reluctantly accepted my words. After Zara apologized for barging into the house, we said our goodbyes and the two were on their way.

«The girl was really worried about you,» Miles commented.

"Mm-hmm. I see that now. She shouldn't have to look after someone else at that age though," I said, dejected.

«She'll be fine. Another breakfast or two and she'll take the hint.»

"Hilarious."

I had work in an hour, so I ate the food, washed myself, and donned my suit. Then I left the house for my first official day of work.

Even though I had never felt out of place in my old clothes, something felt different about walking through the streets in a suit. People looked at me differently. Suddenly, I wasn't a teen running about, wasting my days away. In their eyes, I was an adult. A contributing member of society. I kind of liked it.

When I arrived at the office, Borus was already hard at work. Mirya had arrived a moment before me and was prepping her writing utensil for the stacks of papers waiting for her.

"Let's do it!" came Borus' battle cry.

For the first few hours, Miles and I did the same things we had done yesterday, but shortly after noon, we stumbled upon something that was immensely interesting to him. It was an order form for stones that was due at the end of the month.

«This is it,» he said.

Going by this form, the sender, and other files we found in the archive, it appeared that stones were ordered regularly and always adjusted for current demand. They were ordered from the neighboring town, a place I knew nothing about. To Miles' disappointment, we learned from Borus that there was no reason we would have to travel anywhere. The deals would be made by other departments and experienced merchants. All we had to do was manage the orders.

«The job description lied to me...»

Despite the setback, we still gleaned fascinating details—like the fact that we weren't ordering only blue stones. We were also responsible for ordering white stones for the Calling rituals. And finally, there was one order where we had ordered a black one. It was a stone color I had never seen or heard of before. Unfortunately, Borus knew nothing about it either.

"Some high-ranking jerk wanted it and we sent the order together with the one for blue stones. All orders go through us, but we don't really see where the non-blue stones go," he said.

Because of how dangerous the trip was to the neighboring town and back, every additional bit of weight increased the likelihood of something going amiss. This is why one had to have some measure of sway before ordering random stone shipments on a whim.

During a break, while I was taking a walk, Miles began theorizing what the stones might be used for. We knew the blue ones were used for creating water, and the white ones were used during the rituals. However, those were widely varying applications, and we didn't know the contents of the ritual script. That made it even more difficult to determine what the white stones did exactly.

The black stone was an even greater mystery. Someone had ordered it, so they must've had some kind of use for it. We couldn't just order one ourselves, though, and we wouldn't see another white stone before the rituals next year. The only ones we got on the regular were the blue ones.

With that, all hopes of leaving town or discovering differently colored shards had been crushed for Miles. Honestly, I was glad, as this would make life easier for me. He wouldn't be tempted to risk it all to leave town, or go to a water source for experiments early in the morning again. We had learned how the water source script worked, and there were no more plants or stones for further experiments. There was nothing more to do. We could stay as far away from the beasts as possible.

* * *

I liked my job, even if I didn't understand half of what Miles had me doing yet. I figured that if we did this kind of work for a few years, I might eventually learn enough to do it by myself.

That line I had said to Gean back when I had chosen this job started to sound more genuine in my mind as well. This was an important job, and I was proud that Miles and I were doing it well. For the rest of the day, we worked and occasionally made conversation with our colleagues. Issues came up now and again, but they were resolved. Best of all, it turned out that Borus was a nice guy—just as Mirya had assumed.

After another long day, I left the office late in the afternoon to go home. When I arrived at the main square, my eyes fell on the market in the distance as I realized that there wasn't any food at home.

I would have gone hungry this morning if Zara and Riala hadn't been there... Maybe they should keep worrying over me after all, I thought with an awkward smile.

Since I was alone now, I didn't have much of a choice. I steeled myself and made my way over to the stalls. There was still a decent crowd of shoppers milling about, both coming and going from the various stalls laden with wares. In an attempt to keep away from the deeper streets, I stopped at the first stall that had a decent selection. Despite my best efforts, the pretty hawker immediately locked on to me as she praised her merchandise. When I leaned in for a closer look, she suddenly appeared by my side, whispering a calming deluge into my ear. I heard a warning from Miles, but I was already taking a step back.

She looked at me impishly as she said, "Sorry, got to try with newbies."

How she knew that I wasn't a regular market goer, I didn't know, but I wouldn't make that mistake again—not after Mother's lecture. As an apology, the young woman gave me some helpful tips, like avoiding attractive members of the opposite sex if I wanted to lower the risk. Apparently, they could have a field day with inexperienced shoppers who didn't pay attention—essentially coming close to robbing them blind.

When the items were paid for, I set off on a brisk walk for home. There was a spring in my step, and I couldn't hide the fact that pride was welling up in me.

«Good job.»

"Thanks," I said with a laugh.

This was what my mother had done almost daily. A normal routine.

I was almost on the main street when I noticed the familiar frame of a large man who was waiting for me. Once I had gotten close enough and stopped before him, he spoke up.

"Tomar, do you mind walking together? We need to talk," Gean said firmly.

A little nervous, I agreed. I didn't have any real reason to refuse him, so I gave him a light nod and we matched our pace. He started by giving me his condolences, but the next thing he said made me stop dead in my tracks.

"You're being investigated." Gean motioned for me to keep going, but it took me a few seconds until I managed to will myself to stop staring at him and move forward again. "I don't know all the details, and I don't know your situation, but I've been questioned by a guard captain about your test. He is suspicious about something, and the questions he asked made it obvious what he's thinking."

Gean had already believed it, and now there were more people who thought something was off. I gulped as he leaned closer and asked, "Are you a Mad One?"

Before saying anything, I actually thought about the question for a moment. *I'm actually not, am I?*

I hadn't reconsidered this question since the beginning. Naturally, I thought I had the Mad Calling. Even on second thought, that would've seemed like the right answer to me. But aside from the voice in my head, there wasn't a single thing that would qualify me as a Mad One. And even though my Calling wasn't a traditional one, Miles was helping me with my work, just like a Calling was supposed to. Not only that, he was doing a good job! I didn't know what I was, but I wasn't a Mad One.

"No, I'm not," I answered truthfully.

"But *something* is going on with you. I've noticed that from the start," Gean said and I flinched again. "Listen," he continued, "I was curious about what had happened to you, but I didn't mean any harm. After the test, I didn't consider you a danger anymore. I just wanted to let you know that something is happening. Take care of yourself."

With that, he turned to head toward his house, and I watched him go until his suit blended into the crowd.

"Why did he tell me that?" I asked Miles.

«Shrug.»

"Did you just *say* 'Shrug?'"

«You're right, that was weird. You shrug for me.»

We chuckled lightly before Miles started again. «It's hard to say what his intentions are. That confession only confirmed our suspicions that he was looking into you. Granted, it's unlikely he's doing it to gain an advantage, especially if there's another person snooping. I think he might actually be looking out for you.»

Someone is investigating me. So what? I thought. I was just a normal, young man who had been involved in a weird beast incident. Of course they would look into that, but from then on there would be absolutely nothing suspicious about my life. Just like the past two days.

I would visit the market, go to work, befriend my colleagues, do my part, and occasionally visit Zara and Riala to thank them for all their help by inviting them to dinner.

My normal life starts now, I thought.

* * *

"Any news on the boy?" the High Priest asked.

The black-clad figure kneeling before him spoke immediately. "Yes, sir. Gean Maila met with him. We couldn't get close enough to make out the topic of their conversation, but the two of them spoke for several minutes before parting ways."

"Gean? You don't say," the High Priest mused. Gean still showing interest in the boy after clearing him only strengthened his suspicions. He had to be careful about how he would approach this situation, but if he was right, Tomar could be a huge asset to him.

"Any other interested parties?"

"We've seen activity from the king's agents and the eastern guard. They are following Mr. Remor, albeit less aggressively."

That's good, the High Priest thought. He might be a step ahead of the others. Given the current situation, he hoped to get to Tomar first. He decided to make a move soon as he dismissed the figure in black.

CHAPTER 13
DISAGREEMENT

After two days of work, I had my first day off. On the last day of the week, most people did not have to go to work. The market and the majority of stores were also closed by their owners. Everybody relaxed, spent time with their family, and recharged for the week to come. *Not that I need it after two days,* I thought with a smile.

For the first time in a while, I made my way to the water source in the morning. I wasn't quite as early as usual and a few people were already there, going about their day. I waved at Zara and Riala in the distance and walked up to the water source. As I got closer and looked at the script, I froze a little. Memories of that morning became vivid in my mind and I had a hard time stepping closer to the cube.

«Are you okay?» Miles asked.

I nodded and slowly stepped closer to fill my tub. *I'm fine,* I told myself. *Everything's fine.* Suddenly, I was startled by someone dropping their bucket, and I almost fell to the ground. *E-everything's fine...* I told myself again as I picked up the tub and walked over to a free spot.

«I guess it will take a bit longer,» Miles said.

"Mm-hmm," I agreed.

«It will get easier,» Miles said compassionately. «Your new routine is good for you. And in time, we'll be able to resume our experiments.»

I froze again. *Did he just say... 'resume our experiments'?*

"What do you mean?" I said in a quiet, quivering voice.

Miles was silent, as if he had been surprised by my question.

"We won't do any more experiments!" I said.

«Tomar, I—»

"Are you insane? Mother died! She's *dead* because of these *stupid* experiments! I don't care if we can have the water sources make it rain or whatever, I'm never going to sneak out to a water source again!"

«Please listen,» Miles said. «I'm terribly sorry for what happened, but nobody could've anticipated that! How often do beasts appear within the walls? Once every few months? It's not actually that dangerous, and it's the only way for us to figure out how to get me out of here!»

"Get me out of here," I thought. *Of course.* He was still stuck inside my mind. An unwilling passenger, unable to do anything. Had I gotten so used to him in this short amount of time that I had forgotten our situation? Or maybe I didn't want to remember. He was still looking for a way out. And when he left, I would be...

"I'm sorry, Miles. I just can't do it anymore. Maybe in a few years, when I—"

«A few *years*?! You want to keep me prisoner here?»

His words were ringing harshly in my head as I desperately tried to keep my voice low. "Of course not! I... I..."

We sat there in silence for a minute while life was going on around us. There were children playing, people getting water and doing their laundry. It was a weird scene with me in the middle—crestfallen and unmoving.

«Do what you must,» Miles spat.

"Really? It's okay?" I asked carefully. No response came—except for a mild headache. *Of course it's not okay.*

I felt a rift open between us, but I pushed the feeling away. *It will be fine,* I thought to myself and went about my day. I washed my clothes, briefly talked with the girls, and ate lunch. The afternoon eventually grew late, and I had settled down to relax, when a thought crossed my mind. Maybe there were other ways we could research what happened to Miles.

A brief look at my humble bookshelf didn't reveal any guides on how to separate two minds using Omega, but there was one book that contained some mentions of Mad Ones and the ritual.

"Can I show you something?" I asked. Miles didn't respond, but knowing that he was always watching, I continued. "Perhaps we can learn more about your situation without these experiments. This book here has some mentions of Callings, Mad Ones, and even the town we get our stones from."

Holding it in front of me, I looked at its title written in bold letters on the cover—*The History of Alarna.*

The book spoke about how the neighboring town to the west, Cerus, had started out as a stone mining camp, and an extension of Alarna. Our settlement had been a great place to live, but not many stones could be found around here. On the other hand, the area around Cerus was rich in stones, but a lot rougher to live in. With an increasing demand for blue and white stones, the importance of the mining camp rose, and when they found a ritual platform there, the foreman, Cerus Balart, declared independence and became the town's first mayor. The control over the stone supply allowed him to broker favorable deals with Alarna's leadership, and the two towns came to terms with the new status quo. Cerus would deliver stones, while Alarna supplied the mining town with other necessities that were difficult to find there.

I had always wondered why there weren't more people reading such books, and a hum from Miles seemed to imply that he didn't find it entirely uninteresting either. It was intriguing to learn more about how this place had come to be. And this was also knowledge unavailable to any Calling, including the Ruler one. Funnily enough, the book also spoke about how that Calling had had a different name in the beginning.

For the most part, the first people that stepped onto the ritual platform after it had been discovered received common Callings. Fighters had remarkable strength, Handiworkers were gifted at creating things, and Researchers impressed with their intellect. A Calling that came later appeared much less impressive at first. It was called "Waysider" by the settlers, and the person who had received it was a young woman. She appeared clever, cunning even, and she had become stronger than an average human. She was also more intelligent, dexterous, and charming, and she had received knowledge about the world nobody had known before. Unfortunately, she couldn't compare to dedicated Callings in any single category. At a time, when people were beginning to receive superhuman strength and intellect, someone who was only above average was belittled.

However, people's perception changed when the young woman gathered a following, brought the Fighters under her control, and crowned herself the first ruler of this settlement. Queen Alarna Ragar set plans in motion that would shape the town for centuries to come, and it was eventually renamed Alarna in her honor.

Naturally, another particularly interesting chapter for us was the one about Mad Ones. Ever since the discovery of the ritual platform, there had been only ten recorded instances of them in this town, and the last one had been hundreds of years ago. They appeared to have been more prevalent in the past.

The book included an account of the first time a Mad One had shown itself. A middle-aged man had stepped onto the ritual platform and almost immediately clutched his head in pain. He screamed and pleaded for someone to make the voices stop. He had also screamed words nobody understood as he collapsed to the ground, panting heavily and smacking the ritual platform with his bare hands. In an attempt to stop him from both hurting himself and damaging the platform, other citizens tried to pin him to the ground. Regardless, the man managed to stay on top for several minutes. He injured and even killed several people before more capable Fighters arrived to take him out.

After this event, a group of citizens took it upon themselves to oversee the rituals and protect others from those who were deemed unworthy of receiving divine Callings by the gods. To them, nobody favored by the gods would lash out after receiving such a blessing.

Unfortunately, the book contained little details and also didn't go further back than the founding of the settlement. It didn't speak much about where these "divine instruments" came from, how the water sources were first discovered, nor whether there had ever been any research on the scripts. Of course, if it was all god-given, maybe that was all the explanation people needed.

The gods willed it, and we graciously accepted. Though, if that were the case, why did those sacred things have to be discovered? Why didn't the gods just hand them to us? I certainly would have been thankful if a god put a water source in my backyard. Maybe I would even worship them, which they appeared to appreciate.

The text was quite thought-provoking, though I didn't get too much of a rise out of Miles. I slammed it shut as I made a mental note to look into more research material that might contain some information entirely new to the both of us.

* * *

While preparing dinner, I thought of additional ways we could come to a compromise about our way forward, and I started talking about our theories again, even if we couldn't act on them. Miles had always been happy when we talked about Omega, and I felt it was the one big thing we had bonded over. It also wasn't as if I had suddenly stopped being curious altogether. If we ever found a safe way to work on this again, I would definitely be interested. Even if it took years.

"Hey, Miles? About the stones... I was thinking—the scripts don't define what the mana should turn into, right? What if the stones do that?"

More silence. I hoped that he was just thinking about what I had said. It seemed like a good theory to me. As far as I understood the script, all it did was push mana out of the cube and run a conversion. It didn't define the form the mana was supposed to take. One possibility was that it was the only thing a script could produce. However, the ritual platforms used stones as well and their function was entirely different. It was also unlikely that the stones were just a necessary resource for these tools because it seemed unnecessary to have more than one color in that case.

As I was thinking this theory over, Miles eventually responded. «I've been considering that as well. But it's not like we'd be able to test it. Even under different circumstances.»

It was clear he was still mad, but I didn't want to give up. "The stone is the input, right? Could the script be activated without one?"

«No,» Miles said with a light sigh. «The input is the trigger for the script.»

We continued for a while, but even though Miles appeared less cold as the discussion went on, I was sure it wouldn't be this easy to have him come around. Yet, I was hopeful. If we could find a way to live together, maybe it wouldn't be so bad for him. And maybe, one day, we might find a safe way to get him out.

* * *

The town's four guard captains sat in a room and discussed the recent increase in suspicious sightings.

"Guards report seeing shadows run around the city at night almost every day! They're unnerved. We need to put a stop to it!" one said.

"Quite right. I don't know what's going on amongst the citizens, but the amount of activity we're seeing is highly unusual," another said.

For the past two weeks, there had been sightings, but every time the guards went to investigate, the shadows were already gone. Initially, the first thought had been beasts, but there had been no attacks. Even after one beast had appeared and then subsequently been killed, the sightings continued. The simplest explanation for the lack of attacks was that one or more citizens were running around town at night. However, most common guards weren't exactly the rational kind.

"I understand your concerns," the captain of the eastern guard station said, "but do you have any actual suggestions? You know very well that we don't have the manpower to monitor the entire town."

"As most reports come from the eastern side," the northern captain said, "don't you think it an overstatement to speak of the *entire* town? Maybe only one of us here needs to get up and do something."

"I would agree with the sentiment, Lera," the southern captain said. "It is *your* district, and enforcing the curfew is part of *your* job. I didn't think you were this incapable."

"Maybe we should wait until we know more before pointing fingers," Captain Lera said. "The people may be coming from your districts because they enjoy mine so much more."

Two captains chuckled, while the last one grimaced. There was a constant rivalry between them, and they rarely saw eye to eye. Only when the time to fight came would they unify. Fortunately—or unfortunately, depending on who you asked—there hadn't been any threats dangerous enough to warrant the combined strength of Alarna's entire military in years.

"I will make a concession," Captain Lera said. "I will increase patrols in the areas where the reports were high. With any luck, we might catch someone who can tell us more about what they're doing and where they're coming from."

All of the guards accepted and continued on to the enjoyable part of the evening—getting drunk and arguing with each other.

CHAPTER 14

BOREDOM

Unexpectedly, Miles had been in higher spirits again the next morning and every day since. I would say he just needed to let it sink in over a good night's sleep, but since he didn't sleep, I wasn't sure what had brightened his mood. Whatever it was, I was happy. I didn't want him to suffer, and it would be better for both of us if we got along well.

I started my daily routine. Greeted friends and acquaintances at the water source, ate leftovers from last night's dinner for breakfast, and cleaned up afterward. I was still sad whenever I thought about Mother, but having something to do helped. When Father had died, my mother cried for hours, while I barely understood what had happened. Afterward, she got up again, gave me a brief hug, and moved on. I would try to follow her example.

After putting on my suit, I was out the door, on my way to the office.

* * *

"I should've become a soldier," a figure in black said. "Seriously, this is the most boring target ever. I want to fight something!"

"Relax, Dirra. Sooner or later, something is going to happen. Our time will come," another said.

"'Sooner or later?' Reva, this is the most ordinary guy we've ever tailed! You saw him the other day; he got flustered at a *market stall*. I don't know what the High Priest was thinking when he gave this assignment."

Reva sighed as they watched a boy walk up the main street, greeting passersby. "Okay, I see your point."

"And we didn't even get to see the beast last week."

"Neither did the other guys. They lost him."

"Quite the feat. I still don't understand how they managed that," Dirra said sarcastically.

The boy kept walking, but suddenly took a turn down a path that they hadn't seen him take before.

"Huh? Where is he going now?" Dirra said in surprise.

The two figures were immediately on edge. They went over to another location and kept following their target. It wasn't long before the boy disappeared into a building.

"Come on, Reva, say it," Dirra prompted, exasperated.

"I don't want to."

"Worst. Assignment. *Ever.*"

As they stood there watching the building, another figure in black walked up behind them. "Morning, boys," a feminine voice said from below a hooded mask.

"Berla? Are you on the Remor boy as well?" Reva asked.

"Freshly assigned. Pari's back is acting up again. How is it going?" Berla said.

"You made it in time. It just got interesting," Dirra said. "He went to the *library.*"

"You're not following him inside?" Berla asked.

"What for? It's not like he's going in there to borrow some ancient, forbidden tome. 'One classified relic, please!'" Dirra mocked.

"He could be meeting someone dangerous," Reva said, to which Dirra gave him a sideway glance. "Yeah, yeah... I heard it myself," Reva added.

The three kept making small talk while they were waiting for Tomar to come out of the library.

"How is the wife, Reva? Did she have an easy birth?" Berla asked.

"She's good, thanks. Gave me a boy," he said.

"Oh! A healthy one?"

"Indeed." Reva smiled brightly.

"Congratulations!"

When the boy finally left the building again, the three followed him to his workplace on the eastern side of town. They got into a position where they could see their target through a front window. As soon as they were in place,

Dirra got comfortable and took out a pack of cards. Reva joined him, while Berla kept her eyes on the building. She knew some of her colleagues were less disciplined than others, but these two seemed way too relaxed.

"Aren't you being a little too lax with this job?" she asked.

"I'll tell you what will happen," Dirra said, pointing at a window. "In about two minutes, he's going to sit down at that desk and start working. Occasionally he's going to get a new file from a shelf, but other than that, he won't get up again until noon."

Berla kept watching the building, and just as Dirra had predicted, the boy sat down at his desk and started going through files. "Impressive," she crooned. She watched the boy for three hours, until the bell at the main square rang, signaling that it was noon.

"Ten kira says he'll take a walk again," Dirra said while they were still playing cards.

"Sure, why not," Reva responded.

About three minutes later, Tomar left the building and leisurely strolled through the streets.

"Looks like Dirra was right," Berla said.

"Of course I was. And another win for me," Dirra cheered as he placed his cards on the make-shift table between them.

"Not my day," Reva said grumpily.

"Who's the girl?" Berla asked.

Dirra stood up and walked closer to her to look at Tomar. "That's his colleague, Mirya-something. Lives near the main square."

"She's cute."

"And yet he hasn't made a single move," Dirra said, shaking his head. "She'll probably ditch him right about... now."

Once more, he was right—Tomar headed in one direction and Mirya in another. "She's going home while he's making his rounds during his break. It's pathetic. They're young adults, for gods' sake!"

"Maybe he prefers men," Berla mused.

"Maybe. Hey, I've got it, Reva! We'll place a cute male agent in the office and have him seduce Tomar! *If* there's something off about the boy, we'll get it out of him!"

"It's the Stoner Agency. Our guys wouldn't be able to keep up," Reva said, rolling his eyes.

"I don't care!" Dirra said, exasperated. "As long as I finally see some action! I'm literally dying of boredom here!"

He walked back to the card table, and they resumed their game. Half an hour later, both Tomar and Mirya made their way back to the office and sat down at their respective desks.

"They're back," Berla said before turning around and sitting down with the guys. "Alright, deal."

"That's the spirit," Dirra said with a derisive laugh as he shuffled the cards.

"How long?" Berla asked.

"Two hours," Reva responded.

They kept playing, only occasionally glancing in Tomar's direction to make sure nothing was happening. At ten o'clock, the bell sounded once more and Tomar made his way out of the office and toward the market district, his three shadows packing up and following him.

"What now?" Berla asked as the stalls came into view.

"He's going to stop at the third stall on the left, get some vegetables and a bit of meat, and then he'll head home via the main street, down to the southeast," Dirra predicted, and it happened just like he had said.

"You're not actually that good," Berla said. "Is the boy really this ordinary and predictable? Why are they having us follow him?"

"I have no idea. The big shots think there's more to him," Dirra said.

They kept following Tomar all the way home, where he entered his house and prepared and ate his dinner. They watched him clean the kitchen, reorganize his books, and make preparations for the next day.

"Is he always talking to himself?" Berla asked while looking at Tomar's lips moving even though he was all alone.

"Yeah, sometimes," Reva said. "He was stock silent for a week after his mother died, though."

"Right, the beast incident," Berla said. "Did you guys see it?"

"No, we had the day shift, and the others lost him."

Berla looked suspicious. "If he managed to shake your guys, maybe—"

"Have you ever had a night shift, Berla?" Dirra interrupted her. "It's even more of a snoozefest than this here. I wouldn't be surprised if our colleagues had fallen asleep after they realized nothing was going to happen."

"And all the boy and his mother did was go to a water source first thing in the morning. Not exactly suspicious," Reva added.

When it got late in the evening, Tomar finally sat down on his bed to read the new book he had gotten earlier.

"And curtain! That's it, lady and gentleman," Dirra said while mockingly bowing to the other two. "I'm going home."

"Dirra," Reva said, "maybe we should take this more seriously after all. We can't leave early every night."

"Come. On. You know what's going to happen! He's going to sit there, read without moving a muscle, and eventually fall asleep! I really don't need to be here for it."

"Ugh. You're right," Reva said while Dirra was already walking away. He turned to Berla. "Give my regards to the king."

"Right," she said sarcastically. "And mine to the High Priest."

After Dirra and Reva had left, Berla looked back at the boy through a window. She sighed and finally left as Tomar was nodding off.

Minutes after he had fallen asleep, Tomar's eyes shot back open. He got out of bed, left the house, and disappeared into the night.

* * *

I had gone to bed to read my new book and fell asleep quickly, but I suddenly woke up from a sharp pain in my arm.

"Ow! What—"

«SHIT!»

I was lying on a cold stone floor, and from behind, I could hear an ominous growl.

CHAPTER 15

MILES

Day 1

Sixty-one years. That's how long I had been alive for when I lost control over my bodily functions. I wasn't able to move or talk... I couldn't even blink. Not of my own volition, at least.

«Huh?»

The last thing I remembered was that I had been in the hospital for a routine procedure. The guy before me now did not look like a doctor, however. I wasn't religious, but if I had to say, he looked like a priest.

«What is going on...?»

The presumed priest stepped closer. I tried to speak, but nothing came out. I tried to move, but nothing happened. My head moved by itself and my eyes fell on his face.

"I didn't notice any signs indicating what Calling you received, but the shard has disappeared and the look on your face tells me the ritual is over. Please tell me the Calling the gods saw fit to bestow upon you."

Calling? Gods? Why can't I speak?!

«Hello?!»

A voice did eventually leave my mouth, but it wasn't mine. It sounded like a teenager, and he seemed confused as well.

"W-Was the ritual really a success?" the voice said.

Weird room, an altar, a priest...

I wanted to get a better look at my surroundings, but all I could do was stare at whatever my eyes decided to stare at. It was unnerving, to say the least.

The priest and "I" talked about some kind of ritual failing. But while the voice sounded confused at first, I felt like its owner was hiding something from the priest. The outburst about wanting to help its mother seemed a bit forced.

However, the priest believed the voice or... the boy? *Me?* No—I had to realize. This clearly wasn't *my* body. I was seeing through someone else's eyes as we turned around, walked out of the room we had been in, past dozens of people, and exited the building.

«What the fuck?!»

We walked across a large town square, surrounded by an eclectic mix of architecture surrounding us. There were buildings that appeared to have jumped straight out of a medieval fantasy, while others looked sleek and almost modern. These constructions, reminiscent of the 21st century, felt entirely out of place in this setting.

The collection of people we passed was just as diverse. Some wore simple, homely clothing, and others fine and elaborate garments. The modern-style suits in particular threw me off, not having seen anything like it in medieval depictions before. And then there were the guards, marching through town in glimmering chain mail and dark leather armor.

My mind swam as we left the street we had been walking along on and headed into an alleyway. We sat down and stared at the floor. Was this a dream? Maybe I was in a coma? *Can someone please get me out of this?* I thought.

«Hey! Can anyone hear me?!»

We stood back up and kept walking down the street, then we took a turn down a side street. After a while, we arrived at a simple house built from wood. We walked through the front door and a middle-aged woman in an apron came out of another room.

"Tomar!"

Is that the boy's name?

"I... I received the Mad Calling, Mom."

Tomar sounded like this was the worst news anyone could ever deliver to someone. His mother's reaction was on the same level. She was deeply shaken. They started talking about "Callings" and "rituals" until Tomar said something of vital importance to me.

"Mom... I'm hearing a voice."

«You can hear me?! Please talk to me. What is going on here?»

That's how I met Tomar and Phiona. By all appearances, I was stuck in the boy's body for the moment. The two of them didn't know how to get me out, and the people who *might* have known would apparently kill us at the mere mention of Tomar hearing a disembodied voice. I didn't know how credible these two were, but they sounded genuine. I didn't have much of a choice but to trust them for now, begrudgingly.

I quickly hit it off with Phiona, however. She had been the one to suggest talking to me, and she was more than willing to shower me with information about their world. She seemed intelligent in comparison to her supposedly fifteen-year-old son, who often seemed a little slow on the uptake. As they told me more about the Callings and how they gave people knowledge, I assumed that was the reason. *If you get all that for free, there's not much reason to study. Guess that makes sense.*

The kicker was when they mentioned that the ritual had been at noon, and that Tomar had arrived just on time, at strike eight o'clock. The date and time system they use is weird. They explained that an hour consists of sixty-four minutes, a day is sixteen hours, a week is eight days, a month is thirty-two days, and a year is eight months. It seemed like a prank by some computer nerd. If I had to guess, I would say a minute felt about the same as a minute I was used to. But given the other numbers, a fifteen-year-old would not have been alive for the same amount of time as a fifteen-year-old in my world. Instead, it would be about half that. *In a way, Tomar is only seven-and-a-half years old...* I thought.

I didn't understand much about this world yet, but I grasped the vital importance of Callings. The world was dangerous, and citizens had to do their part. For that, they were expected to start working at fifteen, but that would only be truly viable with the Callings. *Can't build a society on the backs of people that are mentally seven.*

As it was in my best interest to help Tomar with this problem, I agreed to fake a Calling. Unfortunately, I had yet to see a single piece of advanced technology here, and Phiona didn't know what a computer was. Fortunately, I had developed programs for hundreds of companies in dozens of fields over the course of my life and had collected a lot of theoretical knowledge. Additionally, I had one more strength—math.

Then the cruel jokes continued. I was a mathematics major and had been a programmer for almost forty years, but I had never *needed* to calculate in octal before. I found it beyond hilarious.

«Ha! Octal? This is amazing.»

And they were dead serious about it. When their neighbor, Gean, strolled in and demanded we solve problems, he expected us to even calculate floating-point numbers. In octal. That one had thrown me off a little momentarily, but I managed somehow.

The last test he gave us made my imaginary eyes go wide. For the first time all day, I had seen characters I was familiar with. They were part of an esoteric programming language called Omega that uses elaborate drawings and diagrams to design programs that kind of look like magic circles.

He said he wanted us to solve the equation. Its structure was a little weird, but I understood what the mix of math and Omega script was supposed to do. However, I had my doubts that he actually wanted us to solve it. I told Tomar to feign ignorance.

Even though it had been the right choice, I later learned that they do actually use Omega for something here, which threw me for a loop once more. My answer being correct was pure luck. I had assumed he wanted to test us by showing us this, waiting for me to reveal myself. But since Omega existed here, it could've gone either way.

The Callings, the rituals, Mad Ones, and Omega, they all appeared connected somehow. And maybe they would be my way out of this.

Night 1

When we got home, Tomar fell onto his bed and was out like a light. With his eyes closed, I was "sitting" in darkness, waiting to become drowsy myself.

However, that never happened. At one point, I heard the front door open, followed by the door to Tomar's room. His mother had presumably come home, but she let him sleep.

After what felt like hours, I got really bored. Just out of curiosity, I screamed "Hey!" in Tomar's mind, but he didn't react. More time passed before I finally noticed something. Whenever I was bored, I would play around with my hands. Maybe fold them, drum on the table... and I realized Tomar's hands were moving. I willed them to stop, and they stopped. I tried to open Tomar's eyes, and slowly but surely, his room came into view, dimly illuminated by the moonlight shining through the window.

I tried to get up, but I was struggling. Moving this body was incredibly awkward. For one, it felt different from moving my own body somehow. It wasn't as intuitive, as I had to deliberately control every action at first. The other part was that Tomar's body proportions were nothing like my own. He was maybe a hundred and eighty centimeters in height, a little scrawny and young. It was a stark contrast to my old, *old* body. I had been almost two meters tall and was very "dedicated" to my job, making me more chubby than anything else. It felt like nothing was where it was supposed to be. Eventually I managed to rise up out of bed and started looking around. Tomar's room was very simple. A bed, a wardrobe, and a desk. That was about it.

After getting used to moving around a little, I started examining my surroundings in more detail. I walked out of Tomar's room, checked the rest of the house, looked out the windows, and took a peek at some cupboards and drawers. When I found a mirror, I stared into it for minutes, an unfamiliar face looking back at me. It was kind, but the strong jawline and piercing eyes made Tomar look more mature and reliable than my initial impression suggested.

Despite their weird time system, my host *did* look like a fifteen-year-old, and Phiona had looked her age as well. I touched my face, trying to determine if this was real. I had been here for hours, and everything was so vivid and detailed that I could only come to one conclusion. This wasn't a dream.

Day 2

I decided not to reveal my ability to control Tomar's sleeping body just yet. It definitely would have freaked him out, but more importantly, I still didn't know what exactly I was dealing with here. If these two suddenly decided to act against me, this could be my ace in the hole. After all, I was still an uninvited guest, and it appeared that my mere existence caused Tomar pain. If it were me, I'd try to get such a voice out of my head by any means necessary. They needed me for now, but who knew how long that would last.

When we finally arrived at the water source, I was immediately slack jawed.

«Hey, wait! What is this?»

"The water source. This is where you get water."

Do you think I'm stupid? I can see that!

«I mean the Omega script! Those are the sigils you were talking about?»

An Omega script. Just like the ones from my world. I immediately understood about a fourth of the program, but unfortunately Omega relies heavily on pre-defined functions, variables, and systems. While I could *read* the program, I couldn't say what every part of the script did just yet. I would have to study it.

Tomar called Omega "scripture sigils," a term that was apparently used by the temple. He basically knew nothing about the script itself. He couldn't read it, didn't know what it did, and as far as he knew, nobody else knew anything either. To him, it was decorative scribbling.

«Decorative, huh? Hahaha.»

My mission was clear. Learn more about Omega, the water sources, the temple, and anything else that might help me get out of here in one piece. *But theorizing without a rubber duck to bounce ideas off of is boring...* I thought. In lack of a ducky, Tomar would have to do.

Our first tests weren't promising. No matter what we tried to apply Omega to, nothing happened. I was missing something, and I started tuning out anything Tomar was doing, to concentrate on the water source script that I had memorized. I took it apart sigil by sigil in my mind, tried to glean their meaning, how they related, and how they affected the flow of the program.

It was difficult to keep up the concentration when my rental body constantly moved around on its own. Looking here, touching there, talking to people, hearing, smelling... all while I was trying to think. I was regularly interrupted.

"But if it *were* possible, we could have our own water source in the backyard," I heard Phiona say with half a mind.

Flexible water sources would indeed be a revolution to this world that didn't seem to have running water of any kind. All she was considering at the moment was having a cube that gave water in her backyard, but there was so much more one could potentially do.

«Or the kitchen. And the toilet,» I added before tuning them out again.

Night 2

Tomorrow we would go to the Job Agency. That would take some time, so I decided to sneak to the water source in the middle of the night to do more research. They had a curfew here, but as long as you avoided the patrols, it wasn't too difficult to move around. And by the second night, I had a decent amount of control over Tomar's body.

I arrived at the water source and looked it over. There was nothing on it except the script above the hole that the water came out of. I took a blue stone that I had taken from a bowl in the kitchen, placed it on the cube, and inspected the hole. Based on the script, that cavity wasn't exactly defined as the output for the water. I guessed it had just been placed there to let the people know where the water would come from, and my suspicion was confirmed when I noticed the water appeared from the middle of the hole. It didn't really come out of the cube. *This is basically magic...* I thought. Omega was a fitting choice for this application.

I walked around the cube and examined every part. I kicked it, licked it, hid from a guard, and walked around it some more. It looked like some kind of black quartz, and it tasted like quartz too. Assuming that it was, I was missing something else.

Using a knife, I scratched away part of a sigil without damaging its form too much. I tested the water source to make sure it was still operational and then examined the paint I had scraped off the cube, but it looked and smelled ordinary to me. *That's not it either, then?* Unsure of what I was missing, I turned around and walked back to Tomar's home, deep in thought.

Day 3

Tomar wanted to talk to me about our situation this morning, but I cut him off, saying I was working on it. I was sure Omega would be the key to solving this whole thing. They used "magic" to get water, and they used what sounded like a magical ritual to receive Callings. Or rather, based on the description and what had happened to me, the ritual probably merged other people's memories and abilities into the citizen's bodies and minds. Tomar's ritual had simply gone wrong somehow, and I entered his mind as a living merge conflict.

I would study Omega and figure out how it and the rituals worked. And then I could hopefully reverse the process. Though I would make sure that Tomar and his mother would be safe somehow. For now, he needed me as his Calling, to get and hold a job. I was sure we'd find a way around that, though. I was starting to warm up to them, and Tomar's reaction to hearing that I would be one hundred and twenty in his world was hilarious.

Night 3

The next night, I was standing in front of the water source once again. *What's so special about you?* I pondered. I hopped on top of the cube and sat at its edge, my feet dangling in the air. Then I leaned back and laid down on top of the water source, letting my thoughts wander as I stared up at the stars sparkling above. The sky here was always unbelievably clear. It was quite serene.

Suddenly, a pulse against my back interrupted the experience and brought my attention back to the cube. I thought I had imagined it, but after a moment, I felt it again. I put my ear to the water source and kept listening. *One beat every two minutes. Is this thing alive?*

Day 4

Tomar was slowly starting to understand Omega. Since I hadn't been merged properly, I figured my knowledge might seep into him over time. I also decided to reveal the cube's presumed heart. It was more fun to theorize together, and maybe he would have ideas I couldn't think of, being an inhabitant of this world.

Trees, the things I really wanted to test, were sadly out of reach, but while we were at the market, I saw a stand with vegetables and had Tomar buy a tomato. It might not have been the whole plant, but I had heard somewhere that fruits stay alive for a while after getting picked.

"You paid *how* much for a tomato?!"

Unfortunately, the tomato test was unsuccessful, and all we got from it was a lecture about money and prices of common goods. *Sorry, Mom—er, Phiona...*

Night 4

I wanted to at least *see* a tree. If they weren't what I was expecting, maybe it would be pointless to even try to get to them. This world was similar enough to my own, but who knows.

Making my way from Tomar's home down to the south wall, I had to avoid more guards than I usually had to when going to the water source at night. They were more active the closer you got to the wall.

Eventually I managed to get there, but I didn't find a way to get up onto it that wasn't guarded. Suddenly there was a noise that startled me, and I noticed a guard on top of the wall looking in my direction before running toward a tower. I assumed he had seen me, so I ran back home as fast as I could. I heard the guards move around outside after I was back in bed, but it seemed like we were in the clear.

Day 5

A little girl by the name of Riala was accompanying us on our way to the water source. Apparently, Tomar was helping her and her sister from time to time. I wasn't much of a fan of children, but she was kind of sweet. What perplexed me was when Tomar suddenly told her about our experiments. *That's not knowledge you should share so freely,* I thought.

This had been a slip-up on his part. Given his more careful nature, that had been unexpected. However, if I had to say, I wouldn't exactly call myself careful. A little secretive, maybe, but when it came to programming, I would quickly jump into any discussion about it. This new side of Tomar could very well have been another side effect of the ongoing merge, with his confusion stemming from the opposing instincts he was fighting against. *He apparently knows this girl well, he trusts her reasonably enough, why not share?* It was certainly something I might've done.

Before he fell asleep that night, Tomar mumbled about an idea he had. Since I didn't have any other concrete plans for the moment, I waited for him to wake up again.

Day 6

For the first time, we used Omega successfully. All we got were a few drops of water, but it was all the confirmation I needed. Our theory was sound.

Tomar had brought us to this garden and its weird, large plants all on his own. It had been a good idea to include him in my process.

Unfortunately, his newfound enthusiasm was nowhere to be seen when I suggested modifying the water source for further tests, now that we knew that the script was working and doing what we thought.

«I'm certain it will be fine!»

"No."

He wouldn't budge. We talked about trees again, and there was a remote chance that we might be able to see some during our job, but it was just that. A remote chance. I wanted certainty, and I wanted it now. Surprisingly, Phiona had suggested that we use a different water source, one with much less importance placed on it. What was even more surprising was that Tomar ended up agreeing. We were back to theorizing, and for the second night in a row, I didn't go out. Instead, I waited patiently for the morning to come.

Day 7

Phiona was dead in Tomar's arms. He wasn't crying; he wasn't moving; he was just sitting there, holding her.

When the beast had killed Phiona, Tomar was on the verge of blindly running toward her, but I managed to get his attention. At my instruction, he jumped toward the water source, just as the beast was launching at him as well. In those precious seconds where the monster was confused and looking around, I gave Tomar new parameters for the script, which he quickly put in place. Just as the creature turned around to attack us again, an incredibly fast and thin stream of water shot out of the cube and into the beast. It was still moving, but it was in pain and appeared unable to stand up.

It was a lucky shot. The beast had been just in the right spot, we had just the right script queued up, and there were minimal modifications to make. A second less, or a stroke more, and we would've died as well.

Since the beast had ceased its attack, Tomar finally crawled over to his mother and took her into his arms. Minutes later, the guards arrived and dealt the finishing blow to the beast. Tomar was entirely unresponsive to any attempt at communication, both from the guards and from me.

He had me really concerned when, hours later, he got up to get the suit he had ordered, which he would've needed on his first day at work... but it didn't come to that.

Day 14

After Zara and Riala had brought Tomar back home with them, they took care of him for almost a week, until one morning he finally reacted again. It was as if he had been asleep the entire time. In fact, he had been so out of it that I was controlling his body at times. Finally being able to talk to him again came as a relief. He was still mourning, but in time, he would get better. And then we could resume our experiments.

Day 16

Tomar revealed that he had no intention of doing any tests or experiments anymore. He was deeply scarred—I knew that—but I still snapped at him. My situation hadn't changed. Not only was I stuck in his mind, I believed Omega to be the solution to that problem. Not to mention that our experiments were also the only thing I had here. Was this supposed to be my future? Helping a boy do his homework? *That doesn't work for me. Sorry, Tomar.*

Night 16

Finally, I was back at the chained water source. The guards had apparently increased their patrols, but they seemed more concentrated in the south, making it easy enough to sneak around further north. I continued where

Tomar and I had left off a week ago, but I first had to scratch away the script again, because it had been restored with paint.

This had actually been one thing I was interested in. What would happen if the script was damaged? The people here apparently didn't understand the script, but there weren't any special requirements to modify this "magic tool." As long as you painted the sigils on correctly, the water source would work. Apparently they had people who were capable of that much. Not that it would take more than a template on paper and a steady hand.

I replaced the water source script with another one using chalk. When I activated it, I could feel the mana stream out of the cube again. As I waved my hand around, I peered around the square carefully, but I was alone—there were no beasts in sight. I breathed a sigh of relief and continued on with my experiments. *Would've sucked if a beast had appeared again right now,* I thought with a chuckle.

So far, this script has given me the most important hints I had about how the water sources functioned. Based on our experiments, I was assuming that not everything had "mana" inside it. At least not to a degree that would be enough to produce any kind of effect with an Omega script. I could also deduce that mana was not some mysterious force inside the cube that did magical things. It would freely stream out of the cube if you told it to. Combined with the fact that this water source was known to give limited amounts of water, this meant the mana was something that was stored, let out, and then had to be recovered over time.

An important puzzle piece that was still missing was the purpose of the stones. They acted as the trigger for the scripts, but that turned out to just have been for ease of use. You place a stone, you get water—a straightforward and easily understood concept. It was Tomar's question about whether this was actually necessary that made me look into it again. As it turned out, the stones weren't necessary. I was able to modify the script in such a way that made it run indefinitely without a trigger, and as a result, all it did was output mana. That meant Tomar's other theory was probably right as well. If a script running without a stone produced nothing but mana, the stone must be the key ingredient for the conversion.

I missed working with Tomar on this, but for the moment, this was how it had to be. There were only a few hours left until I had to return my shell to its bed, but I was making progress again—at last.

Night 20

Every night afterward, I was out the door as soon as I gained control of Tomar's body. After I had spent an entire week letting him rest, getting back to scripting had been a treat. A boring job during the day and an interesting one at night. I was starting to feel like myself again.

Weaving through the streets and alleyways, I avoided the patrols with ease. The guards really weren't much to write home about. They always took the same routes at the same times, but they were probably more on the lookout for beasts than people. Maybe their routine would work for that purpose. However, for a human, avoiding them became child's play if they paid attention.

I arrived at the water source and immediately set up. Ever since I started working here at night, I'd always clean up after myself, leaving the water source in a functioning state. I figured the citizens wouldn't care much about the chalk, as long as the water kept running. Based on my script still being there, I had probably been right. I took another quick look around, but I was all alone. *Let's see...*

The first test that I had planned for today was what I came to think of as "multi-scripting." Both the water source and the ritual platform had only one script on them. I had kept it that way until now, but it was time to test whether it actually was a limitation. At least I didn't see a reason for that in the script. It defined the surface where the stone would have to be placed and where the water would come out, but I didn't have a reason to believe that it wouldn't work with two scripts at the same time.

I went to the opposite side of the cube and drew the same water source script, but with the output set to this side of the cube. When I placed a blue stone on top, water streamed out of both holes at once. *Eureka!*

In that moment of happiness, I heard a weird noise in the distance. I didn't see anything, but it *did* make me a little nervous. *Late at night... Alone at the water source... No guards in sight...* I thought. *Yeah. Okay. It is a little scary.*

Now that I knew I could run multiple scripts on one cube, I decided to dedicate a portion of it to scripts I could use to defend myself. That had worked once, and it would work even better now that I was prepared for it. After learning that I could activate specific scripts by giving specific input locations, I prepared two in case of an emergency. That should be enough, even if two beasts were to appear. That taken care of, I joyfully went back to doing tests on the remaining sides.

I was just playing around with the output angles of the water streams when I heard a voice behind me. "Tomar, what are you doing?"

My eyes went wide as my head snapped around and I saw a young girl standing there. "What are you doing here, Riala?!"

"I saw you go out and wanted to see where you were going," she said innocently. "Are you researching again?"

"I am... But Riala, you shouldn't be here. It's after curfew."

"You're here too," she said with a pout.

Crap. What should I do? I thought. *Stupid question. I have to get her home.*

"You know what? You're right. We should both head home."

I stood up and took Riala by the hand before leaving for her house. I would have to be way more careful. If even some girl spotted and followed me without me noticing, I clearly wasn't the ninja I was envisioning myself to be. I had been careless because I wanted to get to the water source as soon as possible and only thought about avoiding the guards. *Stupid mistake.*

We hadn't even left the square yet when I heard the weird noise from earlier again. Looking around, I saw nothing at first, but soon noticed two dimly glowing red eyes staring at us from a dark alleyway. I stopped in my tracks and stared back at it, while Riala looked up at me inquisitively.

"What's wrong, Tomar?" she asked, before following my eyes and seeing the two red orbs approach us. Their owner stepped out of the shadows, revealing a black, wolf-like creature.

Again? You can't be serious! This can't be real...

Riala grabbed my arm and was about to scream when I put my other hand over her mouth. Leading her with the arm she was grabbing, I moved her behind my back to stand between the animal and her. The beast was just standing there, staring me down. Based on everything I had heard, they were supposed to attack on sight. Though, now that I thought about it, the creature had just stared at Tomar that morning as well—until Phiona put herself between him and the beast, knife in hand.

I glanced back at the water source. The wolf wasn't doing anything, but I couldn't just stand there. I slowly moved backward toward the cube. With every step I took, the beast took one as well. I froze once again when I heard a deep, scratchy voice. "Human smells funny." It was coming from the beast's mouth.

At that moment, the town's warning bells rang, and seconds later, a group of guards came running into the square, surrounding the beast. Another guard moved protectively in front of us. As soon as the line of sight was broken, the beast started growling.

My mind was racing. *Stay here or move closer to the water source?* Whatever happened, I had to protect Riala and Tomar. And in case the guards weren't up to the task, I would need the water source. *Moving it is.*

I lifted Riala and began creeping backward again, always keeping an eye on the guards and the beast. Four of them surrounded it, keeping it in check, while another tried to get hits in from its blind spots. The tactic seemed to work well enough to hold it off at first, but the beast didn't take any serious wounds. Seconds later, the first guard flew to the ground, deep gashes in their armor.

Fuck.

I turned around and ran to the water source while glancing back at the fight. Formation broken, the guards took more and more hits. As soon as I arrived at the cube, I sat Riala down and rotated it to point one of my attack scripts at the beast—the same script that had crippled the other one. I screamed at the guards, "Out of the way!"

It was unlikely they'd just listen to me, but my scream surprised them, especially the one guard who thought he was still protecting us. They lost their focus and backed away from the beast to regroup.

With a clear line of sight, I put a blue stone to the cube, and a stream of water penetrated the beast's body. It screamed in pain, but it didn't go down. The shot had been good—I was sure of that. It had hit the beast in almost the same location and at almost the same angle as the other one.

Panic filled my eyes. *It should've worked!*

The guards were confused for just a moment but quickly realized that I had attacked the beast. They tried to surround it again, but it made an enormous leap and landed just meters away from me, before launching and taking a swing at us with its claws. I grabbed Riala and tried to jump out of the way, but the beast scratched my arm deep. And with that, I lost control of Tomar's body.

"Ow! What—"

«SHIT!»

CHAPTER 16

AWAKENING

I was lying on a cold stone floor. Riala, who I was apparently shielding from something, was in my arms. Glancing over my shoulder, I saw a beast growling at us.

«Shit, shit, shit!»

My eyes widened as I shuffled back in a panic, only moving centimeters at a time while lying on the ground. Luckily, four guards came running from behind the beast and started attacking it, giving me a moment to get my bearings.

"Miles! What's happening?" I shouted.

«We don't have time for that! The beast has already killed one guard, they can't hold it off!»

I looked back at the fight, and they indeed appeared to be struggling. The beast seemed a little bigger than the other one and got in regular hits while also avoiding the guards' spears. Miles was right—it didn't look like they would be able to keep this up for long. I was paralyzed for a moment. My heart pounded in my ears, making it feel like the earth beneath me was quaking. I felt Riala squeeze my body, her eyes full of panic and fear. *Just like Mother.*

My eyes darted around, stopping on the water source and the chain. I clambered to my feet. Keeping my distance from the fight, I ran over to the chain and pulled the water source over to us. Someone had been hard at work, as the entire cube was full of scripts. "Tell me what to do!"

«Use the one on the left! Point it at the beast and put a stone on the marked area!»

Rotating the cube, I took a quick glance at the script to see where I had to place the stone, then pointed it at the beast. The script was a slight variation of the FRC script we had tried before. I didn't know what exactly it would do, but I had to trust Miles right now.

I was ready to activate it when I realized the guards would get caught up in whatever was about to happen. "Out of the way!" I yelled at them and the guards immediately jumped back as if we had practiced it. *Huh?*

When I put the stone to the cube, it vibrated for a fraction of a second before it crumbled and then blasted apart. A stream of water shot out its front, hitting the creature, while another wave hit me and Riala, sending us flying through the air before violently crashing into the ground.

I looked back at the monster. The stream had hit it square in the face, and a part of its head was missing. It was still staggering toward us, but it was on its last leg, and the guards were on it again immediately. Then I looked at the water source. It had disappeared completely. The only trace left was the chain that was lying on the ground.

"What was that script?" I yelled.

«…»

"Miles?!"

«I have no idea what just happened!» he said finally, the confusion obvious in his voice. «It was a normal script! Though I *did* crank up the force considerably…»

He messed up. Wait… When did we write that script? I had questions, but those would have to wait. "Riala, are you okay?"

"Yes," came a weak voice. She had hit the floor hard, and her arms were all scratched up, but she would be okay. We had protected her. We were alive.

I looked toward the fight again, and the guards were winning. The beast took their hits like they didn't even register, but it didn't try to hit back. It was focused on us, desperately staggering our way.

Suddenly, Riala started screaming. "Waaah!"

She was rolling on the floor while clutching her arms.

"What's wro—" I started, before my entire body started burning. "Ahhh!"

It felt like fire was flowing through me. Just like Riala, I was screaming in pain as I fell to my knees. The sensation quickly overwhelmed the girl, and she fell unconscious, but I held onto my senses somehow. A few seconds later, the pain started letting up for only a bit and I opened my eyes slightly, just for them to burn with the same searing pain. "W-What is this?" I yelled.

«I think...» Miles started.

The pain was lessening, but it still hurt a lot. I thought back to the days when only my head had hurt. That was most definitely preferable.

«Can you open your eyes? I think I saw something.»

I forced my eyes open, struggling through the pain, and ended up staring down at my hands on the floor. A white mist rose from my skin before evaporating into the air. Forcing myself upright, I looked around. Riala, and every blade of grass and flower surrounding the square, was exuding this mist as well.

As I glanced back at the guards, they finished off the beast. It was surrounded by much more of this vapor, while the guards had it to a much lesser degree. *Living things...* I thought.

"Is this... mana?" I asked, unbelieving.

«As good a theory as any right now. I think we should—»

The beast fell, and the guards immediately turned around to face me, weapons at the ready. They didn't approach; instead, they looked at me as if I were a beast myself.

"Don't move!" one of them shouted, a piercing glare in his eyes.

My mind was running a mile an hour. I didn't know how, why, or when, but I had to assume that Miles had modified the water script. I didn't know how I got here, but I had destroyed a water source and proven myself a danger to a strong beast. *If this doesn't scream "danger," I don't know what does.*

I looked around, searching for a way out.

«Other direction!» Miles said, and I turned my head to look at an alleyway. «We can lose them there, I scouted the area.»

"What? When?" I asked, confused by his words.

«Worry about that later! Take Riala. They're looking at her the same way!»

Surveying between her and the guards, I realized he was right. *Is it the mana?*

In one motion, I jumped to my feet, hefted Riala into my arms, and sprinted toward the alleyway. Despite the searing pain, my body felt lighter than usual. I reached the alley in seconds and kept running while I heard the guards give chase, accompanied by shouts.

"Stop right now!"

* * *

Running, running, and more running. I followed Miles' instructions and made my way through the alleys, streets, and small paths he pointed out until eventually, after what felt like an eternity, he told me to duck into a shed. I was panting heavily, but I couldn't hear the guards anymore. It appeared that we had lost them. As I laid Riala on the dirt floor, I sat down to catch my breath.

«We did it...» Miles said, but I wasn't listening properly.

I had yet to recover from what had just happened. The scene played over and over in my mind. Something was missing. *How did I get there?*

"Miles," I said angrily, still panting, "what the hell... did you do?"

I waited for him to say something—*anything*—to alleviate my anxiety. Several seconds passed before he finally answered. «I... Damn it... Your body, I can move it while you're asleep. I... I've been experimenting.»

Shellshocked, I stared at the shed's wooden walls. Confusion, betrayal, anger... It was difficult to pinpoint what I was feeling. A mix of everything, I guessed. I wanted to scream at him, but I had to stay quiet. Stay hidden. The guards were definitely still searching. I ended up just sitting there, fuming, while I was also still in pain. Not only from the mana but also from being flung around by the explosion.

"Since when?" I said in a low, emotionless voice.

«Since the beginning.»

The anger flared up even more. I was furious, but I had to keep pushing it down. "How many times have I almost been killed?"

«If we don't count our last encounter with a beast, this was the first time.»

Deep breaths. "Why?"

«...»

"Why?!"

«Was I supposed to stand idle? I was looking for a solution to everything! I didn't... I didn't think it was actually that dangerous.»

My tone turned venomous. "Even after Mom's death?"

«You didn't remember... We killed a beast! We did! And technically, it wasn't difficult! I thought we would be safe enough...»

Realization struck me like a brick, momentarily blowing away my anger. We had just killed a beast, and it wasn't the first time. Granted, we had blown up a water source to do it, but that was more of a mistake. *We. Have. Killed. Beasts.*

The anger came right back as I looked at Riala in her battered up state. "Why was Riala there?"

«She followed me. I didn't notice... I was about to get her home when the beast appeared.»

This situation was unreal. He told me what "I" had been doing while I was asleep. I had run around town, played around with water sources, and risked not only my life but also hers. I looked at my hands again, which were still exuding this weird mist. It hadn't stopped yet, and it didn't seem to abate. I was hiding in some shed, gods know where, I was in pain, I was exhausted, and the guards were searching for me.

"Was it worth it?" I spat.

«Tomar, I'm sorry. I really am.»

"Did you have *any* plan for this turn of events?"

Miles hadn't thought about it. He thought he would figure out Omega, find a way to split our minds, and as soon as we had found a way for me to live a normal life, he would be gone. That was the primary plan. After I had refused to continue the experiments, the fallback plan was to continue in secret, blasting away beasts should they actually appear, and then making a run for it before anyone saw him.

"That's it? That was your grand plan?"

It would've been funny if it hadn't been so stupid. I thought Miles was smart, calculating, and that he always thought ahead. But this had been idiotic, plain and simple. He had nothing to say in his defense. He even agreed with me.

"Can you move my body while I'm awake?"

«Huh?»

The change in my tone of voice and questioning seemed to confuse him. We were in an unpleasant situation, and as I kept calming myself, I kept coming back to one question. *What now?* I didn't have time to endlessly admonish him. We had other things to worry about, and I would make sure that he did his part.

«Not really. I think. The only time I ever tried was when you were out of it for days... sometimes it worked and I helped you eat or get dressed.»

I needed more information. Would trusting him put me at risk? Would I have to worry about suddenly doing something I didn't want to do?

I raised my arm. "Move it."

Nothing happened. After a few seconds of waiting, Miles said, «I can't. »

I had felt a slight twitching in my muscles, but my arm hadn't moved. It was possible that he was lying right now, but as far as I knew, all cards were on the table. We were screwed if we didn't work together. That much he would understand.

"Try again," I said, after changing how I thought about my arm. I tried picturing that it wasn't actually a part of my body, as if I shouldn't have control over it. Suddenly, my arm, hand, and fingers started moving and clutching. *Huh.*

"You can do it if I allow it..." I said. I took back control of my arm and stared at the floor. *What now... What would Mother do?*

"Ugh... Ow..." Riala said from beside me. She tried opening her eyes, but immediately shut them again as tears started flowing down her face.

I patted her on her head.

"Tomar? Everything hurts..." she said with a sob.

"I know... I'm sorry, Riala."

"What happened?"

"That's complicated... I will try to explain it later, okay? Come here."

She was still keeping her eyes shut, so I propped the young girl up, leaned her against me, and tried to calm her. "Everything will be fine..." I said, followed by an almost inaudible "Somehow..."

CHAPTER 17
NEXT STEPS

"Could you repeat that?"

"Yes, sir. According to our guards, the suspect used the water source as a weapon to attack a category three beast and nearly killed it."

Captain Lera was speechless as he looked at the target of the supposed attack. It had a round hole in its chest, similar to the beast from two weeks ago, and a part of its head was missing. According to the reports, both wounds had been caused by water shooting out of the water source, which had apparently been destroyed during the second shot. His guards couldn't explain how this had been accomplished, but with four eyewitnesses, there wasn't much room for debate.

"And the suspect is Tomar Remor?"

"Yes, sir. The description matches him. A young girl was with him, but we have yet to identify her."

Two beasts, two attacks, similar wounds, and both were linked to Tomar Remor. Captain Lera had already been suspicious after the first incident, but now he had proof.

He looked at the chain that the water source had been attached to. The last time he had been here, the cube was scratched up, and the sigils had partially been replaced with chalk. If the suspect had done something to the water source to make it behave in this unusual way, it might be connected to the sigils. His guards hadn't paid attention to the cube tonight, but he was sure that it couldn't be a coincidence.

"Get me the priest who restored the sigils after the last incident," Captain Lera ordered.

The guard saluted and left immediately.

Based on everything that had happened, the captain had considered the possibility of Tomar being a Mad One in disguise. Now, however, he had no idea what he was dealing with. The boy was a potential threat and had to be apprehended. But if he had really altered a water source, there would be value in catching him alive. Captain Lera left the scene to update his men and the king. It would be a long night for them.

* * *

I woke up in the shed, with Riala leaning against me. It was still dark, so I couldn't have been asleep for long. I hadn't planned to nod off, but it must've happened while I was trying to calm her.

"You didn't move me," I said.

«No...»

We sat in silence for a while. I wasn't sure where to go from here. The pain had subsided substantially, but the mist was still on Riala and me. I couldn't say if it would become harmful, but for the moment, it seemed to be fine. However, the situation was anything but.

I had fled from the guards. Even though I had feared for my life, for our lives, it might've been a mistake. Had there been other options? I could've tried to explain things. Maybe that my Calling gave me knowledge about the sigils. That wouldn't even have been a lie, and I wouldn't have to say anything about a voice in my head. But my mother and I hadn't thought that approach through yet, when we had talked about what could be done with the water sources. The temple would be in an uproar about modifying scripture sigils. In addition to that, what I had demonstrated earlier was not a fun little script, but one that could kill a beast. As weapon possession was illegal for civilians, I couldn't imagine them looking kindly at some kid who could turn a water source into a dangerous weapon. *If you lined up a few people in front of it...*

This led me to only one conclusion. Fleeing, at least for the moment, had been the right choice. Best-case scenario, they would've arrested me, and I could still try to surrender peacefully. Maybe that would even work better when the guards weren't as agitated.

Next question, what would I do now? I looked down at Riala. She would have to be the priority. I couldn't drag her into whatever was about to happen. I would have to get her home. At the same time, Zara had been somewhat of a friend. Maybe I could hide there for a bit to gather my thoughts. Staying in one place for too long would make it easier for them to find me, so I needed to get out of the shed. *Sounds like a plan.*

The last problem was Miles. Just briefly thinking about what he had done made me angry, but I was also stuck with him. Perhaps I would've left him right here and now if I could, but that wasn't an option. And whatever happened next, I would most likely need him, especially if I wanted to pretend to have received some "Sigil Researcher Calling." I didn't have enough knowledge about Omega. I could draw a script or two, but it wouldn't be enough to be convincing. Not to mention that I would also lose the ability to do my job without him, which would be equally suspicious.

As I was contemplating my situation, I had another question. *Was my mind always this clear?* I went through my problems and options step by step and quickly came to reasonable conclusions and solutions. At least temporary ones. Was it just that I was forced to think for myself? Or was there more to it? This I didn't have any answers to yet.

In any case, I needed Miles, and he would need me, one way or another. It would come down to trust. Would we fight each other or cooperate? We both had our advantages over the other, but it would be easier for everyone involved if we worked together. My mind was made up.

"Miles," I said in a quiet voice, as to not wake Riala. "I need you to promise me something. Never use my body like that again. You said you're sorry, right? Prove it. In turn, I promise that we'll get you out of there, sooner or later."

He didn't say anything at first, but eventually responded. "I promise."

Miles was quiet, but it was different from his usual quietness. He wasn't distracted or secretive. Instead, he sounded deeply apologetic. He had royally messed up, and he knew it. Saying that I fully trusted him would've been too much, but I would try. *Like Mother would.*

* * *

Oryn Tilia had been woken up in the middle of the night by a guard and was escorted to the eastern guard station. With a sleepy face, disheveled hair, and a white robe that he had hastily put on, he stood before Captain Lera.

"You restored the chained water source two weeks ago?"

"Yeah," Oryn said with a small yawn.

"Was there anything unusual about it?"

Oryn's ears perked up. *The water source? Unusual?* There had indeed been something unusual, and now he was being questioned by a guard, right after a beast had appeared. He knew something must've happened.

"Well, the scripture was mostly gone, parts of it replaced with chalk. Unfortunately, that happens from time to time. However, the replacement sigils were drawn very well, and there was one sigil I have never seen before."

This was another confirmation for the captain's theory. The scripture had been changed and there had been unknown sigils on the cube. Even though they didn't have all the details yet, they could assume that Tomar would be dangerous while in the vicinity of water sources. This was all the information he needed.

"Thank you," Captain Lera said. "You may go now."

"That's it? What—" the priest started, but the captain had already started to walk away.

Oryn was wide awake now. Something was happening, but he wouldn't get any more answers here. As the one responsible for restoring damaged sigils on divine instruments, his curiosity had been piqued. He would have to send a report to the High Priest.

* * *

A guard stood in front of a house and knocked on the door. It was early morning, when not everybody would be awake yet, but the door flew open right away.

"Have you found my sister?" a young woman asked.

"I'm sorry, Ms. Fera, we haven't found her yet. However, a young girl was seen at the scene of tonight's beast incident. She was with a suspect we assume to be Tomar Remor. Based on your description, it could've been your sister."

When Zara had woken up to the warning bells in the middle of the night, she had gone to check on her younger sister, but couldn't find her anywhere. Even though the curfew had still been in effect, she immediately ran out the door and went to the first guard she could find to tell them that Riala had gone missing. Given the situation, the guard let Zara go, but he asked her to stay home, while promising to update her as soon as he had any new information.

"She was there? Why was she with Tomar?" Her voice was a sullen mix of hysteria and crying.

Zara wanted to run out the door right away and find the two of them, but the guard stopped her. If Riala were to return home, it would be better for Zara to be here. Reluctantly, she agreed to stay back. She gave the guard a brief description of the relationship between Tomar and the sisters, and then the guard left. Seconds afterward, she heard the back door open. She had barely turned around when her sister flew into her arms.

"Sis!"

"Riala!"

Zara was ecstatic for a moment, but fear soon crept onto her face. She started shaking and slowly pushed the girl away by her shoulders to look at her. "W-What happened to you?"

She didn't know what it was, but something felt off about her sister. Her eyes grew wide as they fell onto another person who had entered the house. Whatever was going on with her sister, it was even worse with this boy. She pressed Riala against her again in reflex and shuffled backward to put more distance between them.

"T-Tomar?"

"Please don't be scared. Especially not of Riala."

"I'm okay, sis," the young girl said, hugging her sister.

"I don't have all the answers, Zara. But I'll try to explain as much as I can."

CHAPTER 18
TIME OUT

Zara appeared terrified, but thankfully she sat with me to talk. I kept some information to myself, but was forthright with her in the matters involving Riala. I revealed that "I" had researched the water sources with the help of my Calling, that her sister had learned of my experiments, and that she followed me there the previous night. I recounted the beast attacking us, me using the water source as a weapon against it, and how something had happened to us. It probably wouldn't have sounded very believable if Riala wasn't sitting right there with us, confirming my story—and if we didn't strike fear into her for reasons she didn't understand.

The most important piece of information was that the guards might come looking for Riala. If that happened, I didn't know what would happen next. Based on the reaction of Zara and the guards, I guessed that we felt like beasts to them, a foreboding air surrounding us. Until we found a solution to that, it wouldn't be safe to let her younger sister walk around outside.

I bowed my head slightly. "Zara, Riala, I'm sorry. I didn't mean for any of this to happen."

Zara had listened to everything I had to say in silence and looked scared for most of it. After I was done, however, I noticed her standing before me. I had just lifted my head to look at her when she slapped me hard across the face.

"How could you get Riala involved in that? She could have died! And now you're telling me to lock her up like some kind of monster?"

Riala jumped up and quickly put herself between us.

"Stop, Zara! It was my fault! I followed him!" she said.

I doubted Riala could truly understand what was happening right now. When she had woken up, I told her that something happened to us and that we would have to be careful about meeting other people, but that was about it. She was a little girl. I figured all she would care about was getting home to her sister.

"No, Riala. *He* is the one doing illegal things, and *he's* the one who got you involved. I want him out, right this second!"

Zara tried pushing Riala out of the way, but she wouldn't budge.

"Please let him stay awhile, Sis!"

The two of them struggled for a moment before Zara took a step back. "Why would I let him stay here?"

"Tomar saved me! A-and he saved the guards too!"

I hadn't gone into much detail during my explanation to Zara. Not that it would've made much of a difference coming from me. But from her little sister, it held some weight. Except that I didn't think it was Riala's fault. The way Miles had told the story, the beast had probably watched him for a while, but only showed itself when he was heading back with the girl. I should've corrected her, but the look on Zara's face told me that Riala's pleading was paying off. Desperation beat out honesty. *I have to talk to Riala later.*

Zara was struggling with what her sister had asked of her, but eventually relented. "When are you planning to leave?" she spat.

"Tomorrow morning," I said. I needed some time to think, a bite to eat, and some water. I had yet to come up with a follow-up plan, but if she was willing to grant me that much, it would be a start.

"Tomorrow morning," she said declaratively, taking Riala's hand and leaving the room.

«That could've gone worse,» Miles commented.

"Mm-hmm," I agreed.

* * *

Zara was anything but happy about me being here, but after hours of running, hiding, and sneaking around, her vicious stares were a small price to pay for being able to lean back and relax. Eventually, she allowed me to stay in their parents' former bedroom. She just wanted to get me out of her sight, but I was thankful nonetheless. Even though I couldn't fall asleep, lying on a soft bed and staring at the ceiling in peace was just what I needed.

"Do you think they will kill us on sight?" I asked Miles.

That was my greatest fear. We had avoided other people on the way here, but Zara's reaction had been eye-opening. It would be bad if others saw us the same way. However, if I could explain myself to the authorities, maybe they would be more understanding than I thought. My whole life I had heard stories about Mad Ones getting killed immediately; though that was under entirely different circumstances.

«Honestly, I don't know,» Miles said. «I want to say the worst that could happen is that they lock us up, but in my world, we wouldn't kill Mad Ones either if we could avoid it. If they're really that eager to take down any kind of danger to the citizens, anything is possible I guess.»

"I think I might've liked it better when you were certain about everything. It made me feel safe," I said with a sad smile.

«I won't lie to you again.»

"That's good too..."

The only way to truly get out of this would be to come clean, at least to some degree. I would have to go to the authorities and make my case. We had done something illegal—several things actually—but we didn't have bad intentions, and we didn't hurt anyone. *They have to see that. They just have to.*

"We'll go with that plan. We will surrender and hope for the best."

«Maybe we should prepare for the worst case, though.»

"How?"

«It was your theory that we appear to have mana streaming out of us.»

Mana... He was suggesting that we test Omega on my body again. That we use it as a water source, the "vessel" for a script. However, this brought back memories of the cube crumbling and then blasting apart. Not exactly something I would want for myself.

"I don't think that's a good idea. We don't know what will happen."

«We could start with a very simple script, a tiny amount of output, no force—something that would barely even register on a water source. Maybe it comes with some risks, but if we can truly use scripts, we could defend ourselves.»

Without more information, it would be impossible to say whether this idea was madness or not. Just like we didn't know what would happen once we'd reveal ourselves. However, if this worked, our chances of getting through the second part alive would be better.

"Does this actually make sense, or am I just talking myself into it because I'm curious?" I asked aloud without meaning to.

«If my theories are right, and you are taking over traits of mine, I think curiosity might be playing a big part,» Miles said. I felt like he was smiling a little.

Unfortunately, there was a hurdle. I explained to Zara what I wanted to test, and that I'd like to borrow a few blue stones for it, but she would have none of it. After hearing what had happened to the water source, she thought me insane for even asking, and I went back to the bedroom. There were blue stones at my house, but if the guards were still searching for me, they would probably be looking there. Maybe they were even monitoring the house. It also wasn't early in the morning anymore, and avoiding people would be much harder now.

That's when the door to the room opened and Riala slipped in, blue stones in one hand, ink in the other. She closed the door again and held the items out to me.

"You can have it if you let me watch!" she said.

"Riala... your sister isn't wrong. I have no idea what will happen. I can't let you get hurt again."

Her eyes bounced between her hands and me as she thought about something. With no warning, she sat down and started drawing sigils on her arm. "I will test it then!"

"Ah!" I jumped up and took the quill away from her before she could finish. As I let out a sigh of relief, I examined her arm. The script was practically perfect. "How are you this good?"

"I practiced!" she said with a toothy grin.

What is with this kid? I thought. Would she just try it on her own the moment I turned around? That could have ended very badly. She didn't know the meaning of the sigils, and if she made a mistake, then...

I can't let that happen.

"I will do it, but you need to promise not to try it yourself, okay? I'm serious. It's dangerous," I said.

"Okay!"

Did she just manipulate me? I thought with another sigh. I led her to one corner of the room while I went to another on the opposite side, so we would be as far apart from each other as possible. "Stay there."

I took the quill and listened to Miles' instructions. I was about to start drawing when I looked first at the quill in my hand and then at my arm holding it. "You do it," I whispered.

Goodwill, I thought. He would be faster, more precise, and wouldn't have to dictate everything to me first. Also, our differences had partially come from him being trapped in my mind with seemingly no hope of escape. Maybe this would help us. It was important to him.

Miles waited a moment and then started drawing an Omega script on the palm of my hand. One similar to that of a water source, but a few of the variables were different. It took him barely half the time I usually needed. When he was done, I held my arm forward, with my palm facing the floor.

As soon as I placed a blue stone on the back of my hand, the pain from last night came back. It wasn't as strong, but it was uncomfortable and the shock almost made me drop the stone. The burning sensation traveled through my body and to my hand, before I saw the stone grow smaller and a tiny amount of water streamed down from my hand to the floor. "Wow..."

After catching some of it with my other hand, I examined the water. It looked normal and smelled neutral. A taste test confirmed it was ordinary water.

Riala saw my amazement at the successful test and came running over. "Me too!"

In my excitement, I was happily about to draw the script onto her arm, but forcefully shook myself out of it. *What am I doing?*

"I can't, Riala. Your sister would kill me," I said, garnering a pout. That reminded me—last I heard, she had been ordered to stay in her room, forbidden from approaching me. Would Zara come looking for her?

"Actually, where is your sister?"

"She's getting more water," Riala said with a laugh.

«That's kind of funny.»

"That *is* kind of funny," I said, looking at the puddle on the floor.

* * *

"Captain Lera!" a guard said, jogging toward the captain. "We have received information that the suspect is hiding in a residence in the southeastern part of town!"

"Finally," the captain said. "Gather your men, Jara. We're leaving immediately."

"Sir, there's one more piece of information. We have been told the suspect... believes himself to be a living water source."

The captain was perplexed. "What is that supposed to mean?"

"We don't have any details, but the informant has talked to the suspect, and the boy has supposedly mentioned being able to turn his own body into a water source, that he is capable of producing water on his own."

This information was quite critical. The suspect, Tomar Remor, was believed to have destroyed a water source, as well as having used it as a dangerous weapon. As nonsensical as it sounded, if he could produce water on his own in the same manner, this boy might be more dangerous than he thought. Even without access to a water source, he couldn't take him lightly.

"Tell Eissen to gather his squad as well!"

"Yes, sir!"

CHAPTER 19

OVER

I looked at the puddles, then at my clenched hands. "So far, so good."

We had decided on a script that we would use to defend ourselves. While using them was uncomfortable, I felt fine. Even after repeated use, and with force applied to the water, the sensation didn't change. Meanwhile, Riala was still hopping around me, pleading to try it as well.

"Please, please, please!"

«You know, if we're leaving for the guard station soon anyway... I mean... Zara might be mad at us, but—»

"You're a bad influence."

Riala looked at me in confusion for a moment but jumped in happiness when I gave in to her pleas.

"Alright. We'll try it. But, Riala, it hurts a little—like last night. Is that okay?" I said, but my words didn't even register properly.

"Yes!" she said gleefully.

We got another Miles here...

We sat down, and I wrote a simple script on her hand that would do nothing but spray a bit of water in the direction she would point her palm. She looked on with great curiosity. "This part differs from yours. This too," Riala pointed out.

How attentive is this girl?

The sigils she was pointing at were for the force of the stream and the amount of water. The last script I had tested was for my self-defense. Since we were inside the house, I had kept these values low, but the current script on my hand would produce a much stronger water stream.

"That one is too powerful to use inside. We don't want to break anything, right?" I said, finishing the script. "Just point your hand forward like this and press the blue stone on the back of it with your other hand."

Riala stood up and did as instructed, raising her arm and holding it out toward the door. At the exact moment she used the blue stone, the door opened and Zara looked on in horror as water shot from her sister's hand and landed at the young woman's feet.

Uh oh...

While I was looking at the scene with wide eyes and gritted teeth, Riala ran up to her sister. "Sis! I can make water!"

Zara's eyes darted around between the puddle at her feet, her excited sibling, and me. Her expression turned from horror to fascination. Seeing someone produce water out of thin air, hundreds of meters away from a water source, would mesmerize anyone.

Maybe I should've approached this whole thing differently.

She got to her knees and looked Riala over. "Are you okay?"

"Yep!"

The fascination didn't last long, however. Anger flared back up as she looked at me next. "I told you I don't want you to do that in my house! And you even did it to her!"

"I'm sorry, Zara... I thought it would be better if I supervised her, instead of her trying it on her—"

"You shouldn't do this at all! Nobody should! I knew I should've never trusted you... You're just like him!" she yelled. "I've reported you to the guards!"

"Just like him?" I thought. I stared at her for a moment as I let the words sink in, wondering who she was referring to. Regardless, I understood the bit that mattered. It hurt a little, but I couldn't blame her. Whatever the mana was doing, it scared people. Not only that. I had also endangered her sister and told her every single illegal thing I had been up to.

"I understand," I said. "I'll leave."

As I stood up, I saw a squad of guards already approaching the house. "That was quick..."

«Would've looked better if we had gone to them.»

"Mm-hmm," I agreed.

Zara held Riala tight as she moved out of the way to let me walk toward the front door. I gave a sad smile as I waved at Riala and left.

"Tomar, don't go!" I heard her say from behind, but I walked on.

It'll be fine, I assured myself. I would explain myself to the authorities, and they would understand why I had acted the way I did. I was just a boy who got a Calling that allowed him to modify sigils. It was the first of its kind, and I was scared but also curious. They had to believe me. *They will. It'll be fine.* And as soon as the situation was cleared up, I could talk to them about Riala. I took a deep breath and opened the door.

* * *

A guard captain walked down a street with two squads of his men behind him. Such a display marching through town was rarely seen in these parts, and while the citizens readily moved out of the way, very few of them left. Instead, they watched on to see what was going to happen.

Captain Lera motioned one of his squad leaders to take position behind the house while he and the remaining squad came to a stop at the front. The guards formed two rows on either side of the path leading to the door, spears at the ready. The captain was about to announce his arrival to the people inside when the front door opened and a boy stepped out.

"Mr. Remor. You're under arrest. Raise your hands and come forward," Captain Lera instructed.

The last time he had seen the boy, he was unresponsive and barely functional. What the captain was looking at now was something else. Tomar had a fear inducing aura around him, similar to that of beasts. Yet his body language was non-threatening. He had expected the boy to either cower in fear or try to make a run for it. Yet he just stood there, seemingly at peace with himself, a hint of a smile on his face.

Tomar slowly made his way up to the captain, his feet softly thudding against the stone path. No sooner had he taken his fifth step, when a shout erupted from the house.

"Riala, don't!"

A young girl came running out of the house, raised her arms, and produced a large stream of water that blasted the captain off his feet.

One of the guards immediately incapacitated her with the blunt end of his spear, prompting Tomar to attack the guard in an attempt to protect her. Nevertheless, he was overpowered by the remaining guards before he could do anything.

The drenched captain stood back up and walked up to the children being held by the guards. "Listen, and listen well, Mr. Remor. I have orders to bring you in alive, but these are not strict orders," he said to the boy while holding up his head by the hair. "Handcuffs! And search them!" Lera ordered as he let Tomar's head drop into the dirt.

Their hands were bound behind their backs. The guards found several blue stones hidden in Tomar's clothes, leading the captain to the conclusion that he hadn't actually planned to come willingly. Riala didn't have any more on her, however.

"We're taking both of them!" the captain announced, walking away. His men hefted the boy to his feet and picked up the unconscious girl before marching after the captain in formation. Left behind was a devastated young woman.

* * *

"I don't care what your gods say, Orthur. The boy has broken town laws and will be judged by the authorities," the king said.

"The *town's* laws? He has broken the laws of the *gods*, using the holy scripture as a plaything for himself! It's blasphemy!" the High Priest said theatrically.

"A word spoken by your *ancestor* hundreds of years ago is hardly the word of the *gods*, High Priest Orthur. As much as you would like that," King Hertar said. "Let's be frank, shall we? We both were monitoring the boy, and my guards got to him first."

The High Priest was fuming. Tomar was out of his reach now. None of the major factions could act lightly against the others, and openly opposing another could quickly lead to war. His agents had messed up and didn't notice what the boy had apparently been up to. Had they been there first, they could've taken him into custody and the roles would now be reversed. The agents had already been dealt with, but that didn't change the situation. It also meant that the king would have to be careful about how he acted.

"I demand that you let us study him. Whatever he has done to himself is in direct contradiction with the teachings of the gods, and we will get to the bottom of it!"

Meaning you want to know how to get that power yourself, the king thought. However, the temple was in charge of the rituals and they were the only ones who even attempted to study the scripture sigils. That made his demand hard to refuse.

"Very well. You're allowed to study the boy in his cell, under supervision," the king agreed begrudgingly. This was a compromise neither party was happy with but both agreed to. The High Priest stomped out of the king's reception room, shouting at one of his subordinates to find a certain priest.

Meanwhile, the king turned to Captain Lera, who stood by his side. Just before the High Priest had stormed in, the captain was about to make a report.

"Have you gotten anything out of him yet?"

"He has been quite forthcoming, actually. He claims that his Calling gave him knowledge about the scripture sigils, but since this would be seen as blasphemous, he kept quiet. Instead, he snuck out at night to research the water sources, planning to release his findings to the public."

Tomar's story appeared to make sense on the surface, and unbeknownst to the king and the captain, parts of it were true. Nevertheless, the boy couldn't explain how he had gotten the power to use scripture sigils on his own body. Nor did he have any information on how one would build water sources. If his claims were true, he would know more. Instead, he had partial knowledge, like one might receive from reading books. As neither Tomar nor Miles knew what it was like to receive a normal Calling, they hadn't been able to consider how suspicious this would be to those familiar with the experience. The knowledge you had about a given field should be all-encompassing.

Tomar's crimes—from breaking the curfew to destroying a water source—were numerous enough to execute him immediately. That would've been standard procedure because the town wouldn't waste resources on long-time prisoners. But first, they would get everything they could out of him.

CHAPTER 20

Last Resort

I was chained to the floor inside a cold and dark stone room. The only light came from small slits in the wall that were too high to reach, and the only exit was a heavy wooden door. I had seen this building many times in the southeastern corner of the main square, but my mother had told me to stay away from it and I had done as she instructed.

They had paraded us through the main street like they usually did to criminals on the way to the prison. At first, people had looked curious when they saw the guards, but their expressions changed when their eyes fell on Riala and me. They looked at us with contempt and fear. My attempts at explaining myself and the situation had fallen on deaf ears. All that my repeated pleas got me was a guard punching me in the gut, which brought on cheers from the crowd.

Crimes in Alarna fell into one of three categories. The first were minor offenses, which were often punished with a warning or a fine. Examples of this included overzealous Charmers, not showing up to work, or being outside after curfew. The second category would get you jail time. This was typically awarded to repeat offenders. The last category was for crimes that endangered citizens. This included robbery, murder, attacking people, and whatever else the authorities deemed too dangerous. And this last one was what the authorities made a show out of.

I had wanted to come forth and admit to my category one and two offenses, and depending on how much they believed me, I hoped I wouldn't have to go to jail for long, if at all. Looking back, I had been naïve, and it certainly hadn't helped that I snapped when a guard attacked Riala. The way they had brought us here, separated us, put us in cells, and interrogated me, blew away all hope of leniency.

It was difficult to judge time in this cell, but it was already dark out, indicating that we had been here for the entire afternoon. I told Captain Lera that I just wanted to make people's lives better, and that I had only fled because I was frightened. I greatly emphasized how Riala was just a kid who had only followed and later tried to protect me. It hadn't felt like he believed me.

Miles and I had been thinking about our situation for hours. Maybe it hadn't been the greatest plan in the world, but I had wholeheartedly believed that there was a chance. Now, it felt like we would walk to the gallows in the backyard come morning.

"This time I messed up..." I said with a sad expression.

«The plan wasn't bad on paper. It's just... the execution didn't go smoothly.»

"I shouldn't have told him everything."

«Keeping quiet would've made you look even more guilty. You did nothing wrong.»

"Yet we ended up here."

«But we're still alive. This isn't the worst outcome.»

At that moment, the door opened to reveal two guards and a priest. The guards positioned themselves on either side of me, while the priest put a bucket down and sat on it to look me in the face.

"Mr. Remor, it's good to meet you! My name is Oryn Tilia," the priest said. "I've heard you were the one who altered the water source two weeks ago. I'm very excited to talk to you."

The priest's eyes immediately fell on the now blurred Omega script on my hand. "Oh! May I take a look at that?" he said, taking my hand and looking it over without waiting for a response. "Fascinating! I can't make out all of it, but this is the same scripture as on the girl's hand, isn't it?" he asked me as he compared the script to his notes.

My eyes went wide. "You saw Riala? How is she?"

"Riala! What a nice name. She was well when I arrived. Unfortunately, she wasn't willing to talk to me this evening."

"What do you mean by that? How is she *now*?"

"Don't worry, Mr. Remor, she is resting. Now, let's talk about the scripture. I'd really like to know how the two of you became able to produce water."

"I already told the captain that I really don't know. We were hit by the water source's blast, but I don't know exactly what that did to us."

"Yes, I've read the report. But, Mr. Remor, surely you must have an inkling."

That seemed to be all they were interested in anymore. Only this ability, not the sigils, which I would've seen as more interesting.

"Let me put it like this—would you be able to reproduce the effect?" the priest asked.

"Well—"

«Wait, Tomar. I have a bad feeling.»

Miles' thoughts boiled down to one question. What would they do with that information? We would have to destroy more water sources, but maybe it would give people the same ability. What would happen afterward, though? There were five more water sources in town, and they were vital to the citizens. The one in the southeast also saw too much use already. If you blew up another one, something or *someone* would need to take its place. Maybe they could make a job out of that, assuming it would be safe, but what would happen once that person became unable to do that job? What would they do once there were no more water sources? Would they... try to blow up a person?

"Mr. Remor?" the priest prompted, still waiting for an answer.

"Well," I started again a few seconds later, "that happened by mistake. I messed up the scripture and I don't know the exact sigils anymore."

Maybe our worries were unfounded, but the thought of what they might do was horrifying.

The priest looked at me inquisitively before he said, "You're lying, Mr. Remor. We'll come back to that. For now, I'd like to measure your volume."

"My... *what*?"

"Don't worry, I just want to know how much water you can produce."

The priest stood up and flipped the bucket over. He then took my hand again, washed away the script, and drew on the standard water source script. He then held my hand over the bucket he had brought and placed a blue stone on the back of my hand, producing a water stream.

"No matter how often I see it, this is truly marvelous," the priest said.

Once the bucket was filled, he had a guard dispose of the water and then started anew, filling it again. Then a guard disposed of the water, and he started again. Again. And again. After about fifteen buckets, the pain became worse, and my body tensed up every time he activated the script. After twenty buckets, I started screaming and stopped counting. I didn't know how much time had passed when he finally stopped, leaving me limp on the ground.

"My! Over one hundred and fifty liters! Mr. Remor, I'm impressed! Ms. Riala only made it to five buckets!"

I couldn't think clearly and I wasn't able to move or speak anymore. My body was completely drained. As I was falling unconscious, I had only heard his last words with half a mind, but I locked onto that one detail.

They did this to Riala...

* * *

Light was streaming into the cell when I woke up. I must've slept for hours if it was daytime now, but I still felt exhausted. I struggled slightly when trying to sit myself up.

"Ugh..." I grunted and looked around the cell. The guards and the priest had left. I was alone.

"Hey, Miles... Can you tell me what happened?" I asked, but there was no reaction.

"Miles?" I said worriedly. The silence was unnerving. He hadn't completely ignored me in days, and I didn't think he would do that in this situation. "Are you there?"

I thought I felt alone and helpless after my mother had died, but in this moment, in this cell, I learned what it truly meant to feel all alone. I sat in the dimly lit room, looking at the stone floor, when the door opened and a guard brought in a piece of bread and a cup of water. He put them on the floor a few meters in front of me and left.

"Wait, please! You—" I said, but he closed the door without listening to me. I crawled over to the food and started eating.

More time passed before I finally heard Miles' voice again.

«Tomar?»

"Miles! Where were you?!"

«I'm not sure... I became drowsy when the priest kept drawing water from us. It was kind of like a dream.»

My eyes teared up. "I'm glad you're not gone..."

«Me too... Did anything happen?»

"No. I—"

As if on cue, the door opened once again, and the captain who had arrested us walked in. "Good morning, Mr. Remor. I'd like to continue our conversation from yesterday," Captain Lera said.

"Continue? But I've told you everything!" I said.

"So you claim. But we both know you're lying, don't we? I'd like to give you one last chance to come clean."

The captain looked sure of himself. The problem was that I had told him the truth. The only thing I had kept from him was Miles. Should I risk telling him everything? Even if I did that, would it change anything about the situation? Would it not just add another problem on top of a growing pile? In addition to all the other crimes I had committed, they would probably brand me a Mad One. But what would happen if I didn't talk?

"Captain. Will I be... executed?"

The captain's eyes sharpened. "It depends. That would certainly be standard procedure, but we can't deny that you have a certain value. If you give us what we want to know, your fate might still change."

"What is it that you want?" I asked.

"*Everything* you know about the scripture sigils, the water sources, and your ability to produce water."

Everything...

«If we give them everything, they won't need us anymore, and they'll stay in control.»

They didn't intend to release me. They just wanted what Miles and I had, and then they could dispose of us. If they were to let me go, I would just be a liability. And not only me... Riala as well. She had refused to talk and didn't actually know a lot, but they had seen her use an unknown script. *We'll die if we stay here,* I thought. But whether we could leave wasn't our decision to make, was it? Miles kept giving me his thoughts.

"'Captain, I know you're lying as well,'" we said. "'I can accept my fate... but I want you to spare Riala. Promise me that, and I'll tell you everything I know.'"

The captain looked at me appraisingly, thinking over what I had said. "Very well. I promise the girl will walk free," the captain said.

"'One more thing... I'd like to say goodbye to her. Will you please let me see her one last time? I just want a few minutes to explain everything to her. She's just a kid... and she thinks this whole thing is her fault.'"

"That can be arranged," the captain said, walking to the door. He glanced back at me, but finally left, closing the heavy door behind him.

"Will this work?" I asked Miles while we were preparing for the captain's return.

«I have no idea. I also don't like the time of day, but we don't know what they will do next. We don't have much of a choice, right?»

"No, I guess not."

Minutes later, the captain returned. At his side was Riala, who was staring down at the floor with a blank expression. Her eyes were puffy and red.

"Riala!" I said, promoting her to look up.

"Tomar!" she said, tears flowing down her face as she ran toward me.

The captain stood in the open doorway while Riala hugged me. A few drops of blood fell from my chained hands. I leaned closer to whisper in her ear.

"I will try to get us out of here. When I say 'now,' get behind me, okay?"

She let go of me, brushed away some of her tears, and nodded. As she looked at me, she tilted her head. "Tomar, why are you smiling like that?" she asked quietly. "It looks kinda evil."

I looked away from Riala and fixed my eyes on the captain. "Now."

CHAPTER 21

JAILBREAK

At my command, Riala moved behind me. The captain looked surprised as I jumped to my feet and pointed my palm at him. I added one last bloody stroke to the script on the back of my hand, and a blast of mana erupted from my body, shooting in his direction. With no time to react, he was pushed off his feet and sent crashing into the wall on the other side of the narrow hallway. His body was held in place there until I disabled the script by wiping away part of the blood I had drawn it with.

«That was awesome...» Miles hummed in wonder.

"Awesome..." Riala said, perfectly in sync with him.

"Not the time!" I said, fixing the script to activate it again.

While I had been fast asleep every night, Miles had figured out how to activate scripts without stones. They only produced mana, and running indefinitely, they were difficult to regulate, but it was our only chance. Fortunately, drawing some blood to write the script had worked. The captain was now unconscious and no other guards had stormed into the cell yet.

The next problem was the chain attached to my cuffs. We adjusted the script and tried shooting mana at the metal, but it didn't have any effect. Another shot, this time at the stone floor, didn't yield any results either. The script needed to be cranked up, but I was already feeling the pain.

I yanked at the chain, but it wouldn't budge. Suddenly, Riala ran past me and out of the cell, toward the captain. She approached him carefully and grabbed a key chain from his belt.

"Ugh..." the captain groaned.

"Eek!" Riala quickly ran back to me and shuffled through the keys. "I think it's... this one!" she said, sticking the key into the holes of my cuffs and releasing me.

She must've memorized which key the captain used to release her...

"Good girl!" I said as I mussed her hair and looked back at the captain.

He was slowly coming to, and we needed to get past him before he was back on his feet. I prepared the script once more and moved toward the door, carefully looking into the hallway. It was empty, but even if nobody had heard the commotion, we would inevitably meet another guard.

"Can you run?" I asked Riala, who answered with an emphatic nod. We left the cell and sprinted down the hallway, leaving the captain behind.

* * *

The cell we were coming from had been on the ground floor in the back of the building. We scampered through the dimly lit hallways until I saw a pair of guards walk in our direction around the next corner. They must've seen me peek around it, as I heard them shout "Hey!" and their steps quickened. We fell back, and as soon as they moved around the corner, I blasted both of them into a wall.

"Ahh!" I groaned and fell to one knee from the pain.

"Tomar!" Riala said worriedly.

The priest's experiment had given us a little insight about our capabilities. Miles knew the approximate amounts of water and mana that water sources produced during normal operation. Combined with the knowledge that I apparently had a maximum capacity of one hundred and fifty liters, he had guessed that we could get away with five attacks until the situation became critical. However, we were probably not back to full capacity yet, which the pain I felt made quite clear.

I stood back up and we went on. Luckily, we made it all the way to the front door without any more issues. The guards were generally spread thin, and you wouldn't need a lot of them to watch a few prisoners.

I take back everything I ever said; the lack of Fighters in town is great.

Through a window, I peeped into the main square. It was as busy as you would expect in the middle of the day, but at least there were no guards in sight.

"Okay," I said to Riala. "I need you to run as fast as you can, okay? We need to get out and then off the streets."

She gave me a hesitant nod. Taking a deep breath, I opened the door and started running, while making sure that Riala could keep up. We immediately headed toward the office district in the east, where we would encounter fewer people. On the way there, most citizens quickly moved out of the way when we came closer, but I felt bad when one woman just crouched down in fear, screaming from the effect that our mana had on her.

From the eastern part of town, we headed south, using small paths and running between houses to avoid other people. After a little while, we ducked into a familiar shed. Riala promptly let herself fall to the ground, panting.

"We actually made it out," I said with a huff.

I hadn't noticed anyone chasing us yet. Everything was quiet. However, the guards would surely be on our tail. We didn't have a lot of time. Unfortunately, we also didn't have many options. Hiding in town would be difficult. We couldn't trust anyone, and most people wouldn't want to get anywhere near us anyway. Even if Zara would've changed her mind, that's probably where the guards would look first. We could've tried staying in sheds and abandoned houses, but how long could we have kept that up without getting found?

«This town isn't large enough to stay hidden for long,» Miles said.

"I know, but... what about her?" I said in a whisper, looking at the young girl that was still breathing heavily on the ground.

«Do we have any other choice?»

Unable to think of another way out of this, I reluctantly crouched down next to my partner in crime. "Riala, we have a problem. The guards will keep looking for us, and I don't know how long we can hide from them. We need to head to the neighboring town, hopefully providing us a few quiet days. This is a big decision, but I can't make it for you. Do you want to come with me?"

"Out of town?"

I nodded. "It will be dangerous out there, but I believe we'll have a chance. They can't drive us into a corner in the Wildlands."

She thought for a moment before asking another question. "Can sis come?"

This one I had been worried about. Naturally, she would want Zara with her. But I didn't think that would be feasible. "It will be difficult to get to her. The guards are probably on the way to your house already because they know you'd want to see her. And out there we'd have to protect her. It would be even more dangerous for her than for us."

The girl sat up and looked at the ground, deep in thought. I hated putting her in this position, but she was in as much danger as we were. Regardless of how irresponsible taking her with us would be, this was the best option. But if she didn't want to come... we would stay here and try our best to protect her.

"I'm sorry, Riala. This is all my fault." I hung my head, staring helplessly at the dirt. "I wish I could just clear your name, but right now I don't know how. I know we'll come back here one day, and that our lives will go back to normal... But in order for that to happen, I have to figure out a few things. And for that, I need time."

A few more seconds passed before the silence was broken again. "I want to see the Wildlands!" Riala said.

I raised my head to look at her face and saw her usual bright smile. Did she have a better understanding of our grim situation than I gave her credit for? I didn't know. In an ideal world, I would've gone to talk things over with Zara, but that was the last place in town we should have been.

"Alright. We'll make some quick preparations, then leave," I said, glancing out the shed.

With nobody in sight, we went on the move again.

* * *

"Their abilities are remarkable, sir. I recommend we take them into our custody as soon as possible," the sigil priest, Oryn, said to the High Priest. "While the girl was only able to produce about twenty-five liters, the boy has a volume that's even higher than a small water source. And given both their age and volume difference, I'm hypothesizing their volumes might increase with age. Not only that, their knowledge about previously unknown sigils is groundbreaking!"

Oryn was over the moon. For years, he had studied scripture sigils and divine instruments. He had read everything anyone had ever written about them at least thrice, trying to learn more about the power the gods had granted them. While the temple priests saw themselves as the only ones who were allowed to be involved with the scriptures, Oryn cared little where new knowledge came from, especially if it was as revolutionary as what these children had to offer.

The High Priest grimaced at the report. He had already assumed that this find would be valuable, and had tried to get the king to turn them over, but he had failed miserably. If he used all his power and authority, they would be able to get these two, but that could mean war between the Worshippers and the Rulers.

"What about their application as weapons?" the High Priest asked. If he was to go for this, he would have to come out the other side with more firepower than he had before. He would need to gain a significant advantage over the king.

"Unfortunately, I haven't been able to do any tests in that regard yet. However, based on everything we know and what I learned from questioning eyewitnesses, I believe the boy to be worth multiple guards, as he's severely injured two beasts so far. Even the little girl managed to land an attack unbefitting her age on the eastern captain using the scripture."

With a person he trusted confirming his assumptions, the High Priest concluded that they had to get their hands on the two by any means necessary. He was hopeful to finally stand above the king and the authorities if he gained not only this new knowledge and the potential to create living water sources, but also power rivaling that of the king's army.

"Very well. Gather the agents, Oryn. We have an appointment with two blasphemers."

Only ten minutes later, a group of four priests in white and eight agents in black made their way across the main square, led by the High Priest himself.

Citizens stopped and watched the unusual display, many of them in high spirits, as these repeated events broke up the monotony of their everyday life.

When the group got closer to the prison, however, they saw several guards on high alert, coming and going. The High Priest immediately knew that something had happened. He approached a battered Captain Lera who was standing in front of the prison building. "Captain, what happened?" the High Priest asked.

Unhappy about being questioned by the temple, and guessing what this group before him had come here for, the captain only spat, "The prisoners have escaped. There's nothing for you here," before he left the fuming High Priest standing alone.

"Find them!" he shouted at his agents before making his way back to the temple.

CHAPTER 22
ENCOUNTER

Thinking about it, the turns my life took in the last three weeks weren't ideal. However, as I stood in someone else's house and emptied a bowl of blue stones into a bag, I also felt a bit of excitement that I couldn't quite explain.

"You don't have any qualms about this?" I asked Miles.

«I'm not happy about it, but I think you shouldn't beat yourself up over it either. We don't have much of a choice right now.»

Before we could leave town, we would need food, flint, writing utensils, and most important of all, blue stones. The mana blasts we had been using seemed to work well to throw someone into a wall, but it was far from ideal. Without blue stones, we couldn't properly defend ourselves against beasts. We also wouldn't be able to produce water for our own use. Writing utensils on the other hand were more of a convenience—I didn't want to write with my blood anymore.

Riala entered the house I was in through the front door and notified me that it was time to leave. "Someone's coming!" she exclaimed. Worryingly, her face was full of excitement.

We left through the back door and searched for another empty house. Because of the severe punishments for crimes against the town's citizens, and because everybody had a job anyway, thefts were exceedingly rare. So rare, in fact, that almost nobody even owned a lock for their house, to the surprise and delight of Miles. From the viewpoint of a freshly minted thief, I had to agree. This made it beyond easy to run around and just take whatever you needed. I had never even considered something like this before.

To lessen the impact per family, we tried to take as little as possible from each house, but we also couldn't take too long because of our pursuers. After five houses, I decided it would have to be enough. We had several dozen stones, enough food to last us three days, chalk, and some ink. One reason for stopping here were the people we stole from. The other was the fact that even though stones were relatively light individually. This amount was not only getting heavy but also unwieldy.

I carried the bag under my arm as we made our way to the eastern gate.

«This is the best option?»

"The eastern gate is our best option," I said in a way that it could be interpreted as information for Riala, since I had yet to explain Miles to her. "It's almost noon, and the workers will come back in to take a break before heading back out. That's one of the few times when there's a remote chance to slip out of town, provided that you can make it past the guards."

We arrived at the house closest to the gate and hid in its shadow. I had been at this gate a few times before, watching the workers return and stealing glances of the fields outside. The majority of adolescents were fascinated by the Wildlands at some point in their lives, as all we ever got were stories of the outside world.. These ranged from fun adventures to horrifying tales of beast attacks. Most of the time, however, the workers returned in one piece, thanks to the guards.

It wasn't long before someone on the outside announced the arrival of the workers and their protectors. The two guards on the inside started to open the large, wooden doors to allow the group inside. The first to enter were the workers, a group of about twenty men and women, flanked by six guards. Two wagons followed after them, guarded by two more guards each. The men that had opened the gate stood by, waiting for the group to pass. Afterward, they would close the gates again as soon as possible. It would be tricky to make it through.

I was getting ready after the first wagon had made it inside when Miles piped up. «Wait. I have an idea for a distraction.»

Per his instructions, I took out some ink and jotted a script on my hand. Then I aimed at the first wagon's wheels and used a blue stone to fire a thin stream of water before ducking behind the house again. I heard wood cracking and the guards panicking as the cargo started falling off the wagon.

"Stop! An axle broke!"

The gate wasn't large enough for two wagons to pass through side-by-side, so they would have to clear the way before they could continue. This would give us some flexibility. Almost everybody present started helping with securing the cargo and getting the wagon out of the way, while we went up to the wall and slowly crept toward the gate.

I was a little worried about getting separated from Riala, so I let her climb onto my back. Laden with a heavy bag and a little girl, I jumped around the corner and started sprinting through the gate.

"Hey! Stop!" the guard said as I ran straight toward him.

I shoved him off his feet with a water blast, jumped over him, and entered the Wildlands.

Wide, almost unobstructed grass fields lay before us, dotted by bushes and small trees. A dirt road led into the woods to the east, where the workers had come from. That would be our destination before we went deeper into the forest to shake any potential pursuers. Afterward, we would circle back and make our way west toward the neighboring town. There was nothing between us and our freedom. I kept running, hearing another guard move and shout behind us. I had barely made it twenty meters when a blinding light appeared out of nowhere and I stopped in my tracks.

I don't hear the guard. Did he stop as well?

I squinted as the light abated and I saw a glowing white figure standing before me. It didn't have any face or other defining features. It was slender, and just a little taller than me.

A god...?

Glancing back, I saw three guards stand stock-still just outside the gate, staring at the figure. That's when I realized I felt fine. I glanced to my shoulder where Riala's head was and she only looked at me in amazement. The god stood just three meters away, which should've been deeply uncomfortable for us, but the oppressive air I had felt in the past wasn't there, and it seemed like it was the same for Riala.

I looked back at the god as I heard a sweet, feminine voice say, "You shouldn't leave the safety of the walls. It's dangerous for you out here."

I swallowed hard and steeled myself. "It's dangerous for us inside town as well. We'd rather try our luck out here."

"You're too young to understand the gravity of what you're attempting. I can't allow you to throw your lives away so easily. Let me accompany you back inside. There will be no danger for you there."

Would she talk to the authorities? Maybe throw around her weight as a higher power? I considered it for a moment, but I had never heard of a god directly involving themselves with mortals in such a way.

"Why would you do that?" I asked, eyeing her with suspicion.

"All life is dear to me, and you are inadvertently going to end yours on this path. That would be a shame."

I wasn't sure what to do. Maybe it would work, maybe not. I didn't know if the authorities would even care about her words.

«So that's a god?» Miles asked inside my head. However, the figure seemed to react to it.

"Oh? You're not alone in there?" the god said, followed by a barely audible whisper in a much less graceful tone. "You seriously messed up, Gallas..."

The god of rituals? My ears perked up at the mention of the name, but my confusion was quickly displaced by shock as I realized she acknowledged the voice in my head.

«You can hear me?»

"You identified me as a god. Did you think I wouldn't notice your presence?" she said with a chuckle, returning to her sweet voice.

«Would you have noticed if I hadn't said anything?»

"Of course," came her immediate response, but something was off. She appeared flustered somehow.

I glanced back at the guards, who were still frozen in place. I remembered the feeling. In the presence of a god, it should be difficult to move. To even think. People took that as a sign of their overwhelming power. Public wisdom was that they refrained from appearing more often for our sake.

"Why aren't we affected by you like the others?" I asked her.

"You two are special—precious, even. Which is why I can't allow you to run to your doom."

«You want us to go back that badly?»

"Very much so, yes," she said, followed by a moment of silence.

«Make us,» Miles said, at which the god visibly twitched.

It took her several seconds before she started again. "I would prefer not to use my powers for such a purpose. I might hurt y—"

«You can't, can you? That's very interesting...»

She twitched once more. "I assure you, I—"

«Let's go, Tomar!»

I took off in a sprint, running around the god and toward our destination.

"You'll regret this!" she hissed.

When I glanced back, she disappeared into thin air. The guards started moving again, but they didn't follow us. We were finally, truly, outside the walls. As we ran, we looked around in wonder. Very few people ever got to see this. No houses, no brick roads, no walls... just the open Wildlands.

I wanted to discuss what had just happened with Miles, but that would have to wait until later. In a few minutes, we would arrive at the edge of the woods, and then we'd find out exactly how dangerous our journey would be.

* * *

The escaped criminals quickly became the talk of the town. A prison break would've sufficed to kindle the ensuing gossip, but the appearance of the goddess Shae stoked the rumors tenfold. It was the first appearance of a deity in years, and in an even more surprising twist, she was unsuccessful in her attempt to send the criminals back to Alarna, adding an air of uncertainty about what the authorities had been dealing with.

Despite any feelings of unease, many citizens joined in and shared their theories about the kids who defied even the gods. Each hypothesis was wilder than the one before, but they took another turn when people who had recognized Tomar and Riala came forward to voice doubts about their supposed actions. The odds of these two being dangerous criminals was bordering on being laughable to some.

There were precious few who knew the truth about what happened, and these people now recognized their own carelessness. Not wanting to overreact, they had ignored several warning signs. The price was losing immediate access to the escapees, but they weren't going to let it end here. The abilities and the knowledge these two held were too valuable. Just two hours after their escape, a search party consisting of soldiers and agents moved out through the eastern gate in pursuit of them. High Priest Orthur Syfar and King Hertar Alarna stood on top of the town wall, watching the group depart.

"You'll honor our deal?" the king asked.

"We let something precious slip through our hands while trying to avoid antagonizing or working with each other. I don't intend to repeat that mistake, and I don't intend to fight you. That leaves cooperation. Equal rights," the High Priest said as he extended a hand toward the king.

"Equal rights," the king agreed, shaking the priest's hand.

As the group of Fighters made their way closer to the woods, the two leaders parted ways and walked away in opposing directions, displeasure on their faces.

CHAPTER 23

WILDERNESS

Side by side, Riala and I walked down the dirt path. The edge of the woods was about one thousand meters from the wall, and a path leading deeper into the forest had been cleared, with a buffer between the path and the trees on each side. At first we were running, then jogging, and finally we slowed to a quick walk, while gawking at the surrounding trees. Neither of us had ever seen a tree up close. It was a sight to behold, and we had to raise our heads to see the treetops, some of them dozens of meters from the ground. We took in unfamiliar smells and sounds, from greenery to the birds and insects making the outside world their home.

As we made our way further east, adjacent paths led north and south at regular intervals, splitting the forest into rectangular areas.

"Why don't they just start at the edge and gradually make their way further down?" I wondered to myself. Surrounding yourself with trees like this seemed risky.

«If trees produce beasts, maybe there's a minimum requirement, and splitting them up like this gives the workers a larger buffer. Otherwise they'd always be working right at the edge.»

"Hmm, maybe," I responded without thinking about it.

"Huh?" Riala said, visibly confused by my random words.

I should probably get this over with.

"Listen... There's something I haven't told you yet." Riala tilted her head and looked at me with curiosity. "I can talk to my Calling."

She blinked a few times, beckoning me to explain further. Either she didn't understand the implication or she didn't care. "Can I talk to it too?"

"He can hear you, but I'm the only one who can hear him."

Without missing a beat, Riala waved at me, flashing her biggest smile. "Hello, Tomar's Calling!"

I chuckled at her carefree nature. "His name is Miles," I clarified. "He says, 'Hi.' I just wanted to explain this to you in case I ever say something out of nowhere, or if it seems like I'm talking to myself."

"Okay!" she said contently.

«That was easy.»

Yup. Life is so much easier to accept when you're younger, I thought.

"Can I touch a tree?" Riala said, the topic seemingly already gone from her mind.

"Let's do that later. I want to test something myself, but we have to get further away from the town first." I then forwarded Miles' theory to her. We hadn't seen a single beast yet, so he might have been right about this spacing buffer, but we still had to be careful.

Since Riala didn't seem to have a problem traveling with a crazy person, I brought up the god to Miles.

"What do you think was up with that god?" I said.

"Dunno," Riala said after looking up at me.

"The question was meant for Miles," I said with an awkward smile. "Hmm... How about this, when I'm talking to Miles, I'll put a finger to my head, okay?"

"Okay!" she said, skipping a few steps ahead.

It can't be normal how easily she's accepting this...

«It's hard to tell,» Miles said. «She was too much talk and no action. I was expecting more resistance from a "god." She didn't want us to leave, but I don't think she would've actually helped us.»

"Mm-hmm. I'm thinking the same thing," I said with a finger resting on my temple. "The way her presence didn't affect us... Do you think it was the mana?"

«Since Riala wasn't affected either, that's a reasonable assumption.»

The white light hadn't looked like the mana we were exuding, but maybe that's what it would look like if you had a godly amount of it.

"When I first told you about gods, you said you didn't believe in them. What do you think now?"

«Let me answer that with a question. Originally, you told me these gods had a presence that would make their power obvious to anyone around them. But this one didn't affect us at all. Do *you* think she was an omnipotent being?»

I had to admit, the question had crossed my mind as well. People worshiped them, and the priests told wondrous stories about the gods' many acts of kindness toward us "lowly mortals," but this encounter felt strange. She didn't do anything, we didn't feel her godly presence, and she got flustered by Miles.

"I think I'll wait until I see another one to decide that," I said.

«Heh. Spoken like a true Researcher.»

"Speaking of research... Did you hear what she mumbled?"

«Yeah. 'Gallas,' was it? Do you know who that is?»

"I do. He's the god of rituals. The priests say he's responsible for assigning our Callings. If he 'messed up' as she put it..."

«Then our situation might be on them. Interesting...»

After walking and talking for about twenty minutes, we couldn't see the town's walls anymore, and took a turn to head south. I had expected to be trudging through dense forests by this point, but the workers had done a good job clearing paths to walk on. However, after ten more minutes, we reached a dead end.

"This is it..." I said, slightly worried. I double checked the scripts on mine and Riala's hands. "If you see *anything*, you tell me. And if a beast comes close to you, use that script, got it?"

She was clearly picking up on my worriedness, as she now looked panicky herself. "Will we be okay?"

"Don't worry," I said, feigning confidence. "With these scripts, we're more of a danger to the beasts than they are to us." *At least I dearly hope so...*

Riala nodded, and with that we took our first steps into the thicket.

* * *

"Welcome back, sister," a glowing white light said to a smaller one amidst a vast nothingness.

"Thank you," the other light said.

"You're not even going to deny it?"

"I have no reason, brother. I'm right, and if the council still doesn't see that, then so be it."

"Why are you so obsessed? It's just a human."

"Did you not even listen? It's two! And not only did they awaken, they're using it! Now they've left their town. Please, brother, explain to me why you're not worried as well."

"Because they're just humans. They're going to die, and soon. Your own fate, on the other hand, is uncertain. The council is waiting for you."

"Are you serious?"

"Very much so. I'm here to escort you."

The two lights started to disappear.

"Mark my words, brother, these two humans mean trouble for all of us."

* * *

As the sun disappeared behind the horizon and night fell over Alarna, shadows began roaming through the town, ignoring the citizens that were making their way home. Meanwhile, after an eventful day, the two guards stationed at the eastern gate were eagerly awaiting the arrival of the night shift.

"I still don't understand why they went outside. That's a death sentence," one guard said.

"Maybe they were going to be executed, and they just wanted to see the Wildlands one time in their lives!" the other mockingly expressed.

"Haha! I would prefer dying with a noose around my neck over getting ripped apart and devoured by beasts."

"Oh well. To each their own. I'm just glad we got the gate closed before anything tried getting in."

As if on cue, two shadows appeared from behind the house closest to the gate. The guards' eyes grew large upon noticing them, and they immediately took up battle stances. From atop the wall, a bell started ringing, but when reinforcements arrived only minutes later, the shadows were nowhere to be seen and the town gate stood wide open, the two guards lying in pools of their own blood.

* * *

As it started getting dark, traveling had become difficult amidst the dense trees that let little moonlight shine through. We made camp at a clearing in the middle of the forest, against a small cliff face.

The first few minutes inside the forest had been terrifying. The tiniest noises had me on edge, even if we caused them ourselves. I was constantly looking around to make sure we were safe, but I relaxed after a bit. By all appearances, we were alone. When absolutely nothing happened, Riala started touching every other tree, purely amazed by them just standing around like this. Admittedly, I was fascinated as well. If people could just go into the forest to get themselves a tree, we wouldn't have to pay for firewood anymore. The proof of concept was the free campfire in front of us now.

After a small dinner of bread and dried meat, Riala and I sat in front of the fire, side by side. Even though she had been carried part of the way, she was exhausted and already dozing off. I was getting tired as well, but it was difficult to surrender to sleep.

«You need to rest.»

"I know... But what if something happens in those few minutes until you take over?"

«It's too bad we don't have earth magic,» Miles said with a chuckle.

"What's that?"

«I guess I haven't mentioned this yet. In my world, we have stories about something similar to scripts called "magic." What we are doing with the blue stones could be called water magic. And if we were able to manipulate earth, we could make ourselves a makeshift shelter.»

"Hmm... But we're not manipulating the water, right? We're just producing it. Wouldn't earth magic just be like shoveling dirt then?"

«Heh, I guess. Unless there's more to the scripts that we don't know about yet.»

Miles was a step ahead of me. While I had been focused on this one script, he was considering what lay beyond. Other scripts, other applications, maybe entirely different effects. I didn't see a way to move forward yet, not without another divine instrument to study, but his idea sounded very interesting. As I thought about this, I finally succumbed to my sleepiness and nodded off.

* * *

Tomar fell asleep, and I took control of his body for the first time since the other night. Riala was sleeping soundly, and with a careful look around, I confirmed that we were still alone. After about six hours in the Wildlands, we had yet to see a beast.

False advertising? I thought. Maybe there were other explanations. When I had talked to Tomar about the beast that attacked me and Riala, he was just as surprised about its unusual behavior as me. For one, it didn't attack us at first. It appeared more interested in watching us than doing a taste test, especially when it *spoke* and told us that we smelled funny. Tomar had never heard of beasts being able to talk, or about them watching people. What made this even more mysterious was that the creature's behavior couldn't be explained by our mana, as it had happened before the cube exploded.

I thought back to the god who had been able to hear me. That certainly seemed like a godly ability, but what if the beasts could hear or feel me as well? Maybe they could smell it? The two beasts I had seen looked like large wolves, and dogs are said to have remarkable noses. It seemed plausible, though the thought that we might actually be surrounded by beasts who were curiously sniffing at us from a distance was kind of disturbing in its own right.

I stared at the edge of the clearing where we had tested some scripts earlier. Depending on the unevenness of the bark, writing scripts on trees was a challenge. We had more failures than successes, but we *did* manage to draw water from some of them. It wasn't nearly as much as from a water source or ourselves, but more than enough to use as drinking water. Using the trees as weapons would prove tricky, however. The output wasn't high enough to produce a water stream like the second one we had used on a beast. Ideally, we would be able to do more with the water than just blast it out with varying degrees of force and volume.

Thoughts of us flinging around spells floated through my mind; the dream of any wizard class player. But as much as I wanted this to be a magical fantasy world, the Omega scripts were too simple, too one-dimensional—an input and an output.

An out... and an in?

CHAPTER 24

TRAVELING

When I awoke the next morning, I was sitting at the burned out fireplace. In my hand was a quill, and my entire left arm was filled with scripts that appeared to be chained together. A revitalized Riala sat by my side, a wide smile on her face.

"Do one more!"

"Um... guys? What are we doing?" I said.

"Tomar, good morning! Miles did something awesome!"

"Did he now..."

It was a little creepy to wake up in the middle of whatever this was, but it's not like I hadn't expected Miles to do some tests while I was asleep. We hadn't specifically talked about it, but we had both heavily implied it. *As long as I can trust him not to do something stupid...*

I looked at my arm again. All but one of the scripts were exceedingly simple. The only thing they seemed to do was modify the force of the output, though there was also a sigil I didn't recognize.

"What does this do?" I asked.

«Hold out your arm and activate it,» Miles said expectantly.

After putting down the quill, I picked up a blue stone and put it onto the first script, which was the designated input. The script activated, the stone dissolved, and a stream of water shot up from my palm. I didn't understand what was so special about it until the stream suddenly changed directions. It hopped around us in arcs as it was pushed again and again by the chained scripts. Once it had circled us twice, it shot into the air and then into the cliff face behind us with a high-pitched noise, creating a hole in the surface. One of half a dozen holes, indicating that this had not been the first test.

"Huh," I said in a daze, looking at my arm again. "You figured out an entirely new way to use scripts in one night?"

The sun hadn't risen above the horizon yet, so I had only been asleep for about five hours. I didn't know what I had expected, but this was definitely more than that.

«I had the idea just after you nodded off. The difficult part was finding a way to suspend script execution before changing the trajectory. It's fascinating. I've never used Omega like this before!»

As I listened to Miles' explanations, I saw that Riala's arm was filled with the same scripts.

"It's so pretty!" she said, watching a water stream she had created.

Nevertheless, her small arms couldn't hold nearly as many scripts. The water she had created didn't hop around as long as mine, and instead of shooting into the rock, it just dropped down. Seeing Riala try to catch the water with her mouth made for a funny display, though.

"Should we get going?" I asked.

«Sounds good.»

"Okay!"

After gathering our things, we continued moving westward. Our plan was to use the forest's cover to walk around the town, and eventually head toward Cerus. We had first traveled south and then turned west. It was a little difficult to judge distance and direction in the woods, but based on the sun's movement, we were on the right track, and Miles did his best to estimate how far we had come based on our movement.

"Do you have an idea for our mana problem?"

«Kind of. Though I have to admit that last night's experiment distracted me a little,» Miles said apologetically.

"It is pretty," I said with a chuckle.

Apparently, Riala had been woken up a couple of minutes before me by the first water stream crashing into the cliff. She was immediately enamored by the new skill Miles had shown her. The fact that she wasn't actually talking to me hadn't disturbed her in the slightest. On the contrary, she commented, "Miles is nice!"

By this point, we had been in the Wildlands for over ten hours and hadn't encountered a single beast yet. Even though I was trying to not let my guard down too much, it was difficult to not start thinking about this as a nice stroll through nature. Plants we had never seen, the occasional bunny or deer, and all the trees around us were serene and beautiful enough that I had to wonder how terrifying the outside world could truly be. Though I did scratch my leg on a low-hanging branch.

All my internal joking came to a sudden halt when we came across a trail of blood. We didn't see anything unusual, but the blood was still fresh.

«Could be something other than a beast, right?»

"What—you think a deer hunted a bunny?"

«Another predator, I mean. And I just mentally rolled my eyes at you.»

"I've only heard of beasts hunting animals."

Miles told me about a few creatures that he had expected to live in these woods, but most of them I had never heard of. Granted, my life experience was limited, but from books, I had at least learned about deer, boars, and other species. If there were animals that hunted other animals, I probably would've heard or read about them too.

«A beast then... We should probably get going in that case.»

"Right," I said, and we continued our journey with renewed vigilance.

Maybe the beasts weren't as active east of Alarna. Now, in the south, we were seeing more signs of them: scratched up trees, more blood trails, and even bones. Meanwhile, Miles muttered some nonsense about being curious what it would be like to script on the body of an animal or beast, but I forbade him to pursue that idea.

"Don't."

«I just said I was curious! Not like I would actually try to do it.»

"Just... don't."

About fourteen hours after we left town, we caught our first glimpse of a beast. It was standing in a clearing a few dozen meters away. As soon as we saw it, Riala and I ducked behind a tree. It was upwind from us, so it would hopefully not smell us, but it was looking around as if searching for something.

I kept glancing at it, and after a minute or two, it finally walked away. Luckily, not toward us, nor where we were headed.

Seeing one in broad daylight, especially outside of a life or death situation, was interesting. It didn't look like a monster. It seemed like it was just another animal roaming the forest, even with its black fur and impressive size.

«Definitely looks like a wolf,» Miles said. «Are there other kinds of beasts?»

"I'm not sure. I've heard they could vary in size, but nothing about their exact looks. I guess people don't pay close attention when running for their lives."

"What did Miles ask?" Riala said.

I repeated what we were talking about and she joined the conversation.

"Sis told me a story about a beast that looked different once! She said it's much bigger and much heftier than normal beasts!"

"How did she know about that beast?"

"Hmm... I don't remember."

If Riala was right, there was at least one more kind of beast. Since we had only seen three with our own eyes, it probably made sense that we hadn't encountered every kind that existed. The script Riala and I kept at the ready had proved powerful. I could only hope that it would be enough, should we ever face something even more dangerous than the ones from before.

Even bigger though...

* * *

A group of soldiers and agents from Alarna were desperately fighting a huge beast that towered over them. It had snuck up on a soldier and killed her before the others had been able to react. Most of the combatants weren't used to fighting this deep in the woods and were visibly struggling with the trees obscuring their view, making it difficult to attack.

"Ahhh!" a soldier screamed as the beast got a hit in from a blind spot and slammed him into a tree.

Captain Lera used this opportunity to land a devastating blow on the creature's head. As it staggered, all Fighters converged on it. Spears and daggers penetrated its hide in a frenzy until it finally keeled over. In this fight alone, the group had lost two soldiers and one agent, leaving only three of each.

"This is madness!" a soldier said while resting against a tree. "This was the third category five just today! We should get out of here!"

"We can't go back yet," an agent said. "The High Priest wants those children back in Alarna at any cost."

"You think he'd rather see you dead than come back without them?" the soldier yelled in exasperation.

"Of course," the agent said calmly. "Is the king not the same? We're chasing these criminals for the benefit of our people, after all."

The captain put himself between them before the situation escalated. "Soldier, your personal feelings don't matter here. We're on a mission and we're going to complete it. If you think differently, I'm happy to cut you down for insubordination, here and now. Let's finish up."

At this, everybody became quiet and started preparing simple graves for their fallen comrades.

Captain Lera was aware that this mission had turned out to be unexpectedly challenging, but he couldn't have hoped for a better outcome. He rarely got to go outside town these days, and encountering multiple category fives in quick succession was like a dream come true. He was a man who loved the art of fighting, but was rarely confronted by worthy enemies. As long as there was even a remote chance that they would be able to finish their mission, Captain Lera would use this opportunity to its fullest.

A few minutes after resuming their travels, the group found a clearing with a burned out campfire. The surrounding trees were laden with remnants of hand-drawn signs that had been sloppily erased, and the cliff behind the campfire had several round holes in it.

"This is where they spent the night," the captain mused. "And they're practicing."

The holes—which were nearly identical to the ones on the dead beasts examined in town—were several meters up the cliff face and looked like they had been punched into the stone horizontally. Back then, the boy had shot streams of water from the water source on ground level. To create these holes, that high up, he must've learned a new trick.

"Are they really able to create water? I don't mean to question the king and the High Priest, but... it seems bizarre," a soldier said.

"They're able to do that and more. I've felt their attacks myself. I was essentially defeated twice, and they weren't even trying to hurt me."

While the captain hadn't been badly injured, these scripture attacks had proved dangerous. He had only been knocked out for a moment, but that amount of time would've been enough to kill him without contest.

"Wait, what? That's the first I'm hearing of this!" a female agent said. "They've beaten *you*?! I'd rather fight another cat five than you! How are we supposed to bring them in?"

"They're children, and they don't mean harm. All we need are numbers. Looking at this, though, the sooner we get to them, the better our chances," the captain said, pointing at the holes. He then walked on, the group following after him.

"Maybe I should be happy that I didn't keep following him that night..." the agent mumbled to herself as she trudged after the others.

CHAPTER 25

EXTENT

"What's this one?" Riala asked as we were sitting at a campfire.

"It changes the size of the water stream," I said.

After walking all day, we stopped at another clearing when it got dark. Miles and I were currently explaining different sigils to Riala, who was eager to learn more about the scripts, especially after Miles' experiments this morning. The young girl had a remarkable memory and comprehension, and could replicate our scripts after only seeing them once or twice. While I was a little worried about our blue stone supply, Miles was adamant that it would be good to have fresh eyes on the topic. Chaining scripts and delaying their execution was something he had just figured out by trial and error, and he figured a child might come up with entirely different ideas. That's why he was encouraging her to learn.

Riala finished her first script that she had written entirely by herself and activated it. Apparently she had raised the spread considerably, because instead of a stream of water, a wall of water droplets appeared, falling down over a large area.

"I can make it rain!" she said excitedly.

"Good job!" I said with a smile.

«Hmm... That reminds me—it hasn't rained since I got here, has it?»

"It almost never rains in this area, and the summer is particularly dry," I said.

«We haven't seen any rivers or ponds out here either...»

"Of course. You only find those in areas with a lot of rain. I've only read about these things."

«You mean you don't have springs? What about wells?»

"Not around Alarna. I've read there isn't enough water."

«That's very interesting...»

I got a little nostalgic when Miles went quiet to think. I returned my attention to Riala, who was just about to activate another newly created script. I expected another nice, little water spray. Instead, a stream of water shot a ten-centimeter-wide hole into a nearby tree. And the one behind it.

"Oww!"

I quickly checked on her. "Are you okay?"

"Yeah…" she said with a grimace.

I examined the script she had used. It used too much mana, and since she had played around for a while already, she had exceeded her safe-use limit.

"Riala, you need to be careful with that one. It uses a lot of mana, remember?"

"I just wanted to test it. For when a beast attacks us," she said.

"Okay," I said, patting her head. "Let's stop for today."

"Wait! I want to know what this one does!" she said with pleading eyes.

I didn't allow her to use any more scripts, but I kept teaching her theory until she eventually got tired and laid down. I wished I could've taken a book with me. When you're used to falling asleep while reading, it's very boring to just lie there, and it didn't help that I kept thinking about our travels.

In the late afternoon, we had reached the southwest corner of the fields around Alarna. From here, Cerus was a three-day-journey and since the road shouldn't be in use, we wouldn't have to trudge through the forest anymore.

In total, we had only seen two beasts today, and we had avoided both of them. Technically, this was great, but I was admittedly a little curious about how our scripts would do.

"An attack like Riala's should kill a beast in one hit, right?" I asked Miles.

«Mm-hmm,» he agreed, but didn't elaborate.

"Alright, talk to me. What are you working on?"

«Honestly, I'm not sure yet. It's just a random idea.»

I let him think in peace and closed my eyes again, trying to fall asleep. Seconds passed, then minutes, but I just didn't feel tired at all.

"This is weird," I mumbled.

Even if today hadn't been as exhausting as yesterday, we had walked all day. I should be spent, yet I felt fine. Before this moment, I hadn't actually thought about it, but ever since we got mana, I felt less tired than usual. That first night, I'd had a brief nap in the shed and was fine for the remainder of the day. The last time I slept normally was two days prior to last night.

Okay, I was unconscious. Maybe that helped, but...

«Can't sleep?»

"I wonder..."

I told Miles about my suspicion. He hadn't considered it yet. Maybe because it was *my* body, and I felt the difference more strongly. Since that night, my mind felt clearer and my body lighter. It was difficult to not assume a connection to my tirelessness. Riala didn't seem to be affected, but she also had less mana.

«I guess it's possible,» Miles said. «Mana seems to be some kind of energy after all. Oh, and when there was no energy left, we both fell asleep.»

The theory that we were running on mana was interesting, but being unable to fall asleep late at night was also somewhat worrying. It didn't feel right. Since we had barely used any scripts today, I decided to test it out, and drew one with a significantly high output onto my hand. The amount would be fine, but it was still the script with the largest effect we had tried so far.

«You seem adventurous today. We don't know exactly how much damage that will do,» Miles said.

"Tell me you aren't curious."

«You must be joking. Hit it.»

I turned in the opposite direction of the town and aimed at a random tree. As soon as I activated the script, a large stream of water shot out. I immediately crossed the pain threshold and fell down in agony.

"Ahh!"

As I writhed on my side, I heard the unsettling sounds of wood cracking and heavy objects falling.

"Wah! What was that?" Riala said after being woken by the loud noises.

I opened my eyes and propped myself up just in time to notice that a large tree was slowly tilting toward us. Hopping to my feet, I grabbed Riala and jumped out of the way as the tree trunk crashed into our campsite. After cowering for a moment, we both stared at the scene, trying to make sense of what had happened. With curiosity, my eyes wandered to where I had fired the water. A trail of broken trees was left behind. The one I had targeted was split in two, and the water had kept traveling through several trees behind the first. The last trunk that was hit belonged to the tree that had fallen in our direction.

«Holy shit.»

Punching holes into trees and beasts was one thing, but this blast was on another level. Even though I had put half of my mana capacity into it, neither Miles nor I had expected this kind of destructive power. According to him, a water stream that was several meters wide shouldn't have had enough force left to shoot through multiple trees.

"Are you okay?" I asked Riala.

She was still staring wide-eyed at the destruction. She briefly glanced at me, nodded, and then looked back at the trees again.

"This is why we have to be *tremendously* careful with scripts," I said with a sad chuckle. I noticed her gaze snapping to my hand, but I quickly covered the script. "Oh, no! Forget it."

Ignoring her pouting, I got up and looked at the fallen tree again. Somehow, the trunk had just barely missed our campfire and luggage. "We were lucky there."

«It was really impressive, though... and useful for our research.»

"Don't you dare!"

«I know, I know.»

I'm surrounded by children!

* * *

When I woke up the next morning, I was leaning against the fallen tree. Looking to my left, I could see the carnage I had caused in the light of the early day. It was a little disturbing that I could cause such a high amount of damage with ease. On the plus side, I slept like a baby. Curiously, I didn't have a quill in my hand, there were no new scripts on my arm, and Riala was still asleep.

"Quiet night?"

«Ah, morning. Still working on that idea.»

I admired that he could work out all of these ideas and theories just in his head, but I had to wonder if it wouldn't be easier to test them instead. Apparently, I was mistaken in thinking that I was the only one worried about our stone supply.

«It would be easier, but I don't want to waste all our stones on unimportant experiments. Riala needs the feeling of accomplishment, but who knows when we'll get more of them.»

The sun was already peeking over the horizon, so I shook Riala awake. After a quick bite and some self-produced water, we heard a loud roar in the distance, whence we had come.

"That didn't sound like a beast," I said.

«At least not one like the previous ones...» Miles added.

We could hear it roar and rampage through the forest.

"Maybe two beasts are fighting," I guessed.

Wanting to get going before they made their way over to us, I urged Riala to help pack our things, and started walking away from the ruckus. That's when we heard a woman's scream.

"Was that...?"

«Tomar, nobody should be in these parts of the woods, right? If that's a pursuer...»

Unsure about what to do, I stood there for a moment—until I noticed Riala's expectant glance.

"Let's at least take a look," I said.

Trekking back the way we came, the commotion grew louder. And just when the forest became quiet again, we spotted the beast. It was twice the size of the ones we had seen before—and much burlier—but it had the same dark fur and red eyes.

The creature was walking over to a masked, black-clad figure sprawled across the ground. There was nobody else in sight.

"What do we do?" I said in a whisper.

«It looks tough. Much tougher than the other ones. And we don't even know if she's still alive.»

"We'd be leaving her behind to get eaten!"

Riala looked shocked at my words. A few more steps and the beast would be upon the woman. *We can't just leave!*

"Miles, which one?"

«Damn it... Okay, I suggest one-third, make it wide, and aim for the head while it's distracted. You better not miss.»

"Riala, stay here!" I said, quickly adjusting the script that was still on my hand.

I moved closer to the monster, and when it was about to grab the woman, I started aiming. Upon noticing that it was already too close to her, I whistled to distract it. The beast raised its head, gawking at me.

I fired.

The water stream wasn't as strong as the previous one, but it was still remarkably powerful. It shot through the beast, creating large holes in the trees behind it. Fortunately, they didn't topple over; unlike the now headless beast, which dropped to the ground with a heavy thud.

I waved Riala over, and we carefully approached the dead beast and woman. As we got closer, I saw that half of her left leg was missing, the wound still bleeding.

"What now?" I asked Miles.

«She's breathing, but she'll probably bleed to death like that. Quick, raise her leg and take off her top, the hood, and the mask.»

Doing as Miles instructed, I propped her leg up on a piece of wood and partially removed her clothing. After using a script to superficially clean the wound, I ripped a piece of her top to press onto the wound, binding it with the string that once kept her hood in place.

«This is far from ideal, but maybe it will be enough. We're only trying to stop the bleeding.»

I studied her features and concluded that she was young, but a little older than me, and about the same height. The black clothing in her possession was only worn by agents of the authorities and the temple, who didn't usually leave town. "She probably *is* after us…"

«The ninja girl we found mere minutes behind us in the middle of the woods at this time of day? Yes, probably. But it's weird that she's alone, isn't it?»

"Maybe she got separated from her group."

I didn't think they would send a single Fighter after us. Not into the woods. As far as I knew, the town never sent out groups smaller than four; it would be difficult to handle stronger beasts otherwise.

"Will she be okay?" Riala asked.

"I don't know. I hope so," I said.

After a few minutes, the bleeding had slowed considerably, but I kept up the pressure. At the same time, I regularly looked around in case someone or something else came looking for us.

«That looks like a bear,» Miles said as my gaze fell on the beast.

First wolves, now bears. It appeared that he recognized the beasts, but they were a little different from the variants he knew. They were larger, more eerie-looking, and more aggressive.

Suddenly, the woman's injured leg started twitching.

"Ugh…" the woman groaned.

"Don't move," I said as she tried to pull her leg away.

When she heard my voice, her eyes suddenly shot open, and she looked at me for a moment before pulling out a knife and pointing it at me.

"You!"

I quickly took Riala by the hand and moved away.

"We're just trying to help you!"

Confused, she looked down at her body to see the bandaged wound. Afterward, her eyes darted to the headless beast. She lowered the knife, her expression teetering between disbelief and distrust. Her confusion, on the other hand, only seemed to grow.

"Why?" she asked.

"We couldn't just do nothing."

She wasn't able to fight and finally laid back down. Her eyes darted around as she thought about something. After a few seconds, she looked back at the beast and suddenly started laughing as she directed a question at us.

"What are you?"

CHAPTER 26

SIDES

The group of soldiers and agents that were in pursuit of Tomar and Riala had been separated when they encountered three beasts fighting over a dead deer. It was exceedingly rare to walk into a situation where one would have to fight multiple beasts at once, and it was one of the worst things that could happen out here.

Similar to humans, beasts put aside their differences when they were attacked, and they would work together to eliminate any threats. Unless they were weak, there was only one way you would get out alive—you had to separate them. Unfortunately, the group that had started out with ten members was now down to six, leaving only two per beast. Everyone knew that their chances for surviving this mission had just plummeted, but they still acted swiftly and split up into three groups, luring their enemies in three different directions.

The two agents, Berla and Pari, continued on the path the group had been on, and fought valiantly, but Pari fell minutes into the battle against the category five. When Pari was hit, Berla immediately distracted the creature and lured it away again, on the off chance that he might've survived the hit. She kept up the fight, and thanks to her agility, she successfully avoided the attacks. However, in a moment of carelessness, she tripped over a root. The beast used that opportunity to grab her by the leg, clamping down on it with great pressure. She was shaken side to side until the leg ripped off and the woman was tossed several meters through the air. Landing with an audible *thud*, she fell unconscious on the ground.

One of the other groups did not fare any better. Two soldiers had tried to reach open ground to the north, where they could fight without getting hindered by the forest's trees, but they never made it that far. The beast picked them off, one after the other, and then made its way deeper into the forest, content with the prey it was carrying in its mouth.

Only the last group, consisting of another soldier and Captain Lera, survived the encounter. Thanks to the captain's prowess, they had barely managed to defeat the monster, though they had both been wounded. Their foe had only just been confirmed dead when the captain looked westward.

"Captain, I implore you, we need to retreat," the soldier said, his right arm hanging limply at his side. "We will die in this forest!"

"You would abandon your companions?" the captain said.

"*We* barely survived, sir! The others are either dead or running for their lives!" the soldier shot back.

The captain slipped into thought. He was enjoying the fight, and was determined to catch the criminals, but he was also reaching a point where he couldn't be sure about his chances of survival. If they were to run into another category five, they would struggle. Still, he couldn't in good conscience leave people behind like this. If they fell in the line of duty, that would be one thing, but he wouldn't let someone die through his own inaction.

"We're going back to the meeting point," the captain said decisively. "After meeting up with whoever else made it there, we'll retreat and gather new troops."

Based on the movement of the targets, he assumed that they were most likely heading toward Cerus. It would be difficult to intercept them, but as long as he knew where they were going, he would still have a chance to catch them.

Captain Lera walked off without looking back at his subordinate. The soldier was angry, but he knew what would happen if he refused to follow orders. Begrudgingly, he followed his superior.

* * *

"You're Tomar, right? I'm Berla," the woman said after she had calmed down a little.

"Um, nice to meet you," I said awkwardly.

We had successfully rescued her from the beast, but I was at a loss for what to do now. If we just left her like this, the next beast that came along would definitely kill her. On the other hand, helping her any more would be a risk to us.

From behind me, Riala glanced at Berla, and the woman waved at the young girl. "Hello, Riala."

I was perplexed at how casual she was acting. She had just been fighting for her life and had lost a leg, yet it felt as if she would jump to her... foot at any moment, and walk over to us.

"Doesn't it hurt?" Riala asked.

"Oh, it does. A lot. But Fighters are tough," the woman said.

"Tough enough to follow us in that state?" I asked.

"Maybe not quite that tough," Berla said with an awkward laugh. "Could you do me a favor?" She sat up and pointed east. "A friend of mine is lying about fifty meters that way. I don't know if he survived. Will you check on him?"

The situation didn't feel right. Toughness or not, she was acting like nothing had happened, and if her friend was injured, I would expect her to be more concerned.

«Might be a trap,» Miles said.

When the guard captain arrested us, he told me that he would kill me if necessary. Assuming nothing had changed, it could be dangerous to let our guard down. Nevertheless, standing around wouldn't get us anywhere.

"I'm sorry, we can't do that. Was there anyone else with you?" I asked, trying to determine how much danger we were in.

"There was, but we were attacked and split up."

"Will they come looking for you?"

"Probably not," she said with a sad smile. "If anyone is still alive, they will head back to town after this. You aren't planning to go back by any chance?"

"No, we aren't."

Even if she wasn't trying to trick us, we couldn't risk going anywhere near Alarna. And, since she wasn't alone, staying here would be dangerous as well.

Her eyes wandered to the beast once more. "You killed it with the scripture sigils, right? Can you do that at any time?"

We were both trying to get information out of each other. She probably wasn't as calm as she was acting. If I told her that I could only execute that script one more time before I would fall to my knees in pain, what would she do?

"I can," I said, trying to act confident.

"What about you, Riala?" she asked my partner in crime.

Riala looked up at me, and I answered for her. "She can, too, but her attack would be a little weaker."

A sliver of truth. Believable.

Berla looked us up and down for a moment, her expression changing from a friendly, careless one to a grimace. "Ugh, I'm not good at this," she said. "You can go if you want. No games. Bringing you two back would be difficult, even with two legs."

Her facade was gone. She sounded genuine, and she was giving us permission to go. However, as much as I wanted to, we couldn't just leave. Rescuing her would've been entirely pointless if we abandoned her now.

We took a few steps backward as she nodded in understanding. Her look quickly changed to one of confusion when I sat on the ground, several meters away from her.

"I don't know what to do. We can't just leave you, but we can't really help you either," I said.

Her eyes went wide, and she started laughing again. "You really are a child—no offense."

I awkwardly looked away. "Help me out, then. What would *you* do?"

"Leave me," Berla said matter of factly, Miles simultaneously suggesting the same simple solution in my mind. "You saved me, treated my wound... You've already done more than you should have," she continued. "Sitting here, waiting for some kind of divine inspiration, isn't going to help you."

If she was expecting someone to come for her, she would be trying to keep us here. Instead, she was mocking me.

"Are they really not going to look for you?" I asked with a frown.

"Don't worry about me. Just get going," she said as she tried to stand up.

"What are you doing?" I asked in surprise, getting up as well.

"My friend, Pari, really is lying back there. I need to check on him. Good luck to you two," she said, hopping in the direction she had pointed.

She only made it a few meters before she toppled over and fell to the ground, groaning in pain. The bleeding miraculously seemed to have stopped already, but she definitely wasn't in any condition to move on her own yet.

«Don't...» Miles said, still worried about her intentions.

I hurried toward her as she got up again and helped her stand. She looked at me in exasperation but didn't say anything. Motioning for Riala to come along, we made our way through the forest, and soon found a man lying on the ground. He was dressed just like Berla, and his gray beard peeking from behind his mask was evidence that he was much older than I had imagined.

As we got closer, Berla let go of me and hopped over to him, sitting down by his side. He wasn't moving and the look on Berla's face when she listened for a heartbeat told me that he was gone.

With sad eyes, she pulled off his mask and caressed his cheek. Though she stayed like that for quite some time, Berla never cried.

"Would you help me bury him?" she asked, turning to look at me.

I didn't know who the man was to her, but I was sure she wasn't trying to trick us.

"Of course," I said.

Per her instruction, Riala and I started looking for rocks to bury him under and carried them over to gently place on him. In town, all people would get cremated due to the lack of space for graves. Out here, it was custom to bury people in a tomb of rocks if getting them back to town wasn't feasible.

There were more than enough stones lying around—something I hadn't really paid attention to before. What surprised me was when we found a curious-looking pebble under one of the rocks. It looked just like a blue stone, but it was as black as a water source.

"Is that a black stone?" I said, eyes wide.

«Looks like it could be. Let's take it with us.»

I would've never thought to search for them under random rocks in the forest. They were only supposed to appear in special places, where they would then get mined.

I slipped it into my pocket before continuing with my task of burying Pari.

It took us about half an hour to cover him from head to toe. After helping Berla up, we stood at the grave for a moment longer, until she finally spoke up again.

"Have you made a decision yet?"

I wish...

CHAPTER 27
Trust

«Listen. We can't stay here. If someone comes for her, we'll be in trouble. And taking her back to town would send us running right into their arms. We don't have a choice.»

The logic behind it was sound. She herself had told me that we had done more than we should've already. It was not in our best interest to help her; a sentiment Miles wholeheartedly agreed with. However, there was that one remaining option that we hadn't talked about yet.

"You could come with us," I suggested.

Her response came with an utterly bewildered expression. "And then?"

"We'll leave you somewhere relatively safe, where you'd at least have a chance. We just can't go back to Alarna."

Our intention had been to go to Cerus, hopefully stock up, and maybe even stay for a few days to rest. With Berla in tow, this would probably not work out. She could easily alert the authorities as soon as we hit the town gate, so staying in Cerus wouldn't be an option.

We weren't doing bad out here, however. It had been three days, and we didn't have so much as a scratch. If we could get some food and stones, we would be able to look for another town or settlement to take shelter. It was a compromise, but it would solve my conundrum.

To me, it sounded like a decent plan, but Berla looked at me as if she didn't comprehend what I was saying at all. After a moment, however, she seemed to realize something.

"You don't understand my situation, do you? My life is over. It doesn't matter where you leave me."

Not once in my life had I ever thought about what would happen if someone couldn't do their job. I had never seen a guard that wasn't in peak physical condition, not to mention one that was missing a limb. There were also very few old people in town. I didn't know anybody who was taking care of their older family members, and there was no official place for them to go. It came as a shock to me when Berla explained that the old and the disabled were "put to rest" when they could no longer contribute to society. Apparently, this was something most young adults would learn from their parents after their ritual, but this hadn't been the case for me.

Mother hadn't gotten the chance...

When Berla tried to get us to go back, she was just trying to fulfill her mission—her *last* mission. "Now, if you aren't planning to do me one last favor of becoming my prisoners, you can leave."

Still stunned by this revelation, I stood there, staring at the ground with a sad expression. Riala seemed to pick up on my feelings, but I didn't think she truly understood what Berla and I had been talking about. She took my hand, trying to soothe me.

«You want to take her with us, don't you?» Miles said, slightly annoyed.

"Come with us."

«Of course you do...»

Berla rolled her eyes at me. "I get that you mean well, but even *you* should be able to realize how ridiculous that sounds. What's your plan? Do you want to take care of me for the rest of my life? Carry me around? And where exactly would that take place? Here, in the woods? The authorities established these laws for a reason. It's better for everyone."

Her no-nonsense attitude reminded me a little of my father. She was living for her job, and now she considered her life to be over. However, she shouldn't have anything to complain about in that case.

"If you think of yourself as dead, you might as well come along, right? Every additional minute is a bonus."

I walked over to the tree she was leaning against and offered her my shoulder. She looked at me in disbelief, but seemed to consider my offer. Eventually, she resigned and leaned on me without saying another word.

Together, the three of us made our way back to our camp from last night, where I had left our heavy bag. When we arrived, Berla's eyes went wide.

"What happened here?"

I almost forgot about this...

"Um... It was kind of an accident. The attack I tested was stronger than expected."

She was even more slack jawed than we had been, evident by her eyes bouncing between me and the fallen trees.

«She's going to love hearing about me.»

* * *

When Berla joined us, the sun had just risen above the trees. I didn't want to lose any more time and we immediately started moving again. Originally, I thought we would reach the road to Cerus today, but with Berla in our group, we weren't able to move quite as fast anymore. We had to make camp again in the evening, but I was hopeful we'd get out of the forest by tomorrow afternoon.

We knew that she would inevitably see us using scripts, so we didn't even try to hide it. While she stared in wonder at Riala producing a cup of water with a script on her hand, I stood a few meters away, arguing with Miles.

«I'm not necessarily saying we shouldn't have taken her with us, but you could've thought this through first. You have no idea what she'll do. Also, one reason we didn't go back for Zara was because we would've needed to protect her. And she could've at least run from a beast!»

"I know, but the alternative was not an option for me. We also couldn't stay there, so this was the simplest solution. Think about it like this—we can still leave her behind at any time?"

«Riiight,» Miles said sarcastically, «and when you go to look at puppies, you won't take one back home with you.»

"What?"

«I'm saying you won't leave her behind now that we have taken her with us.»

"No, probably not…"

«And you told her that we're on the way to Cerus. What if she alerts the authorities once we get there?»

"I don't think she'll sell us out after we saved her and we got to know each other."

«But you don't know. That's the issue.»

"I didn't know whether I should trust you either, Miles. But I chose to. *Twice*."

At this, he became quiet. Meanwhile, Berla and Riala were sitting at the campfire. My ears perked up when I heard Riala say something I had asked her not to mention.

"He's just talking to Miles," she said.

Uh oh…

"Miles?" Berla asked as the girl at her side hurriedly covered her mouth with her hands.

Sooner or later, I would have had to tell her. However, I had hoped to get to know her better before I did. Riala had readily accepted Miles, but I didn't think that it would be the same with an adult, especially not a Fighter. But now that his name had come out, I thought that I should get it over with. I needed to be able to talk to Miles, and it would be much easier if I didn't have to hide it.

«Go on. Tell our travel companion,» Miles said. He was certain this conversation would not go well.

I sighed and walked closer to them.

"I'm sorry," the young girl said.

"It's okay, Riala," I responded with a gentle smile.

I turned to Berla, who was looking at me expectantly.

"Miles… is my Calling. I'm hearing his voice in my head."

It was difficult to judge her expression, but she appeared confused and worried. It was obvious that Berla immediately understood the implication, unlike when I had told Riala. I was a little anxious about what she would say, but at least she wouldn't be able to do any harm in her current state. That's what I had thought, at least. But when she suddenly jumped up, tackled me to the floor, and held a dagger to my throat, I knew I had been mistaken.

"You're a Mad One?" she shouted.

"I'm not!" I said in a panic. "Look at me… I'm not insane!"

"You aren't normal either! Not with that air around you and the ability to create water."

"I swear! I'm not dangerous!"

"'Not dangerous'? Are you kiddi—"

Her manic words were cut short when a stream of water pushed her off of me. It wasn't enough to actually hurt her. All it did was give her a push. Riala had chosen the script that Miles and I had initially written to defend ourselves against the guards.

I quickly got to my feet and grabbed a blue stone from my pocket in case she tried to assault me again. Riala rushed to my side, keeping aim on Berla, as did I.

"Not dangerous, my ass! Are you going to kill me now?"

"I saved you and brought you with us. Why would I want to kill you?" I snapped back. "Does anything you've ever heard about Mad Ones match me?!"

She was agitated, but I felt like she was at least listening.

"Mad Ones are killed as soon as they appear because they're aggressive and try to hurt people," I said. "That's not me!"

"Then what are you?" she asked apprehensively.

"I honestly don't know. Miles has some theories, though."

She twitched at my mentioning of him, but didn't otherwise move.

"My ritual was over three weeks ago, and it didn't come with these abilities. All I had was the voice in my head. I was terrified when I thought I was a Mad One, that I might hurt people, but nothing happened."

"What is this voice telling you? Did it instruct you to destroy the water source? Does it want to hurt people?" she asked.

It hadn't occurred to me that this would be one way to interpret everything that had happened. I was hearing a voice, and one way or another, it had caused these incidents, or at least contributed to them. For a brief moment, I started to question myself. What if Miles wasn't real? Was I just imagining him?

Maybe that's what happens to Mad Ones... I thought. *The voices tell them to do things... to hurt people. What would Miles be considered in this case? A well-mannered Mad Calling?*

"Miles is nice! He wouldn't hurt anyone!" Riala said all of a sudden.

Berla wasn't happy about her joining in, however. "Shush! How would you know?"

"I talk to him when Tomar is sleeping!"

It hadn't been an easy day for Berla. She almost died, lost a limb, and now we were throwing more and more weird information at her. It was clear that she was starting to get lost in the craziness. When she slowly started to lower her weapon, I lowered my arms in turn.

"How can I trust you?" she asked me.

"If we meant you any harm, we wouldn't have saved you, and we definitely wouldn't have taken you with us. You said it yourself, it's not in our best interest. And why am I the one who needs to justify myself, anyway? *You* just tried to kill *me!*"

It took several seconds of scrutinizing looks from Berla until it seemed like I had gotten through to her. She kept eying me warily, but she at least put away her dagger.

This reaction was what I had always been afraid of. The mere mention of voices or the Mad Calling terrified people, and a Fighter's first instinct would be to eliminate any danger. I cautiously walked to her and offered to help her up.

"Give me a chance."

Berla took my hand, and I walked her back to the campfire. The rest of the evening, I noticed her occasionally glancing at me, but she didn't say anything. At my explanation that Miles would keep watch, she only nodded briefly.

When Riala was already fast asleep, Berla and I sat there in silence. *Will it be safe to sleep tonight?* I thought, nodding off before my thoughts could answer me.

CHAPTER 28

Ready, Set

"Hi," I said.

Berla looked away from the fire and toward me.

"You're supposed to be Miles now?" she asked.

"Yup."

She hadn't jumped up and tried to kill us again right after Tomar fell asleep, but she didn't look like she was okay with the situation, either. Even though I had expected the talk to go over poorly, her initial reaction had admittedly surprised me a little.

"This is so stupid..." she mumbled.

"Huh. You don't quite believe him, but you're curious, aren't you?" I concluded.

Tomar was probably right. At least to some degree, he had gotten through to her. She wanted to know more.

"What Tomar said is true. His experience doesn't sound like the Mad Calling. That's assuming he's telling the truth. I wanted to see what would happen once he fell asleep, and here 'you' are. I can't imagine why anyone would make something like this up, but even if I were to accept what you're saying, what *are* you two?"

"Well, I can't give you any concrete answers. We only have theories."

I told her what I assumed was happening during the rituals. That, somehow, people's experiences and abilities were transferred to the inhabitants of this world. I also told her how something had presumably gone wrong during Tomar's ritual, causing us not to merge, and that the Mad Calling might be related, but not quite the same. In my mind, the connection was indisputable, but for some reason, Tomar had been fine.

"You're not affecting him then?" she asked.

"We talk, just like you and I are talking right now. That's it. I will tell him what I think, but I'm not controlling him. Except for right now," I said with an awkward expression. "But that's different."

"Tell me, then... What was your opinion about helping me?"

After Tomar's efforts to get her to trust him, I wouldn't lie to her now. I mentally prepared to defend myself, should she take what I was going to say next the wrong way.

"I was against helping you, and especially against taking you with us," I said, but Berla didn't show any strong reactions. "Tomar doing the exact opposite of that should tell you something about how much control I have over his decision making."

When I met him, Tomar was readily going along with most of the things I suggested, but he was changing. He would consider my advice, but ultimately, he made his own decisions.

Berla was looking inquisitively at me. We had piqued her interest. I was never very trusting of strangers, and I certainly wouldn't have risked my life to save an enemy, but I had to admit that this turn of events was interesting to me as well. And, if she truly became our companion, her knowledge could be exceptionally useful to us.

"If this is all a trick, you're a great deceptionist," she said. "You two *do* feel like different people."

"Can I ask you a question?"

"That depends," she said with a raised brow.

"Just something I haven't been able to ask anyone yet. What do we look like to you?"

From the moment the water source had exploded, it appeared like we were scaring people. Even the guards who had been present at the time seemed somewhat frightened. Zara hadn't been willing to talk to us more than absolutely necessary, so all we had to go on was people's reactions. However, Berla hadn't looked scared even once.

"I assume you mean that beast-like air around you?"

Apparently the soldiers and agents had been briefed on us. They had been told that being around Riala and Tomar felt similar to being around beasts. They couldn't see mana like we could, however. It was more of a feeling, a primal fear that rose up inside you just by standing in front of a beast. And we were similar.

"That's really what it feels like?" I asked.

"Yes. We Fighters aren't affected by it as much, and you get used to it as well."

"That's very interesting, thanks."

Confirmation of our theory. This meant we definitely needed a solution to our mana streaming out of us before we reached Cerus, otherwise they might not even let us in. Or maybe they would think we were humanoid beasts and try to kill us.

I had ideas for solving the issue, but I was still working on the sigils for it. The chaining of scripts had given me important hints about how we might be able to control the mana around us, assuming that it could be affected at all. Being able to control a script's input after the mana left the body was crucial. I was deep in my thoughts when Berla interrupted them.

"You seem like the rational one. Can you tell me what the plan is? He wants to help, I get that, but that can't be all."

Tomar hadn't given her a satisfactory explanation to this question of hers. I considered my response for a moment before answering with a counter question. "What would you have done in his stead? *Before* you got your Calling, I mean."

The realization dawned on her. "He didn't get an actual Calling…"

"I don't know how much it really changes a person, but you're supposed to become more mature, right?" I asked.

Tomar was still very young, and the ritual was supposed to turn you into an adult, which he missed out on. If he had gotten my cynicism, he most definitely would not have acted the way he had. I've known people who would go out of their way to help others in my own world, but jumping into it with no plan at all was something I couldn't imagine a lot of adults doing, especially in a dangerous world like this one.

"I'm relying on literal children here? Now I almost wish you had a little more control," Berla said with a sad chuckle.

We talked until she finally got tired and laid down. I had enjoyed our conversation, and maybe I would even go so far as to say that Tomar had made the right decision. Regardless, I was sure this wouldn't make our travels easier.

Maybe I can at least optimize our walking speed a little, I thought.

* * *

Captain Lera knelt in front of King Hertar in the royal reception room. It was late in the evening, but the captain had just returned and wanted to make his report as soon as possible. With him was the one remaining soldier that survived the incident.

"Your Majesty, I'm ashamed to report that we couldn't apprehend Tomar Remor and Riala Fera. We hunted them through the woods and made it all the way to the southwest, where the beast situation became untenable."

The captain gave a full report, including the continued training on the boy's side, and the unusually high concentration of beasts they had encountered. He explained their decision to return to town to recoup, noting that on their way back, they found a dead soldier and a blood trail, indicating that the rest of the group had most likely been killed.

"I take full responsibility," the captain said.

King Hertar sat in silence, his fingers drumming the plush arm of his ornate chair.

"Every Fighter provided to you had been carefully chosen for their experience in fighting within the Wildlands. Ten of the best set out into the woods, and only two came back alive. Yet, you're telling me that two *children* wandered through unscathed? To Cerus, no less?"

The captain had wondered about this as well. Not only had they not found their dead bodies, but they hadn't found any dead beasts either. Even if the criminals could kill beasts with ease, there would've been signs. It defied common sense.

"I don't know if the boy is doing something to avoid the beasts or if maybe they're scared of him, but we haven't seen any signs of them getting attacked," Captain Lera responded.

The king was unsure how to proceed. The more he heard about Tomar, the more he wanted control over him. Yet, the boy was slipping further and further away from his grasp. Going back into the woods to follow them would be a fool's errand, though. In that case, they would have to be smarter about it.

"I assume you'll want to assemble more men."

"With your permission, my king."

Now, the situation was different. If they were headed for Cerus, they would use well-established roads. They could bring more soldiers, more provisions, and if they traveled through the night, they might even arrive before their targets. The king and his men were going to make one last push.

"Assemble the captains and take one platoon each," the king instructed. "I've had enough of this peasant making a mockery of us."

The silver lining in this mess was that he could exclude the High Priest from his plans once more, arguing that the criminals had left the jurisdiction of Alarna. Their joint effort had failed, and everything the king gained away from town would not be part of their pact. Instead, he had to worry about the mayor of Cerus, but the king believed himself a negotiator. The mayor was a businessman, and even if he got ahold of the boy first, it wouldn't take much to buy him back.

"I know you will do your best as always, Lera, but tell your men that they will be compensated generously if I have the boy in front of me within a week."

"Yes, Your Majesty. They will be delighted," the captain said as he stood. After saluting the king, Lera and the soldier left to make preparations.

The race toward Cerus had begun.

CHAPTER 29
Two Sides

The captains of Alarna assembled their troops in the middle of the night and set out for Cerus within two hours of receiving their orders. Traveling during the night wasn't without risk, but the impressive size of their forces would all but guarantee that any losses sustained would be minimal.

Even though most people were fast asleep at this time, a certain group of agents had been persuaded to stay ever vigilant, and they didn't miss the troops assembling and setting out westward. Their contacts within the king's mansion were tight-lipped about what exactly was going on, but after seeing that the captain had returned with only one other soldier, they could infer that the joint venture to capture the criminals had failed. Unless King Hertar was now suddenly declaring war on Cerus, there wouldn't be many reasons to send such a force their way, especially at this time and with such urgency. They knew the king was going after the targets again. Alone.

"We have to report this to the High Priest..." Nier said, peering out from a window as the troops disembarked.

"He will immediately send us after them," Reurig responded with a frown.

"If we don't, we'll end up like Dirra and Reva!"

"I hate this so much. My parents told me to get a nice, safe guard job. Why didn't I listen?"

The High Priest had made an example of their predecessors when they had failed to monitor Tomar. He was not one to overlook such errors, and the king getting his hands on the boy had further fueled his anger.

"You know we don't have a choice. At least we don't have to go to the woods like the others."

"*Great*, but we still have to go after that water source freak. He knocked out Captain Lera! What does that make him, cat six? Maybe seven? And who knows what that little girl can do!"

"I hear you…"

Not all Fighters were happy about their jobs. Some were born combatants who lived for the fight, but for many of them, it was just work. They had their reservations about going up against strong beasts, but they did it nonetheless. The current events plaguing the town were unusual. Increased beast activity, criminals with unknown abilities, task forces being decimated in the woods, gods getting involved… All of it was a lot to take in. They felt inept, even more so when their Callings were of limited help.

"Did you know Reva had just become a father? Now he's gone, just like that."

"Let's not go down that road. This is our job. Any of us could die at a moment's notice."

A somber mood fell over the duo.

"Have you ever thought about leaving Alarna?"

"Reurig…"

"I'm serious, Nier. All that forest, all this land… Surely better places are out there. I never wanted to be a Fighter," he said, interlocking his fingers nervously. "Do you suppose we're next to die? The king's men at least have a proper force. How many of us will the High Priest send?"

The two of them sat in silence for a little while.

"It'll get better once they're caught, right?" Nier said. "Everything that has happened was linked back to them. And you saw the forces. There's no way they'll get away this time. This is the end. We'll survive this one mission, and maybe we'll even get a chance to capture the two. After that, everything will calm down. Let's go make our report, hm?"

Reurig looked at Nier with sad eyes, but he eventually nodded. Deserting wouldn't be a real option. He knew little about what lay beyond the lands surrounding Alarna and Cerus, except for more woods, filled with more monsters. And this place at least had comparatively weak beasts and a strong wall. He wasn't going to join a town where citizens were regularly sacrificed to category tens, just to appease them, nor was he going to try to live in the woods by himself.

Both of them left their assigned location and headed toward the temple. They knew the High Priest would be furious about being woken at this time, but that would be the most welcoming part of their visit. Information about his lost agents and the king's lead would certainly send him reeling, but they would endure it in hopes of better days to come.

* * *

I didn't know what Miles and Berla had talked about, but it must've been effective, because she was much more open toward us in the morning. She didn't say another word about my unusual Calling, she was friendly, and I had been woken by her playing catch with Riala. That last part had possibly been the biggest surprise, giving me a new perspective on just how resilient Fighters were.

«They're called crutches,» Miles explained.

With the help of scripts and my knife, he had used a few thick branches we had cut from trees to use for firewood to build a walking aid for Berla. All I had ever seen before were canes. Those could've helped her a little, but with the crutches, she was surprisingly mobile; so much so that Riala had a hard time escaping or catching the agile Fighter.

"One more time!" the young girl said enthusiastically after being caught again.

Berla was starting to get tired. "Let's stop for now," she said with a smile. "This is more exhausting than just running around."

She walked over to where I was sitting and looked at me with a smile as well. "Thank you, Miles."

"He says, 'You're welcome.'"

After getting ready for the day, we left our camp behind and made our way northwest, where we would eventually reach the road to Cerus. Berla and Riala were in high spirits now that we were back to a more normal walking speed.

"That was nice of you," I said to Miles as I was walking a few meters behind the girls.

«It solved the movement speed issue.»

"It did, but it was also nice."

«I guess.»

After what happened last night, I had come to realize that Miles hadn't been entirely wrong. Helping Berla was a good deed, but not only didn't I have a real plan, I had actually endangered us. I had also underestimated her, thinking that she wouldn't be much of a danger in her injured state.

"It seems like you made peace with the situation. I'm happy about that, but I also see that I was a little hasty yesterday… Thanks for covering."

«To my surprise, it appears to be working out. It's hard to say "I told you so" in this situation. Maybe we'll find more of a middle ground in the future. And you shouldn't let your guard down.»

"Sounds good."

As we were making our way through a clearing, Berla turned toward me. "I've been wondering—why haven't we encountered any beasts yet?"

"We've seen a few before, but we were able to avoid them," I said.

"A few? We saw several category fives every day!"

"What's a category five?" I asked.

"The one that got me was cat five, one of the strongest beasts in this area."

It was the first time I had heard the term, but it made sense that the Fighters would have a ranking system for the different kinds of beasts. These bears being one of the strongest also meant that we were able to kill the strongest beasts around, which filled me with some sense of safety.

"And you've seen several of them? With how dangerous the woods are supposed to be, we *did* find it weird that we barely ran into any beasts, but we didn't really think about it anymore after a certain point," I said.

"Beasts rarely kill other beasts," Berla mumbled, giving me a suspicious side-eye.

"Miles says, 'That's one theory.'"

Berla chuckled. "The dynamic between you two is quite bizarre. Can he talk through you while you're awake?"

"Honestly, we've never tested it."

Knowing that Miles controlled my body at night was creepy enough, but my own body moving around on its own while I was wide awake was something I struggled with. I knew that Miles had been stuck with that sensation for weeks now, but I hadn't been ready to give him that much control yet.

"Let me watch—if you try it," she said.

Berla's vastly different demeanor made me feel slightly uncomfortable. I hadn't expected Miles to work a miracle last night, but it seemed he did just about that. "What did you two talk about last night?" I asked.

"Nothing special. Boring adult stuff," she said with a chuckle.

I raised my brow. "Adult stuff?"

«She's just making fun of you.»

Maybe I should've been concerned about how quickly they bonded, but I didn't care at that moment. It was nice that everyone was happy. We continued on for a few hours, and shortly before noon, we reached the path that would lead us westward toward Cerus.

"Finally out of the woods," I said.

The road we were standing on was similar to the dirt road that had led us into the woods east of Alarna. It was wide enough for six people to comfortably walk side-by-side, with a generous buffer zone between it and the forest.

"I would say 'we're safer now,' but you guys are apparently scaring away the beasts anyway," Berla said with a shrug. "It is nice to travel under an open sky, though."

From here, it would take less than three days to reach the mining town. All I knew was that it was similar to Alarna in many aspects. Unlike our hometown, however, Cerus was a merchant town and more open to letting people come and go.

"Have you been to Cerus before?" I asked her.

"I've accompanied the caravan a few times, but we never stayed longer than a night."

"Will they just let us in?"

"As long as you fix your mana, it shouldn't be a problem."

She was well informed. Apparently she and Miles hadn't only made smalltalk. He didn't have a definitive solution yet, but he was getting close to finishing a prototype script, which we would then test.

"Can Berla learn to use scripts like us?" Riala asked.

Berla looked at the young girl with surprise. It seemed like she hadn't considered the possibility, even though it had been all the captain and the priest focused on when they questioned me.

"I don't know if I'd actually want that, but I am curious about the answer," she said as she looked at me.

Miles and I had talked a bit about what happened with Riala and me, but we only had theories. One was that the water source had infused us with its mana, but since we were actively regenerating it ourselves, that seemed unlikely. The other theory was that the blast had somehow enabled or unlocked our mana. However, when we blasted the captain into a prison wall, we had used a considerable amount of mana as well. If it were that simple, he should've started exuding mana. Aside from not knowing enough, Miles and I had decided to keep these particular theories to ourselves for now.

"We don't know the exact steps yet, so she can't at the moment," I said in response.

Both seemed content with my answer. Giving others our abilities was certainly an interesting prospect, but it would have also changed the world as we knew it, potentially turning even children into dangerous weapons.

As we traveled along the road on this mild summer morning, I thought back to how I had assumed my life to be over just a few days ago. Now, walking under the sun, talking and laughing with Riala and Berla, it seemed like a bad dream, and I was excited for what might come next.

CHAPTER 30
On The Road

"Everything okay?" I asked Berla.

She had been looking down, examining the dirt in front of her for a while.

"Yeah. It's nothing," she replied, fixing her eyes ahead.

All I saw was a well-used dirt road, but I felt like she had been looking at it for a reason. I was expecting Miles to chime in and say something about my observations, but he said, «We should test the black stone tonight.»

You're in your own little world again, aren't you?

"I am curious about it as well," I said, gesturing to the others that I was talking to Miles, "but don't we have more important things to worry about?"

«You mean the mana? We can test that as well; I just finished the prototype.»

"And onto the next one already," I said with a snicker.

I could hardly blame him. He enjoyed scripting, and it was probably pretty boring up there otherwise. It wasn't like he had anything else to do, after all. I was wondering once more what it would be like to be just a voice in someone's head, when Berla suddenly stopped, pulled out a dagger, and turned around, letting one of her crutches fall to the floor.

I quickly glanced behind us and saw a beast standing in the middle of the road, about ten meters behind us. Just like the two times we had seen beasts back in Alarna, it just stared at us, unmoving. Me and Riala each grabbed a blue stone and raised our arms, when a voice came from the beast's mouth.

"You are the anomaly?" it said in a raspy voice, looking straight at me.

Even though I had heard from Miles that the second beast back then had said something to him, actually hearing it was still mind-boggling. I glanced at my traveling companions, who were similarly staring at it with their eyes wide, and mouths agape.

"Did that beast just... say something?" Berla said, unbelieving.

It was good to know that this wasn't common and surprised a seasoned Fighter just as much as it did us. I had a clean line of fire, but I was so startled that the thought of shooting had momentarily disappeared from my mind. From my right, I felt a tug at my clothes. Looking down, I saw Riala staring at something. I followed her eyes and saw a second beast positioning itself behind us.

"I asked you a question, human," the first beast said.

A question? I thought. It hadn't registered. Still in a daze, I sputtered, "W-What was the question?"

"How is this beast talking?" Berla blurted out.

It snarled at her, then focused on me again. "Why do you smell like that, human?"

Riala was aiming at the second beast, while I had my arms pointed at the first. It might've been smarter to kill them, but curiosity overcame me.

"Smell like what?" I asked.

"That's what I want to know. You do not smell human, human."

"I don't know what I'm supposed to say to that. I am one."

I had no idea what was happening. I briefly considered whether this creature was talking about the mana or not, but Miles reminded me that we didn't have it when he heard a beast talk for the first time.

«The other one said we "smelled funny."»

The beast's ears perked up when Miles said that.

"That's why... How did you get in there?" it said.

Just like the "god" before, this beast was able to hear Miles. *Is this good or bad?* I wondered. The god didn't seem happy about it, but a god being able to hear him seemed fairly reasonable—unlike a wild beast.

«Before I answer that, would you mind answering a question?»

"You're in no position to be asking questions," the beast snorted.

«It would help if we knew what position that was.»

"Can we just take care of them and be on our way?" the other beast suddenly said.

Great. Both can talk, and they do want to kill us.

"Riala," I whispered, "aim carefully."

She nodded and prepared herself.

"Just a moment," the first said in response to the second. "You. Why were you in that town? And inside a human, no less?"

"We don't know what you're talking about," I said in place of Miles. "Where *should* he have been?"

The beast grew quiet as it looked us over. It knew something we didn't, but it wouldn't freely share. I considered ways we could make it talk, but we didn't have the right scripts prepared for immobilizing such a strong enemy.

«Maybe we can help each other out; we both have questions.»

Reading the facial features of something with a snout wasn't an easy feat, but if I had to guess, I'd say it looked like it was smirking.

"If you don't have an answer to that particular question, your answers have no worth to me," it said, before addressing its partner. "Let's get this over with."

Both creatures launched themselves at us. Riala and I used our scripts, but only one of them reached its target. She hit the beast straight on, leaving it with more empty space than face. It cratered into the ground, its forward momentum finally giving out when it came to a stop before us.

The other beast managed to evade my water stream. In the split second before contact, it stepped to the side and kept coming at us. I froze in surprise and the monster was upon me in no time. The only reason I'd kept my head was because Berla shoved me out of the way. I stumbled over Riala and we both fell to the ground.

It immediately lunged for me again, but Berla jumped onto its back and repeatedly drove her dagger into its spine to create a distraction. Riala and I got to our knees and tried to shoot it point blank, but a fraction of a second before we fired, the beast jumped out of the way, with Berla still on its back.

«Damn it!» Miles spat in frustration.

We had been at full capacity, and we weren't using our strongest scripts, but we didn't have the luxury of infinite mana. We had never had a situation where a beast managed or even tried to evade our attacks.

«We have to catch it off guard!»

"Riala, stay here and shoot when I tell you to!" I instructed.

The creature tried to shake Berla, who was doing her best to stab through its thick hide, but for all her efforts, there were only shallow wounds and bruised fur. Failing to free itself from the Fighter's mount, the beast ran straight at a tree and tried to ram her into it. At the last moment, she released her grip, and the beast slammed into the trunk alone.

"Now!" I instructed Riala, before making some distance between us.

With Berla out of the way, she had a clean shot. When it saw her shoot, it immediately evaded in the only free direction, turning away from my traveling companions, where I was waiting for it. With a shocked expression, it saw a stream of water erupt from my palm, and the monster was unable to change its direction quick enough with its current momentum. The water sliced through its face and parts of its body, leaving a twenty-centimeter-wide hole. It dropped dead in the grass at the side of the road.

I was panting heavily and glanced around to make sure Berla and Riala were uninjured. "Are you okay?"

"Yes," answered Riala. Berla just nodded—both had labored breaths.

We all checked our surroundings, but we seemed to be alone with the two dead beasts. Exhausted, I collapsed to the ground, my heart pounding in my ears. "What the fuck was that?!"

* * *

We rested for a little while and talked about the attack. Everything about it seemed strange. Even putting the "talking" part aside for now, these were the first ones that had attacked us directly out here.

"What category was this one?" Berla said, confused, looking at the one we had struggled to kill. "It looks like a cat three, but it was way too tough," she mused. "I couldn't slash its throat and my dagger could barely penetrate its flesh. This isn't normal."

"Talking beasts aren't normal either, right?" I asked her.

"I don't even want to think about that. I've heard of intelligent beasts before, but never about ones that could talk… And why were they looking for *you*?"

It seemed like the creature had been specifically interested in Miles being inside of me instead of somewhere else, perhaps as a mistake. Not in Alarna and especially not inside my mind. I told Berla about the incident where Miles had heard a beast talk before, as well as what he had said to this beast now.

"You said you weren't dangerous, but you do seem to attract unusual and dangerous problems," Berla said with a frown.

«That's not exactly our fault,» Miles said, and I forwarded it.

"Maybe not… But at what point does it become a problem for others?" she said. "An entire group of soldiers died trying to catch you. Little Riala over there got roped into everything, and she could've easily died today as well."

She was telling me that it might be better for everyone if I was gone. If I had become a Mad One, I would've been killed, and none of this would've happened. All those people and my mother might have still been alive, and Riala would be safe within the town walls with Zara.

I looked over to the young girl who was… petting the dead beast…?

"It's fluffy!" she said with a bright smile. It was a surreal scene.

"We can't change the past," I said, laughing at the absurdity of what we were looking at. "If", "maybe", "perhaps"—none of it really mattered. We had done our best, and we would keep doing so.

"Are you really okay with dying for the greater good?" I asked Berla. "I'm not. And what would become of Riala? Do you want her to kill herself as well?"

Berla looked at the girl with a sad expression. In a way, we were three dead men walking. Back in Alarna, Riala and I would've been executed, and Berla would have been thanked for her service and then "put to rest," whatever that meant, exactly. We would have to fight to turn our life around, but I believed that we could do it.

CHAPTER 31

Meanwhile

In the past two hundred years, no one had made any progress in researching the scripture sigils, and Oryn Tilia had been the first priest in a hundred years to resume it. He studied the water sources, the ritual platform, the stones, and everything his predecessors had ever written about the sigils.

In all recorded history, there had been one successful attempt at using scripture sigils not given to them by the gods. It incorporated a black stone which, in combination with modified sigils, would produce an effect unlike anything anyone had ever seen. It had been pure luck that a priest had stumbled over these sigils, and even using a black stone hadn't been his intention. He had clumsily tripped over his robe, blurred part of the sigils he had been experimenting with, and dropped the stone he was holding onto the water source he was testing the sigils on. The produced effect had been fascinating, but unfortunately it didn't have any practical usage.

Oryn had once reproduced the experiment successfully, but he had come to the same conclusion as the priests of the past. He also was discontent with the way this discovery had been made. He didn't want to rely on luck. He wanted to actually decipher the sigils and learn how to use them, just like a certain boy had done recently.

A leather-bound notebook filled with dozens of hand-drawn iterations was proof. Sigil after sigil. Page after page. Again and again, with slight variations.

"Attempt sixty-eight..." he said to himself.

The sigils Oryn had seen on the hands of Tomar and Riala hadn't been complete, but after combining them, there were very few gaps to fill anymore. If he could just find the right sigils to make the scripture work, he would become the first priest to have ever discovered something new on purpose.

During his years of research, he had developed many theories as to what certain sigils could mean. A single scripture was nigh useless for this kind of analysis, but in combination with the black stone experiment and the sigils on the ritual platform, he had at least been able to make out certain patterns, even if they had never led him to success.

"Come on..." he said as he placed a blue stone on the small water source on a table before him.

With bated breath, Oryn looked at the cube. After a few seconds he let himself fall backward into a chair and started staring at the ceiling.

"I've tested every combination..." He let out a loud groan.

Based on his notes and theories, one of the scriptures should've worked. With disappointment plastered on his face, he mentally went over everything he had seen and heard once more. He wouldn't give up so easily.

While playing with a blue stone in his hand, Oryn stood back up and paced around the room. He tried to reenact the scenes of how the boy and the girl had used the scripts. He raised his arms, he ran, and he jumped, but no idea would come to him. When he made another small leap and tried to do a pose, he messed up the landing and tripped over his own foot, stumbling head first into the table with the water source. It toppled over and Oryn ended up on his back, with one hand on the cube beside him.

"Ow...." Suddenly, a large stream of water shot out of the water source and propelled the cube upward into the ceiling.

He was barely able to roll out of the way before the heavy source crashed where he was just seconds ago. Oryn's eyes went wide, and he jumped to his feet to examine the water source. *How did I do that?*

He grabbed another blue stone and desperately placed it onto the water source, but nothing happened until he went over what had happened again. He realized that the cube had landed with the scripture facing upward. He had placed the stone *on* the scripture, not on top of the cube, like you usually would.

A *squish* sounded from rotating the cube on the wet carpet as he recreated how it had been positioned before. He placed another blue stone on the source and quickly stepped away. Once more, it blasted into the ceiling and fell to the ground with a wet thud.

"I did it... I did it!"

He was over the moon, but his repeated cries of joy did not go unnoticed. A priestess hammered on the door from outside his room.

"Shut up, Oryn!"

It wasn't unusual for him to bother the other priests with frustrated shouts when his experiments didn't produce any results, but the ruckus he was causing today was on another level. The door flew open and an ecstatic Oryn came out of nowhere, tackling the priestess into a hug.

"Wah!"

"I did it, Aelene! I discovered a new scripture!" he shouted into her ear.

She did his best to pry him off of her, but with his tight grip and erratic movements, it proved difficult.

"Let go of me!" she yelled, finally managing to push him away, making him fall onto his wet floor. "What is wrong with you? And why is your whole room wet?"

"I did it!" he said, laughing like a maniac.

It wasn't until now that his words finally registered in her mind. "You... you did? Are you serious?"

"I restored the sigils the kids had on their hands! Wait, I'll show you!"

He quickly got up and ran over to the water source, almost tripping over himself. Aelene hesitantly walked into his room, her every step producing a *squish*. As she entered, she looked around the room, seeing a mess of papers, books, and stones, most of it drenched.

"The High Priest is going to rip you apart if he sees what you did to the temple's books," she said.

He only briefly glanced behind him to look at her while he rotated the water source into place again. "Huh? Oh, it doesn't matter. I know every single word in these books. I'll just rewrite them. And then I'll add one of my own!"

Oryn motioned for her to stay where she was and used the script a third time. Aelene looked on with wide eyes as she watched the cube fly up with a strong gust of water. Even the fact that some of it sprayed onto her, and that the ground below her feet was becoming more pond than carpet, didn't bother her.

"That's amazing, Oryn," she said in a daze. "How did you do that?"

He was about to explain his process when he froze. "I..." he started, but he said no more and fell to his knees, looking at the carpet, crestfallen.

"Hey, what's wrong?" she said with worry.

"It was just dumb luck, just like him," he said, not quite realizing that it had been more than that.

* * *

"Hertar! You have to send someone to look for her!" a woman said to the king. "She might be all alone in the woods, without any food or water!"

"Berlotte... The soldiers searched for survivors, but they didn't find anyone. I'm very sorry, but the chances that she is still out there—"

"Don't give me that!" Berlotte said, interrupting King Hertar. "You encouraged her to become an agent, and you sent her on this mission! I don't care about chances. I expect you to not rest until you have found my daughter! That's the least you can do!"

"You have been holding that over me for years," the king said. "She got the Fighter Calling, and we all had to live with that. I was hoping to make her my successor! The least I could do was to make sure she would have a good life!"

"And you think part of that good life was going after criminals out in the Wildlands?" she asked, exasperated. "Please, Hertar, I beg of you... send someone to look for her. If there's even a sliver of a chance, we have to take it."

King Hertar had no reason to believe that his niece, Berla, was still alive. Lera hadn't found her body, but even together with her partner, Pari, she wouldn't have stood much of a chance against a category five beast. And if she had miraculously survived, she would've been able to make her way back home—unless she was gravely injured, that is. But the last thing he wanted was for his men to find her disabled. She would not be able to do her destined job anymore, in which case town law would require him to send her to her death.

He wasn't able to exempt himself and his family from the town's laws. Over the years, he himself had sentenced hundreds of people to be put to rest, and not following the same rules could lead to riots like it had when rulers had tried to do so in the past. Should they actually find an incapacitated Berla, his sister would never speak with him ever again. On the other hand, he had a hard time ignoring her pleadings.

"Berlotte," he said, "I will send a few guards to search for her, but please, prepare yourself for the worst."

"I feel that she's still alive, Hertar. You will see," she said before thanking her brother profusely and leaving the room in high spirits.

After she departed, the king begrudgingly turned to a guard that was standing in a corner of the room. "Get me Eissen."

The guard quietly saluted the king and left the room.

He would have to do *something* to get his sister off his back, but he didn't intend to execute any extensive searches. Unless Berla was still alive and had just decided to not come back for some reason, nothing good would come from finding her. Giving the job to a trusted subordinate of his childhood friend, Lera, would be the safest way to see his requests fulfilled.

About half an hour later, there was a knock on the door.

"Come in," the king said.

Eissen entered and knelt before the king with his head bowed. "Your Majesty."

"I need you to assemble a squad and head to the southern woods where Lera had last seen my niece Berla. You know her, right?"

"Yes, Your Majesty. It is a tragedy that she did not return. My heartfelt condolences."

"Thank you... but I want you to do another search for her. If you find her well despite all odds, bring her home safe. If not, I expect you to come back alone. Do you understand?"

"I will do what's necessary," the guard said without hesitation.

"And don't put the search above your own lives. You, too, are expected to return safely. Should the beast situation still be out of control, retreat immediately."

"We will. Thank you for your concern, Your Majesty," Eissen said before leaving.

* * *

A direct order from the king was a great opportunity for the young guard. All he had to do was ensure Berla wouldn't return, and he would be one step closer to one day succeed Lera as guard captain. If everything went well, it might even put him above Jara, the current second in command of the eastern guard.

He assembled a group of four trusted guards, and they left for the southern woods posthaste.

CHAPTER 32
CAMPING

Once evening hit, we made camp in a wide clearing that housed a water source. Places like this were scattered at regular intervals along the route, made to ensure that merchants and guards who frequented the journey would have easy access to water and a campsite.

«Feels kind of nostalgic to see one of these cubes.»

"If only people knew that trees can give water. The only reason they need water sources during these trips is because the default script doesn't work as expected on trees," I said.

"What? Trees can give water?" Berla asked incredulously.

She had seen us produce water a few times now, but not from a tree. We had stopped using them just before meeting her because I wanted to expend some mana during the day to be able to sleep at night.

"Most of them can. But the water source script doesn't work because of the input location."

"I'll show her!" Riala said excitedly, pulling Berla away. I watched her draw and execute a script, while Berla looked on in amazement.

"Riala would've been a good match for you as a Calling," I said to Miles with a chuckle. "Then again, you probably would've gotten into trouble even sooner."

«Or we might've advanced faster, become much more powerful, and then taken over control of Alarna,» Miles said jokingly.

"Now you want to be king? Or I guess it would be *queen* with Riala? Praise be to Queen Miles!" I said, laughing.

«Granted, that might've been a little awkward.»

The three of us passed the time in relative peace after that. I gathered some dry twigs and moss to start a fire. The older woman had a hard time following

Riala's ramblings, but she listened with interest, marveling at the water streams hopping around in the air.

I thought back to what Berla and I had talked about after we defeated the beasts. She had been in good spirits in the morning, but the strange events surrounding us seemed to have brought her back to reality.

"I know it's weird for me to ask this now, but do you think we can fully trust her? Her questions earlier seemed a little ominous."

«You should never trust someone until you really know them. That said, she *did* help us with those beasts.»

"Her mission was also to bring us back alive."

«True. Does it really matter though? You considered the possibility that we won't be able to rest in Cerus. You're prepared for it. And if she doesn't betray us after we get there, we should be safe. Might be best not to teach her attack scripts, though.»

"Unless she's faking it, I don't think we have to worry about that," I said with a giggle, looking at Berla. The expression on her face as she tried to grasp Riala's explanation of chaining scripts was priceless. "Speaking of Riala... her progress isn't normal, is it? I have some of your knowledge at least, but she's absorbing all this as if it's nothing, and she hasn't even properly learned to read yet!"

«Children do learn faster, but no—she definitely isn't normal. Maybe she's a prodigy. At least she hasn't managed to come up with any completely new scripts; that would demotivate even me a little.»

It took a few more minutes and some rigorous work from me to get the fire roaring. The other two made their way over to prepare dinner. Berla insisted that we make enough to last us another day, but I wasn't entirely enthusiastic about what we were eating.

"Are you really sure this is edible?" I said, taking a meat skewer from Berla to cook over the fire. She had done most of the work, butchering the beasts into various cuts of meat.

"You have so much to learn about life. What do you think the meat you ate in town was?" Berla said.

I froze. "I've been eating beast all my life? My mother always called it deer!"

"Your family wouldn't have been able to afford venison," she said with an eyebrow raised. "I guess it's not entirely your own fault you're this innocent. Your mother might've—"

She stopped, realizing that her next words would shake me more than eating beast meat did.

I clenched the skewer in my hand. My knuckles grew white with tension as I held the meat over the flames, trying not to let the sadness overtake me.

"Tomar, I'm sorry..." Berla said.

"It's okay."

An apology. Apologies are good. ADD[TRUST;1], I thought.

Silence loomed over our group until dinner was done. After a few minutes of the meat sizzling away, I took a bite—juicy, tasty goodness oozing out. On my right, Riala tried to eat gracefully, but quickly burned her tongue.

"Ah! Hot!"

"Drink something," I told her while chewing.

Grabbing her cup and a water stone, she scampered over to the water source, making me giggle lightly. In her pain, she must've forgotten that she could've just used the script on her arm.

"How is it?" Berla asked.

"A bit greasy, but good," I said, smiling slightly. "It isn't so bad out here, is it?"

"Aside from the talking beasts, you mean?" she said with a chuckle.

"'Isolated incident,'" I said, gesturing that it came from Miles.

"I have to admit, with you guys around, one could almost forget that these woods are filled with dangerous beasts. Sitting here, in nature, looking at the stars... It's nice."

"It could be a life."

"Maybe..." she said.

* * *

"This is weird, isn't it?" Eissen said while walking through the southern woods, flanked by four other guards. "I heard the last group was practically stumbling over beasts every few hours, but I've never seen the Wildlands more quiet, especially at night! It almost seems wrong, doesn't it?"

"Definitely. I thought you were crazy for suggesting that we should keep going at night, Eissen," another said. "Did you know we wouldn't encounter anything out here?"

Their leader peered carefully around the forest, using a lantern to fend back the inky darkness. The forest was indeed eerily serene.

"Honestly, I'm as surprised as you are. Even if the category fives are gone, I would've expected the usual ones to appear."

Before setting out for Cerus, Captain Lera had advised caution. The complete lack of beasts was a small miracle, and it would make the squad's job much easier. The group kept a tight formation, traveling through the forest until they came upon the place where the captain decided to retreat. The actual search would begin here. The party fanned out, combing every blade of grass and unturned rock in hopes of picking up a trail. Eventually, one presented itself, and they followed it west until one among them noticed something slightly off their path.

"Hey, Eissen. Is that a grave?" the guard said.

Cautiously, the group walked over and examined the mound of rocks piled haphazardly.

"This is Pari, Berla's partner," Eissen said after they had dug up the contents of the makeshift grave.

"She buried him? That means she's alive," a guard said in surprise.

As the group continued, they came upon a clearing. Between it and them stood several damaged trees.

"What happened to these trees?"

"You've read the reports, haven't you?" Eissen snapped. "The boy probably did this."

"The boy?! This hole is a meter across! What did he—" he started, but as he looked around, the guard's eyes fell on a large, dark lump, lying on the other side of the clearing. Holding his lantern in its direction, he realized it was a beast. "Enemy!" he shouted.

The guards immediately readied their spears, but quickly realized the creature was motionless, and a critical body part was missing.

"Its head is gone…"

They carefully approached, monitoring their surroundings as they moved. One guard startled the others when he tripped over something on the ground.

"Ah! Is that… a leg?"

Eissen crouched down to examine the slender limb partially covered in black cloth. "This must be hers," he said.

The pieces were falling into place. Berla's leg had been ripped off during the fight, but instead of her body or a blood trail, they found a dead beast. She wouldn't have been able to decapitate it or bury Pari in her state, and a lack of a grave for her suggested that she was still alive.

Someone had come to her aid.

"She's with the boy," Eissen declared.

It made sense. She had chosen life and went with the guy that could blast away a category five beast's head.

"That's it then. They probably left yesterday. We won't be able to catch up to them," a guard said.

Their mission wasn't going according to plan. Eissen had wanted to make a good impression on the king, but he had neither found Berla's remains nor been able to kill her. If she was with the boy and didn't plan to come back, she would be branded a deserter, and if she showed herself around Alarna again, she would be executed.

I need to report this to King Hertar, Eissen thought.

The group started heading back to town, relieved that they hadn't encountered anything that threatened their lives.

"If the Wildlands were always like this, we wouldn't need walls," one of the guards said in wonder.

CHAPTER 33

FAILS

"Before we start, I want us to test something else," Tomar had said after dinner.

We had a few different things to try out tonight, such as the black stone, but he had another item to add to the list. I had no idea what it was, and I was startled when Tomar suddenly started tilting to the side as if his strings had been cut. I barely managed to catch us, preventing our forehead from becoming intimate with the ground.

"Tomar!" I cried in panic.

I was suddenly in control of his body, but something felt different from how it did when he was asleep. As if the body was truly mine. It was easier to move around, and my senses were stronger.

"Did you—"

«Wow…» came Tomar's voice from inside my head.

"What's going on?" Berla said with worry.

"Tomar gave me full control," I told her.

«This feels disorienting.»

I stood up and stretched—a youthful body was something else.

"Miles? Did Tomar fall asleep?" Riala asked.

"No, Ria. Now *he's* the voice in *my* head," I said with a laugh. "You should've given me more warning, Tomar. Everything okay?"

«I think so. It's surreal. I'm wide awake, all my tiredness is gone.»

"Yeah, it's right here," I said.

The need for sleep was presumably tied to Tomar's physical body. Whoever was in the back seat didn't get tired. At all. Ever.

It's not as fun as it sounds, I thought. Right now, it felt like I had been walking all day, and I felt exhausted for the first time in weeks.

"I kind of like it. I could go for a few hours of sleep. Being wide awake that first night was really irritating."

«Believe me, I remember. The headache the next morning was something else,» Tomar commented grumpily.

Berla looked at me curiously as I talked with Tomar. "You're in full control now? What's it like?" she asked.

"It's... normal. As if this were my own body right now. When you're up there, you feel kind of like a puppeteer, and during the day, the puppet does whatever it wants," I said. "Although, this tingly feeling is weird..."

«Hmm? What do you mean?» Tomar said in confusion.

Since shortly after I had been given control, there had been a slight prickling sensation throughout my body, and it was growing stronger. I didn't recognize this feeling, and it slowly started to unnerve me how it got worse over time. It didn't feel normal.

«Maybe my body just feels different from your own?»

"I'm not sure. It's actually starting to hurt a little. It's kind of like... my body is on fire! Let's switch back! How do you do it?"

Tomar quickly explained to me how he had been picturing his own body not belonging to himself, and following his instructions, I was suddenly back to being only a voice and felt almost nothing anymore.

«Is the pain still there?» I asked.

"No. I feel fine. Just like always," Tomar said. "It was burning? Like the mana before?"

«I think so. Maybe your mana doesn't like me,» I said, crestfallen.

After the water source blew up, Tomar was in a lot of pain. I only slightly felt it at the time, but he had said it was like fire flowing through his body. The pain had subsided over time, and eventually it disappeared completely. It coming back as soon as Tomar gave me the wheel probably wasn't a coincidence.

«Well, this sucks.»

* * *

Based on Miles' experience while being inside of me, he was assuming that foreign mana could be a problem. We guessed that the burning sensation back then was either us getting used to our own mana, or that a bit of mana from the water source had gotten into our systems. With that knowledge, we concluded that my body considered Miles as an invader.

"Still want to do some tests?" I asked compassionately.

«Yeah, let's,» Miles said with a sigh.

"Me first!" Riala yelled.

"No, not you first. Tree first," I said.

The main test for today would be a script that was supposed to suck up external mana and funnel it back into the vessel. We had yet to find a way to execute a script without it running indefinitely or requiring a stone, but for this particular application, an infinite loop would actually be ideal. The idea was that the mana would be removed from the air and infused back into our bodies before it could cause any issues for other people.

I drew the script onto a tree, per Miles' instructions, and it activated automatically after the last stroke. Riala and I looked on in fascination as the mana emitted from it lessened. Meanwhile, Berla stood at our side, taking everything in.

"How do you know if it's doing anything?" she asked.

"We can see the mana, and it's definitely doing *something*," I replied.

A short time later, the mana around the tree disappeared completely. I was about to declare the experiment a success, but something unexpected happened.

«Does the tree look darker than before?»

"It's difficult to say in this light," I replied. But when the trunk started to crumble away, we knew something was wrong.

"Get back!" I instructed.

We quickly put some distance between ourselves and the tree. From there, we kept watching as it slowly disintegrated.

Within seconds, the middle part of the trunk was no longer able to support the rest of its canopy, causing it to topple over with a deafening crack. Dazed, we stared at the fallen tree and the script on its trunk that had felled it.

«Volunteers?»

* * *

When Aelene had left Oryn in his room in the afternoon, he was unresponsive and continuously mumbled something about being a fraud. Physically, he appeared fine, so she hadn't been too worried about her eccentric colleague. It was normal for him to fluctuate between enthusiasm and frustration at a moment's notice. But when he hadn't come to the dining hall that evening, she started to become a little concerned.

She made her way back to his room and knocked, but no answer came. Aelene put her ear to the door, managing to catch some noises from within.

"Oryn?" she said, carefully cracking open the door to peer in. "Are you okay?"

She could see him standing at his table, working on something, but he obstructed her view. In an attempt to get his attention, she raised her voice.

"Oryn!" she called, and he finally turned around.

"Aelene? What is it?"

"I just wanted to check up on you. When you didn't come to the dining hall, I thought you might still be sulking."

"Oh, no. Don't worry," he said, turning back to the water source on his table. "Now that I know what I did wrong, I just have to continue. I will have my success, come what may."

"So you haven't reported what happened today to the High Priest? I imagine he would be delighted, even if you got lucky."

"Perhaps, but he would send me back to continue right afterwards, anyway. I might as well make a big impression," he said, putting the finishing touches on the cube. "This is the one, and it will be my own accomplishment."

"What is this one supposed to do, then?" Aelene asked, looking at the scripture variant.

"The boy had another one on his body, and I noticed a certain pattern between the sigils in that one, the water source scripture, and the one I tested today. If I'm right, this will change everything."

Oryn finished his work and put down the stick of chalk. He took a deep breath to steady himself and grabbed a blue stone from a bowl.

"Theoretically, this should put a decent-sized hole in the wall."

"Wait, what? Oryn, you—" Aelene started, but he was so fixated on his test that he didn't hear her.

Oryn held the stone to the cube, staring intently at the wall.

Aelene's eyes widened as the cube started vibrating and appeared to implode. A stream of water shot out from one side of the cube and into the wall, while an invisible force hit Oryn and Aelene. Both were thrown backward onto the floor.

With a groan, Aelene propped herself up before looking at the hole in the wall. "You maniac! What were you thinking? There are rooms on the other side of that wall!"

Oryn didn't react to her admonishments. He was entirely focused on his experiment. In a whisper he said, "I understand it, Aelene. I actually understand the change I made to the scripture. My theory is correct."

As he lay on the wet floor, Oryn marveled at the fact that he had made a purposeful change to the scripture. Something that, to his knowledge, no priest had accomplished before.

I finally did it, he thought. *All those years, all the time I spent on researching the scripture sigils, all—wait...* The realization of what had actually happened struck Oryn like a brick. He looked at the empty table where the water source stood moments ago. He hadn't intended to destroy it, but he realized that Tomar had probably done the same thing.

The chained water source disappeared, a stream of water injured a beast heavily, and then...

Aelene was about to yell at him again when suddenly, both of their bodies tensed up, and a searing pain made them scream in agony. It didn't take long for silence to fall over the room. Other priests who had heard the ruckus peeped out from their offices, but an eerie aura seemed to reach from the room into the hallway. At first, nobody dared to approach. A priest with high curiosity slowly walked up to the open door and looked inside. He saw Aelene and Oryn motionless on the floor. He didn't understand why, but he had a hard time formulating a clear thought in his mind. He stumbled backward, struggling to even look away.

"G-G-Get the High Priest!" he finally managed to blurt out, panic bleeding in his voice.

CHAPTER 34
BIRTH OF HOPE

I stared at the script that had made short work of a tree, now drawn into a patch of dirt with a stick. It hadn't quite worked as intended. It *did* make the tree's mana disappear from our vision, but there was another issue we couldn't pinpoint. While Berla was doing maintenance on her weapons, Riala sat down by my side, listening in on my one-sided discussion with Miles. As always, he wasn't short on theories about what might've happened.

"You think the tree overloaded itself with mana?"

«It's a possibility. We saw the mana vanish completely, and it was all put back into the vessel immediately, but maybe the mana needs to be able to leave the tree. And without that outlet, the mana destroyed it from the inside. The water source, on the other hand, was destroyed under the strain we put on it... I think the mana needs to be balanced carefully.»

"What's the alternative, then? Could the amount be reduced instead of stopping it completely?"

«We could test that, though I'm not hopeful.»

The problem with my idea was that it would presumably still lead to an overload. If you put all mana that streams out of the vessel right back in, it would destroy itself. Slowing this process down would give you more time, but it would most likely still happen.

Regardless of the chance of success, we decided to give it a try and went back to the tree line. At first, the results produced looked promising, as the tree's visible mana lessened by about half. But eventually it, too, died.

«Back to the drawing board.»

It was clear that this idea wasn't going to work. We couldn't stop the mana, but just letting it stream out of us wasn't going to work, either. We needed to do something else with it.

"Can I do the next tree?" Riala asked, her eyes signaling that she wanted to fell a tree as well.

"I think this was the last one for now," I said.

Looking down at her, I thought back to a script she had tried two days ago. She had used it to create a wall of water droplets, thinly spreading the effect over a large area. If we were to apply this to our mana, would that solve the problem?

"Hey, Miles. How about spreading the effect like Riala did with the water the other day?"

«Huh... Interesting idea. The concentration might be a factor, like on those "gods." Let's try it!»

We walked over to the next tree, and I handed the chalk over to Riala, knowing that she wouldn't be happy until she could test a new script as well.

"Can you draw one like your rain script, but with the external mana as the input?"

"Okay!"

She went to work immediately. I didn't quite understand how she was improving this quickly. It had only been a few days since she started studying, but she understood Omega almost as well as me. *I can't let her beat me*, I thought.

With the last stroke she made, the script activated, and the mana scattered over a wider area. It resembled fog. The tree appeared healthy, just with less mana surrounding it. While we marveled at the promising result, Berla startled us when she suddenly appeared at our rear, dagger at the ready.

"What did you do?" she yelled.

"We're just trying different scripts," I said in confusion as I glanced back at her. "What's wrong?"

"It feels like a beast is here!" she said.

Interestingly, the scattered mana around the tree did not have the desired effect. Instead of making something less threatening, we had created a "tree beast." *This could be useful for distractions*, I thought. It was fascinating how much of an effect different mana concentrations would have on normal humans.

«I think the idea is good, it just needs to be tweaked. We should try scattering the mana even more to see what happens. Either it will get worse, or we'll reach a point where the mana isn't perceivable anymore.»

"Should we try it on us?"

«Sounds good.»

Since this script didn't have any negative effects on the vessel, it would be safe to test it on ourselves. With Berla, we'd get an accurate reading about how frightening the new results were.

I walked over to the fire, took the ink, and carefully drew the new script on my arm. After leaving most of the experimentation to Miles over the past couple days, it was a lot of fun to be directly involved once more.

As I made the last stroke, the mana around us lessened, just like it had on the tree. Instead of our mana, I could see an almost unperceivable fog around us. There was a limit to how much we could stretch the output, so if this didn't work, we would need a new plan. I looked over at Berla to see what her reaction was, but instead of looking at me, her eyes darted around, not focusing on anything in particular.

"How is it, Berla?" I asked.

"It's weird. You don't feel dangerous anymore, but it feels like there's something in the air," she said. "Do you know how Rulers sometimes feel? It's similar, but not quite the same. Does that make sense?"

"I think so. Does that mean... this would work?" I asked with hopeful eyes.

"You'll still draw attention to yourself, I would imagine, but nobody will flee from you," she said with a smile. "Good job."

It felt like an immense burden had been lifted from my shoulders. Not being able to enter a town ever again had been one of my greatest fears. I teared up slightly as I took a deep breath.

"We'll be okay..."

«You won't inspire confidence if you start crying now.»

"Oh, shut up," I said with a groan of happiness.

* * *

When the High Priest arrived at the living quarters, he saw a slew of priests praying in the hallway. They were kneeling a few meters away from an open door, which he knew belonged to Oryn Tilia. He hadn't been given details on the situation, but this display was clearly unusual.

"Out of the way," he said, and the priests in his path quickly moved to the side to let him through. As he got closer to the doorway, he started to feel the ominous air that had been described to him.

This air... out of his room... he thought.

The High Priest knew what Oryn was spending the majority of his time on, and what the boy's knowledge could mean for their research. Nevertheless, the High Priest had never expected Oryn to make any meaningful progress; not after their knowledge hadn't advanced for hundreds of years.

Did he do it?

Despite his nervousness, he tried to move as gracefully as was expected of him, and approached the door to look inside. The first person his eyes fell on was Oryn, sitting on the floor, staring at his hands. Focusing entirely on him, the High Priest didn't feel anything particularly special. Oryn seemed a little different, but if he had become a living water source, like the criminals, he should've been as frightening as a beast.

The other individual was a woman by Oryn's side. She didn't feel like a beast either. Instead, she felt divine. Not quite like a god, but still somewhere far beyond a human being. She was the reason the priests in the hallway were praying. They thought her akin to a newly born goddess.

"Oryn, w-what happened here?" the High Priest stammered.

Worshipers were less affected by the energy that beasts and gods were giving off, but even the High Priest couldn't stand before a god and feel nothing. And while Aelene's current state wasn't quite on that same level, he was already struggling slightly.

"Sir," Oryn said as he looked up at the High Priest, a mix of disappointment and confusion in his eyes. "I believe I have recreated the scripture that turned Mr. Remor and Ms. Fera into living water sources. But... it didn't work on me."

He explained to the High Priest what he was seeing. He told him about the mist that surrounded everyone, and especially the vast amount of it around Aelene. To his dismay, his own aura wasn't noticeably different from others, and the script that he had hastily written on his hand after regaining consciousness had produced an amount of water so miniscule, that he might as well just spit on the floor instead. With a hanging head, he glanced over at the unconscious Aelene.

"She is different from the other two, right? What does she feel like to you, sir?"

The High Priest was stunned silent. Oryn's experiment had turned one of his priestesses into a divine being. None of the clergy would believe her to be anything less when they saw her like this.

In an instant, the rug that was Orthur's world view had been pulled out from under him. Ignoring Oryn's inquiry, an abundance of questions flooded his mind. Of this power's nature, the gods' involvement, their divine existence... or lack thereof. Queries no Worshipper should ever think about suddenly appeared of vital importance and occupied his mind.

"Sir?" Oryn asked after a moment.

Slowly coming out of his daze, the High Priest finally responded. "She is divine. The priests are already praying in the hallway."

"That's what I thought," Oryn said with a sad smile.

He looked at Oryn, sitting on the floor, with downcast eyes and disappointment in his voice. However, to the High Priest, these feelings were misplaced.

"You have done this, Oryn Tilia. Be proud of that."

He looked at the High Priest in surprise. Oryn had never seen him so out of it. Instead of his usual pompous self, he seemed overwhelmed and compassionate. The priest's expression quickly turned to one of happiness as he came to realize that the High Priest was right. He had accomplished something remarkable, and this wasn't the end.

CHAPTER 35

First Light

«Ready for the next experiment?»

"Do you have any idea what might happen?"

«Not a clue, and I love it.»

With a nervous sigh, I shook my head. Was I the weird one for being apprehensive? Miles was excited, as was Riala, but Berla... she only looked at me in confusion.

"What are you going to try now?" she asked.

I pulled a stone out of my pocket and showed it to her.

"We found this in the woods yesterday."

"A black stone..." Berla marveled.

«We should call these things something else. It sounds kind of silly to say, "Oh my, a stone!"»

"Let's discuss that later," I said to Miles before turning to address Berla. "I've heard about black stones at the agency, but I haven't seen one until now, assuming this one is genuine."

"It certainly looks like it is. Do you know what it does?" she asked.

"No. You can imagine what a certain someone wants to do, though. If he were here, he would look like that," I said, motioning at an expectant and wide-eyed Riala.

Berla looked less enthused and glanced back at the two demolished trees a few meters away. "Is that how your experiments usually end up?"

"'Hey, that was my first—okay, maybe second miscalculation,'" Miles said through me. "'But we would never learn anything new if we didn't try new things.'"

One could hardly argue against that. It was unlikely that we would find someone who would be able and willing to tell us what this stone would do. Though, it didn't mean we should be reckless.

"Still, let's be more careful. Okay?"

«Don't worry, I'm not crazy enough to suggest that we use an unknown stone without safety precautions,» Miles said. «I say we look for a low-hanging branch, draw the script on its surface, put down the stone, and then wing it.»

I was honestly a little surprised at how reasonable his plan was. Then again, Miles had also been careful to not damage the water source in the beginning until he was sure he would be able to fix whatever he broke. *I should probably explain this way of approaching experiments to Riala later.*

"Alright. I'm going to look for a rock to break this stone into smaller pieces. With more fragments, we'll have more attempts, meaning more chances at success," I said.

After my task was complete, we selected a nearby branch that was big enough to script on. While I was preparing it, the girls waited at a safe distance.

"Low power, right?" I asked Miles as I arrived at the tree.

«Yup. Like the first ones we used on you and Riala, I'd say.»

"Sounds good."

I drew the script onto the branch with chalk. If we were to use a blue stone with it, we'd only get a trickle of water on the underside of the branch. However, with an unknown stone, we couldn't even hope to predict what would happen. *If blue stones make water, and white stones give Callings, what will a black one do?*

I dropped the stone onto the branch and quickly stepped back several meters. A second passed, then several, but nothing happened. I thought that maybe it hadn't been an actual stone after all, but when I walked closer to the tree again, the piece I had dropped on the branch had disappeared.

"Huh. So it is a stone, but it doesn't work with this script?" I said.

«Seems like it. Let's try it without conversion.»

I wasn't sure what that was supposed to do, given that it was my understanding that the conversation plus the stone equaled something other than mana appearing, but I did as Miles suggested.

After adjusting the script, I dropped a piece of black stone onto the branch once more and stepped away from the tree. Just like before, nothing seemed to happen, but the stone was no longer there.

"What a pointless test."

«If you don't know anything, you might as well test everything. I'd like to test it without force.»

"But with conversion?" I asked.

«That's right.»

Even though I had a solid understanding of what our scripts usually did by this point, Mile's process for figuring out new functions still felt random to me. *I wish there were more scripts that we could study.*

I adjusted the script a second time, dropped the stone, and distanced myself from our test subject. While moving away, I could already tell this attempt was not without effect by the expression on my companions' faces. When I turned around, I could see *something* happening.

"What is that?" I asked in a daze.

«I have no idea.»

Neither water nor Callings were falling from the branch. Instead, a shower of prismatic flakes floated down to the ground, their shapes and sizes varied. Despite the low light conditions, these iridescent particles appeared to be glowing brightly, though they didn't illuminate their surroundings.

As we watched on, mesmerized, I soon realized that several seconds had passed already. That script would not usually run for this long, especially not with a stone that small.

"Miles... why hasn't it stopped yet?" I asked with worry.

«I have not a clue,» Miles said in fascination.

After well over a minute, the amount of flakes slowly lessened. When the last one had fallen, it softly landed on the dirt, disappearing into the ground as if it never had been there.

* * *

A translucent, humanoid figure stood on a grass field that went on as far as the eye could see. The sky, colored a majestic violet by the sun floating just above the horizon, was cloudless and calm.

The figure began drawing sigils in the air with their fingers, starting with a large one in the center, and branching off into a web of smaller ones until their entire vision was filled. They looked over their work, corrected a mistake here and there, and then snapped their fingers. The sigils started to glow, and with a loud rumbling, the ground slowly changed shape as hills and ravines started to form. The earth below their feet started to rise as well, and when it stopped moving, they were able to oversee their work from a higher position.

They looked around with a satisfied smirk on their face. "So far, so good."

When they started drawing more scripture sigils, the air around them whipped and swirled until another translucent figure appeared. They looked around appraisingly, squatted down to touch the grass, and gazed up at the purple sun.

"How's it going?" they asked.

"I finally got it working. Want to see?"

The first figure finished their drawings, which were even more intricate than the previous ones. Again, they snapped their fingers, and an empty riverbed formed, winding through the terrain.

"What do you say? A river with a single snap."

The second figure tilted their head and looked on in confusion. "You know a river is supposed to carry water, right?" they said, returning their focus to the sky. "And what is *that* exactly? A sun? Why is your sun purple?"

"Can we concentrate, please? I created a river! Just like that!" they said in exasperation.

"It's a nice party trick, but I fail to see how that's going to be useful to anyone. You shouldn't even bother with shaping the world. Let a few gods handle it."

"I fail to see how *that* would be any fun," the first spat. "If I'm going to create a world, I will actually create it *myself*."

"Please tell me you're going to have gods. You can't just let nature take its course. Don't you remember what happened to that one universe that only had a single god? There's like two planets with intelligent life and they're a *mess*."

"Don't worry. There will be gods, but not the traditional kind."

The second figure looked down at the grass tinted purple by the sun. They were frustrated and irritated at the newcomer they had become responsible for. Usually, new architects would be eager, but less bold. Over eons, all the building blocks one needed had been painstakingly perfected to be fast and simple to use, and even though some architects chose to mix things up from time to time, most of them didn't attempt to restructure the fabric of time and space on their first try. Beginners would usually play it safe, build their first world, and then marvel at their creation.

"If you scrapped this new system, you could be done in no time. You know it will fall back on me if you dawdle too much, right? I won't let that happen."

"I spent the last forty years creating it. I'm not going to trash it now. What would be the point of that?"

"I'm certain that you do know what the point would be, though you don't seem to care. You have about five hundred years left. Will you be able to fix everything by then?"

"Of course," the first figure said, as if it was only natural.

They then snapped their fingers again, activating the scripture they'd been drawing while the two were talking. However, instead of the world further taking shape, flakes of shifting light started to rain down from the cloudless sky.

"Tsk, that stupid glitch..." the first figure said.

The translucent shapes that made up the second figure's eyes went wide at the display. "Tell me you didn't seriously put that into your system."

The first figure looked away, as if they had been caught during a prank. "I didn't *'put it in'*... I completely integrated the system into the universe. Technically, it has access to everything. That's how it can do what it does."

The second figure was getting noticeably mad at this point. "You're going to lock that away, you hear me? I don't care what kind of mess you make here. It's your first world after all, but *that* is dangerous!"

"Don't act as if I didn't know that. Of course that energy is not going to be accessible."

"It better not be. I'll check back in later," the second said, disappearing into the wind.

The first drew a new scripture in the air and snapped their fingers once more, making the rain stop. "It definitely won't be accessible," they said. "As soon as I figure out how to make it stop appearing randomly."

CHAPTER 36

UNCERTAINTY

"Ngh..."

When Aelene woke up, her entire body felt like it was burning. Disoriented, she opened her eyes, but a sharp pain shot through them, forcing her to close them again.

"Ah! What's going on?"

"Aelene! It's good to finally see you awake. How are you?" she heard a man say.

"Oryn?"

She struggled to pry her eyes open through the pain. Between her squinted lids, she could vaguely make out the objects in her room, with Oryn sitting on a chair by her bedside.

"My entire body hurts... What happened?"

The last thing she remembered was her crying out in pain after the water source had been destroyed. She didn't know how much time had passed, nor how she had gotten here. As she opened her eyes a little more, she could see a white mist around Oryn.

"What... What is that?"

"You have it as well," he said with a warm laugh. "And much more than I."

Aelene looked down at her hands and noticed they were emitting the same mist, but in considerably larger quantities.

"Oryn, tell me what this is!" she snapped at him.

"You've become like the boy and girl," he replied. "This energy allows them to use scripture sigils on themselves. When the water source was destroyed, you received the same ability. Actually, that's not quite accurate. You appear to be much stronger than them. The other priests believe you to be an angel, sent by the gods."

Aelene looked at him, barely able to comprehend what he was saying. She didn't look physically different, nor did she feel different, except for the pain. Shifting her eyes to Oryn, Aelene compared the amounts of energy the two were giving off.

"Why do I have significantly more?"

"I don't know. Perhaps not all people are destined to become divine beings," Oryn said despondently.

Aelene was still confused, but she was slowly coming out of her daze.

"Wait, what does this mean? Those brats were going to be executed! And before that, you... You!" she shouted, grabbing him by the collar. "Oryn, if you experimented on me, I swear to you, I—"

"Wait! I swear I was only waiting for you to wake up! You were asleep for an entire day. I was worried you wouldn't wake up at all. Nobody else was able to stay around you for long, that's why—"

"Why can't others be around me?"

"Well, you know how Mr. Remor and Ms. Fera gave off a beast-like aura? I believe that was because of this energy, but you... you don't feel like a beast to others—you feel almost like a god. The High Priest himself confirmed it. I think people who possess this energy aren't affected by each other. I only see it, but I can't feel it. That's why I brought you here and stayed with you."

"The High Priest?" Aelene asked and fell into thought.

She wondered what was going to happen to her. Her boss had been obsessed with getting his hands on the two fugitives, specifically because of this ability. She was scared, but her worries were quieted by her colleague's next statement.

"He wants to announce that you have been chosen as a divine messenger 'sent by the gods to bring prosperity to the citizens of Alarna,' as he puts it. You really are going to become an angel," Oryn said with a wide smile.

Aelene was stupefied. Instead of being in danger, she would be paraded around for the sake of the temple as an embodiment of the will of the gods. She understood why the High Priest would want to take advantage of a miracle, but this had all been an accident. She wasn't a divine anything.

"But I'm neither of those things! Can't you reverse this... this curse?!"

Now it was Oryn's turn to stare at her in shock. "What are you talking about? Why would you want to *reverse* it? I would give everything to be in your position! You can use the scripture!"

"I don't care about the scripture, Oryn! I care about my life! Oh... What about my family? How bad is this energy for others? Can I still see my parents?" She was almost hysterical.

"Please calm down, Aelene. I'm sure everything will be fine. I don't have all the answers, but we'll figure it out!" Oryn said, holding her firmly by her shoulders. "For now, we should report to the High Priest. He's looking forward to talking to you."

Aelene thought his suggestion over and came to the conclusion that she didn't have any other choice but to accept it. Nothing would come from staying in bed, and she wanted to hear from the High Priest what exactly his intentions were.

Oryn helped her up, and they slowly walked over to the door. Upon opening it, they were greeted by a dozen priests, praying in the hallway. Aelene looked surprised at the display, but not as surprised as the kneeling priests, who opened their eyes when they felt Aelene's energy. The blood drained from their faces and they scurried out of the way, creating a path between them.

The two made their way down the hallway as the priests cowered on the floor. Shortly after they had passed, the priests got up and started following them at a safe distance. Aelene glanced back at them with uncertainty.

"I hate this already."

* * *

Lacking an adequate amount of black stones, we paused our experiments after one more attempt. The colorful flakes passed through everything they came into contact with, leaving no trace they had ever been present. Despite that fact, I didn't dare touch them—a decision Miles wholeheartedly agreed with.

"How likely is it that they don't affect anything at all?" I asked as we walked along the road. "That's impossible, right? Could we be using the wrong script?"

«It's hard to say when you have absolutely no idea what that effect is exactly. It could be nothing, or everything,» Miles said in an ominous tone.

"What's that supposed to mean?" I asked in confusion.

«Just a hypothesis. These flakes took on every color imaginable, and the way the script executed was perplexing. It ran way longer than expected. What if... No, I don't even have a what if. It's just a feeling.»

"Are you somehow becoming *less* certain about how things work in this world?" I said ironically.

«Heh, I guess. Maybe we can get our hands on more black stones in Cerus.»

I was excited to see a different town for the first time in my life. From out here, life back in town felt very isolated. Being able to go as you please and deciding your own path was an incredible feeling.

My thoughts swirled into an illusive daydream. I wanted others to be able to experience this as well. I didn't know how we would do it, or if it was even possible, but I guess that's the whole point of a daydream.

"Tomar?" Berla said, interrupting the mirage painting my thoughts. "Resting in Cerus might be possible for a few days if you have enough capital, but what comes after that?"

"That's up to you," I said.

She remained silent, but seemingly understood what I was implying. Over the past two days, I came to realize how naïve I had been in trusting her, through Miles' admonishments and Berla's behaviorism and utterances. One minute, she was happily playing with Riala or joking around with me and Miles, and the next, she was somber, quiet, and contemplative. Could she truly become attached to us after a few short days? Would she put us above her original mission?

I still wanted to believe that Berla's desire to stay alive was greater than her wish to see us in a prison cell. By her own account, she wouldn't be able to become a citizen in any of the surrounding towns, and to the best of my knowledge, there weren't any ways to earn money without a proper job, and she wouldn't be able to survive alone in the wilderness. As far as I could tell, coming with us was her best bet.

* * *

Two shadows were hiding in the woods, watching Tomar, Riala, and Berla travel to Cerus. They did their best to stay hidden, but they were uncertain whether this was actually working.

"Do you think she noticed us?" Reurig asked.

"I doubt it. We're downwind and she seems distracted," Nier said.

The two of them kept moving, always staying a few meters behind their mark. Reurig and Nier had left Alarna after the soldiers, but to their surprise, they had encountered the fugitives before the small army.

"It's three against two now. The odds aren't improving, and you've seen those trees... I don't even want to know what they did there. Are you still eager to capture them?" Reurig asked.

"The two children we could've surprised, but Berla is certainly an issue. I don't understand why she's even with them."

"Seriously? Look at that young, one-legged woman, and tell me you don't understand."

"Reurig, I've had about enough of your antics. *You* know the laws! *She* knows the laws! What is she going to do? Play house in the woods with some kids?"

"That's just it—they're *kids*! Kids with no Callings, surviving in the wilderness. They should've been dead days ago, but still they stand."

Nier stopped and looked at his friend. "I don't like where this is going. Please don't say anything stupid, Reurig."

The two of them stared at each other, ready to act at a moment's notice, but when neither did anything, Nier ushered Reurig along. "Let's go. We don't want to lose them now."

CHAPTER 37

RESIGNATION

The High Priest had instructed Oryn to bring Aelene to him as soon as she regained consciousness. It had already been an entire day since then, and he was starting to wonder whether she would ever wake up. If she didn't, the plans he had for her would fall flat, although he could also work with an unconscious miracle if there was no other way. He lit up when he heard a voice from the hallway outside.

"Leave me alone!" he heard a woman yell before someone knocked on his door.

"Sir, it's Oryn and Aelene," a male voice announced from outside.

"Come in."

The door flew open, the two of them hurried inside and Aelene slammed the door shut. "Why won't they go away..." she said in frustration.

The High Priest laid down the papers he had been reading and looked her over. He was once more in awe of the aura around her, though he didn't understand what she was so agitated about.

"What's the matter, Aelene?" he asked.

"Good day, High Priest. I'm sorry about this. A few of the others seem to take me as a literal goddess and *won't leave me alone*!" she said, yelling the last part at the now closed door.

The High Priest laughed. "I'm certain you will get used to it. Come," he said, gesturing for them to sit across from him at his desk.

The two accepted, but Aelene did not look pleased. "Sir, I would rather not 'get used' to it. I don't want any of this... Can we try to reverse it, please?"

Oryn lowered his head in exasperation, while the High Priest looked at her in astonishment. "You would deny this most holy boon? Don't be ungrateful, Aelene. You will be the key to everything!"

"Sir?" she said, uncertain. "This isn't a divine gift; it was a failed experiment. I'm not a goddess!"

"That matters not, dear priestess. What matters are the optics, and if those among our order believe you to be a divine being, what do you think the common peasantry will see you as?"

"Will you please reconsider? At best, I would be deceiving people, and I'm not comfortable with this creepy following."

The High Priest looked at her with understanding, but shot down any attempt at changing his mind. Aelene receiving the same *gift* as the children was an enormous blessing for him and the temple. "Think of all we can accomplish for our people and for Alarna as a whole! You need only to assist with Oryn's experiments and let them worship you. Of course, you will be relieved from your normal duties, and your belongings will be moved to the third floor. This will ensure that you have more privacy."

Resigned to her fate, Aelene slowly nodded.

"These experiments," she said carefully, "aren't they dangerous?"

"Worry not, Aelene. You are as precious as you are irreplaceable, and we would not risk harming you. Oryn will approach your examination with the utmost care. Don't hesitate to come to me should there be any issues, and we will resolve them."

"Except for when I don't want any of this..." Aelene mumbled inaudibly.

Orthur continued unperturbed. "Further, I will assign Oryn to be your attendant, so you won't have to deal with the common clergy worshiping you in your off time."

It seemed he wanted to accommodate her, and she feigned a thankful nod, but it did little to sway her opinion on her situation. Their exchange continued for a moment, during which Aelene was told the details of how her life was going to change.

Her complaints and worries hand waved away, the High Priest eventually leaned forward in his chair, a bizarre glint in his eyes as they bore into Aelene.

"Before you go, tell me one thing. How does it feel? This power coursing through you?"

A frown formed on her face. Everybody expected her to be grateful for this supposed gift, but if she was being honest, there could only be one answer to this question.

"It sucks."

* * *

Leaving the High Priest's office, Aelene and Oryn made their way through the hallways of the temple's third floor. It was reserved for the upper clergy, and anyone lower generally wasn't allowed, giving Aelene a moment of peace and quiet to think over the plans that had been laid out for her.

Her new life would begin with a public announcement at the end of the week. High Priest Orthur wanted to pull more citizens into their beliefs. Not with vague statements like, 'the gods are always watching,' but with a bona fide angel living among them. Since the last public appearance of a god had been years prior, fewer people felt inclined to offer their support to the temple, and the new generation had never once even seen one. This put the temple in a bad place, but according to the High Priest, all this was about to change.

"So... what now?" she asked as they walked to her new quarters.

"I know you have your reservations," Oryn said, "but if you don't mind, I would very much like to measure your volume."

"*Excuse you?!*"

"I need to know how much water you can produce. We'll need to test whether or not all scriptures work the same on you as it does on a water source, and if this amount of energy lets you do anything by itself. Weaponization will come after, of course. Oh, and we should also look into 'miracles' that you can perform for the citizens to—"

Oryn stopped his ramblings and froze when Aelene suddenly stopped in her tracks, a heavy pressure radiating around her. An aura he shouldn't be able to feel.

He swallowed hard. "Aelene?"

After a few seconds, the pressure subsided, and she looked around in confusion. "Hmm?"

"You don't know what just happened?"

"You were blabbering on, and on, and on," she said in displeasure.

Aelene resumed her walk, and Oryn followed after her in silent trepidation until they arrived at her new room. As she opened the door and looked inside, Oryn carefully tried to approach the subject of his experiments again.

"Aelene, maybe we could—"

"You're my attendant, no?" she interrupted him.

"Well, yes, I suppose I am," he said with hesitation.

She turned to look him in the eye. "I've had a strenuous day, and I would like to relax. Make sure nobody disturbs me, please," she said. And with one swift motion, she slammed the door in his face.

Thinking about the perplexed expression Oryn would be making on the other side of the door, Aelene stifled her laughter with the sleeve of her robes.

"That felt good and normal," she said with a quiet giggle.

* * *

This would be the last night we would spend sleeping on the ground, I thought as I picked up a piece of firewood. Tomorrow we'd arrive in Cerus, hopefully giving us a reprieve from our travels and worries. At least until the monthly caravan from Alarna would arrive five days later, at which point we might not want to be in town anymore. Within that time we'd have to come up with a plan and gather the necessary resources and information to execute it. Additionally, we had to get our hands on some white stones to advance one important aspect of our ongoing research.

As I contemplated our next steps in that direction, a question lingered in my mind that I had not yet felt comfortable asking. "Say, Miles..." I began.

«Hmm?»

"What will we do if you can't get back to your world?"

He was hoping to find a way to reverse the entire process and travel back to where he came from, but we had never talked about the possibility of us failing.

«Honestly, I'm trying not to think about it. Don't get me wrong, I'm not completely miserable here, but I'd very much like to go back.»

It wasn't quite the same, but I wanted to go back home someday as well. Both of our futures were uncertain in that regard. However, while Miles was trying not to think too much about this road potentially being a dead end, I was considering a mountain of possibilities.

"Hey. If the ritual moves people, or souls, or whatever, couldn't we put you in another body?"

«The thought occurred to me, but I'm surprised you would consider that. Whose body would I take over, though?» he said with curiosity.

"I wouldn't mind too much if the people who tried to kill us were gone."

Wait, what am I saying?

It had been a random thought, but I wasn't sure where it had come from. Miles seemed just as perplexed as I was.

«Do you mean that?»

"I... don't know."

Two days ago, I had rescued an enemy and was actively trying to befriend her, and now I was considering robbing people of their bodies? It seemed weird, but while thinking about the people who had harmed us, I felt something rise within me. Something I had never felt before. I tried to shake the feeling.

"There could be other options! What about those talking beasts?" I said, in an attempt to quiet my impostrous thoughts. "They're clearly intelligent. What if you could occupy one of them?"

«Oh, good. Now you want to turn me into a furry,» Miles said, laughing, and lightening the mood again.

I didn't understand why he didn't want fur. It would keep him warm during winter, and he even acknowledged that it would practically groom itself. Other than that, he was having none of it though.

CHAPTER 38

CERUS

As we rounded the last bend in the road, the town's gates came into view in the distance. They were set into a stone wall reminiscent of the one around Alarna. Its height was nothing compared to the mountain behind it, which was hugging the town from all sides. A natural, impregnable barricade. It seemed implausible for humans to be able to hollow out a mountain to the point where an entire town would snugly fit inside, but by all appearances, they had done just that in their pursuit of mining stone, ores, and shards.

"Is that Cerus?" Riala said with sparkling eyes.

Walking through nature might've been nice, but seeing signs of civilizations had all of us excited.

"It sure is," I said with a smile.

We continued toward the gate. I kept glancing around us, scoping the area and guard towers. Based on Berla's intel and the amount of time we had spent on the road without seeing anyone else, it was highly unlikely that anybody could have arrived before us, but I still wanted to be careful. "So far, so good," I said.

Berla, who had been keeping an eye out as well, gave me a confirming nod. Of all the things that could go wrong now, she was the biggest wildcard.

As we got closer, I could see two guards standing on either side of the gate. *Another similarity*, I thought. Guards would not leave the walls in groups smaller than four. They had also noticed us by this point, and one walked over to the center of the road to receive us. Curiously, the closer we got, the more flustered the guards seemed, which put me on edge.

"Do they see us as beasts?" I whispered to Berla.

She shook her head. "I don't think so. You two haven't felt like beasts to me ever since the new script was activated."

When we were three meters away from the guard, my eyes widened in surprise when he saluted us.

"Welcome! It's not every day we see a Ruler from Alarna here. If you don't mind my asking, are you okay?"

Ruler? I briefly looked at Berla questioningly before clearing my throat and giving the explanation that we had decided on beforehand. "We were attacked by beasts on our way here. Nobody else made it," I said, lowering my head in feigned prayer.

"You have my condolences. Unfortunately, we weren't expecting the caravan from Alarna for another week, and we certainly didn't expect royal visitors. You will have to give us a few hours to prepare accommodations," the guard said.

Him thinking that we were part of the caravan was within expectations since this road only led to Alarna, but him treating us like royalty hadn't been a part of the plan.

This is great, isn't it?

"'That's quite alright,'" I said at Miles' instruction. "'If you could just point us toward the inn, we will be on our way. We would not want to cause you good people more trouble than necessary.'"

"Much obliged, sir. I'd be glad to assist you once the matter of the entrance fee has been cleared."

There's an entrance fee? Why didn't Berla mention it? I thought in surprise.

"Will all three of you be entering Cerus today?" he asked, glancing over at Berla's missing leg.

"We will," I declared.

"Very well. That will be three hundred kira, please."

Three... hundred?! I tried to not look too shocked, but I ended up staring and blinking at the guard for several seconds before Miles shook me out of it.

I shuffled through the contents of my bag in search of the stack of money we had taken from a house in Alarna.

If Miles hadn't convinced me to steal this, we wouldn't have nearly enough to get into town.

After handing almost half of our money to the guard, he quickly counted it, nodded, and stepped aside, motioning us forward.

"Welcome to Cerus. I wish you a pleasant stay. If you'd like to arrange an escort back home, please talk to the captain at the guard station."

As soon as I thanked him, he shouted, "GATE!" and the large doors slowly swung inward, revealing the high street for the first time.

We had finally made it.

* * *

Our eyes darted around as we made our way up the main road and towards the town's center. Both familiar and unfamiliar sights greeted us at every corner, though it all seemed fresh and new in this unknown environment.

The high road and all of its branching paths were dead straight—a clear sign of a master architect's meticulous planning—and far less busy than Alarna's roads. The houses on the other hand seemed far simpler, most of them not more than two stories tall and the majority made of simple wood. It was not at all what I would've expected of a town manufacturing stone bricks.

Upon further examination, we noticed that their designated marketing district was situated along this very street, with residences located deeper within on the side streets, like a mirror image of our hometown.

But the town's most striking feature was undoubtedly the mountain and all the tunnels, ladders, and pulley systems etched into its rugged faces. The sight of workers' shadows moving effortlessly along its surface almost made it feel alive.

Enamored by the display, it took me a moment to realize that an increasing number of people were staring at us. *I haven't had this many eyes on me since we were paraded through town...* I was relieved to find none were looking at us in contempt or fear though, but apparent curiosity.

Content, I turned toward Berla to ask her about what had happened at the gate. "Why didn't you tell us about the entrance fee? We're lucky I had some money with me," I whispered.

"I didn't know either! I've only ever been here as part of the caravan. Maybe the leader paid the fee for everyone."

"And what was up with that 'Ruler' thing?"

"*That* I told you! Don't you remember?"

"I didn't think you meant it literally!" I said in exasperation.

Berla blankly stared at me before shrugging.

"Whatever. We're inside, and that's all that matters."

The closer we got to the center, the busier and louder the street grew, until we finally entered the main square about ten minutes later and experienced a sensory overload. The entire area was filled to the brim with market stalls, and voices of merchants praising their wares assaulted us from all directions. I looked in wonder at everything on display: food, materials, blue stones, and clothes abound. You could essentially get whatever you wanted without walking more than a couple of meters.

"The market takes place during the last week of the month, with goods supplied by various merchants from the four surrounding towns," Berla explained. "And on the last day, the caravan from Alarna arrives to do its business. There will be even more people then."

I had read that Cerus was a merchant town and a trading hub, but actually seeing it in person was something else. We joined the market-goers, practically bumping elbows with them, on our quest to find the inn that was said to be situated on the opposite end of the main square. At my side, Riala constantly pulled at my arm in an attempt to scout alone, but I had firmly gripped her hand in advance, knowing she would disappear the moment anything caught her eyes.

Curiously, I could see a lot of people who didn't seem like merchants to me, but at this time of day I couldn't imagine all of them being citizens of Cerus either.

"It's kind of nice, isn't it?" Berla noted. "Other towns allow their citizens to attend," she said.

"Why isn't Alarna like this?" I asked, traces of frustration evident in my voice.

I had never realized this before, but now that I thought about it, Alarna was like a prison. Citizens weren't allowed out of town without permission, and guards wouldn't let outsiders in without a permit either. The authorities dictated our day-to-day life, down to the clothes we wore.

"Don't get the wrong impression. Alarna is far superior to the other towns," she said, admonishingly. "It's by far the safest and most prosperous one. You might be thinking the Wildlands aren't such a big deal after the last couple of days, but you haven't seen anything truly terrifying yet."

"Like what?" I asked.

"What lurks beyond category five."

* * *

"I have to admit, Lera, you did good," Captain Bern said, glancing at Cerus' gate from behind a tree. "Who would've thought that they would actually come here *and* get in?"

"It was a reasonable assumption," Lera said. "There are only so many routes to take when you rely on blue stones as much as they do."

The two captains moved deeper into the forest to meet their platoons and immediately started giving orders to get into position. The soldiers had left Alarna three days ago, but had fought the entire way with no respite. Beasts harassed the column relentlessly, delaying progress and making sleep a sorely missed luxury. Since arriving, they had been lying in wait for the fugitives to arrive.

"We should've included Cerus' authorities in our plans," Bern said.

"You don't know Mayor Cerus, Bern. That old bastard is as greedy as they come. He'll want an arm and a leg for his cooperation. This plan is solid. They're trapped inside a town with only one exit. They'll feel safe and secure when they fall into a bed tonight for the first time in a week, lowering their vigilance. And they surely won't use their more lethal powers in a densely populated town, either. All we have to do is take a squad inside and get them. It's an ideal situation."

"Except that Berla is with them," Bern mused.

"That wasn't part of the plan, but she won't be an obstacle in her state. To think that the king's niece would fraternize with criminals. Her mother will be devastated."

"She should be happy to be rid of the black sheep," Bern said.

"Let's not get into that now," Lera said before calling another guard. "Jara!"

Jara jogged over to the two captains and saluted them. "Yes, sir?"

"Prepare your squad. We're leaving in three hours. This ends tonight."

CHAPTER 39

SURPRISES

It wasn't obvious at first glance with how packed the space was, but the path centering the square led us straight to the inn. The building rose three stories off the ground, and as one of the larger buildings around, its exterior was impressively decorated to match.

We found ourselves in a reception room, and were relieved when much of the noise died down once we were through the inn's doors. The interior was mostly made from plain, unpainted wood, just like the houses. On the other side of the room stood a counter with a grumpy-looking, old man behind it. Though he was busy reading his ledger, I was a little surprised when he didn't show any kind of reaction to our unusual group.

"G'afternoon," he said. "What can I do for you?"

"Hello. We'd like a room with two beds."

He grunted, and with a stiff turn, he took a key from the cubby behind him. "Fifty kira," he said, slamming the key on the counter.

The price seemed reasonable enough, and we were really looking forward to sleeping in a bed again. After the horrendous entrance fee and the cost for the room, we still had over four hundred fifty kira left, which would buy us ninety blue stones if we got nothing else, although I was also looking to buy some water skins to reduce our stone usage. While I was going over our finances in my head, the receptionist became impatient at my silence.

"You gonna pay or not, boy?"

"Sorry," I said, taking some money from my bag. "Here you go."

He quickly counted it and motioned at the staircase toward the right of the counter. "Second floor, room twenty-three. Have a good one." The man returned his attention to his notebook, vigorously writing something.

After taking the key, we climbed the stairs to the second floor and quickly found our room. It was just enough space to move comfortably between the two beds and dresser, but it was cozy.

Riala immediately jumped on a bed and buried herself in the blanket. "Good night!" she said gleefully.

I had barely stored away our things and sat down on the other bed by the time she was on the verge of nodding off.

"That was quick," I whispered to Berla with a smile.

I slept relatively well in the Wildlands, but I knew that Riala regularly woke up at night to chat with Miles. She certainly hadn't gotten as much sleep as she should have.

"Berla," I started, "are there truly beasts that are stronger than category five?" I asked Berla.

"The most powerful ones I've ever heard about were category ten, but the strongest I've seen myself was a seven. That one... That one needed to be taken down by an entire platoon. Beasts above *that* are living disasters."

"Why have I never heard about them?"

"Because the Alarnian authorities don't want their citizens to fear beasts even more. It's unknown why, but almost no high category beasts ever appear around there. That's what's so great about Alarna," she said with a sad expression. "What the priests always say, that we're 'blessed by the gods,' isn't idle talk. The price for living anywhere else is fearing for your life every single day. Not just because a category three *might* get into town, but because walls barely make a difference against category sevens and above."

It was hard to imagine that the beasts we've encountered weren't the worst of them. The ones that killed my parents were supposedly weak when compared to true threats.

"Then how can people live elsewhere?"

"I'm not sure you're ready to hear this, but there is a solution to that problem. High category beasts are very territorial, and if they claim an area for themselves, they won't let others of their level trespass. The towns within these areas are safe from these calamities, so long as they give sacrifices to the beasts regularly."

"Sacrifices?" I gulped. "Like... people?"

"Yes. As far as I know, most towns choose them randomly. Others have the beasts choose them. As long as the citizens don't resist, these high category beasts can be reasoned with."

I was stunned into silence. When Berla had asked me about our plans, she had already known this. We could hardly stay in this area for long, because they might come for us, but going anywhere else would be extremely dangerous. That is, if these beasts were actually a threat to *us*.

"I should've told you sooner," she continued. "I thought you would leave me behind after a day or two since I was dead weight. Then I figured we wouldn't make it all the way here on our own anyway, and I didn't want to worry you unnecessarily. But now that we're here, you need to know what you're getting into."

"You were trying to protect me? And here you accused my mother of coddling me," I said, tossing her a playful scowl.

"I guess there's something about you," she said, poking out her tongue.

"Do you think they're a threat to us?"

"Your ability is remarkable, but if you can't surprise your enemy, you could die in the blink of an eye. The fight the other day was proof. We need to do something about that."

"Then what shall we do?" I asked.

"Improve, overcome, and adapt. That's the only thing we can do."

* * *

Sharing a body with someone was irritating sometimes. One moment you would be happily experimenting with a script, and the next you lost control and would have to take the backseat again for a while. Or you might want to say something to someone, and you have to tell your buddy to do it for you. All of that I was getting used to. However, when Berla had Tomar do crunches, squats, and pushups for an hour, I was plagued with a sore rental body, and *that* I felt very vivid.

If I feel like this, Tomar must be way more miserable, I thought.

"You could've waited until morning," I said grumpily.

"Why wait?" Berla said with a giggle. "If he's to get into shape, he'll have to work hard. You'll survive it, old man."

Now that we were in Cerus, it was like a burden had been lifted off her shoulders. She was making plans for the future, and all her somberness was nowhere to be seen. Berla looked genuinely happy. Not wanting to put a damper on her good mood, I didn't question her.

The blanket on the bed Berla was sitting on moved, and a sleepy-looking Riala crawled out from under it. "Hi, Miles," she said, rubbing her eyes.

"How do you do that, Ria?" I asked her.

She tilted her head. "Do what?"

"How do you know I'm not Tomar right now?"

"Hmm..." she said in contemplation. "Dunno. You're you."

I glanced at Berla, hoping for insight.

Staring at me, Berla squinted her eyes and crinkled her nose before shrugging. "I don't see a difference."

I shook my head. It was late into the evening and only the dim moonlight illuminated our room, making it difficult to experiment with scripts. We had forgotten to buy candles while we were at the market, but Tomar had refilled our blue stone reserves before his training session.

I finished a new test script and executed it with a stone. Instead of simply shooting water, I used a series of chained scripts to keep the water in one place and give it a little spin to create a ball. This resulted in a rotating ball of water floating a few centimeters above my hand. After a certain amount of time, it flew forward and hit a wooden bucket in the corner of the room.

"Wow... I didn't expect that to work, especially not on the first try," I said with a wide grin. In this moment, I actually felt like a wizard. Still, there was little reason to use water "magic" this way.

As usual, Riala sat off to the side, looking at me expectantly. I, being unable to resist her silent pleas, showed her the script and guided her with its use.

With a splash, Riala hit the bucket as well. "Yay!"

"Since we're all awake, how about we go for a little walk?" Berla said. "I want to show you something, Miles."

"Don't they have a curfew here?"

She shook her head.

"Well, then sure. Why not?"

Gathering a few necessities, the three of us made our way downstairs. When we arrived in the lobby, the innkeeper was sitting at a table behind the counter, resting his head on his elbow, fast asleep.

Maybe he was in a bad mood because of all the visitors, I thought. *All-nighters suck.*

We quietly left the inn and made our way north, passing dozens of vacant stalls that were still set up for the next day. Continuing past the main square, we eventually took a turn east.

Even though I had looked forward to being in a town again, it felt a bit confining. Being outside was more natural to me now. *How the times change. I was never one to venture outdoors much...*

After about fifteen minutes, we arrived at an empty square and Berla came to a stop. It looked like the water source squares in Alarna, minus a cube. I looked around in curiosity until I noticed a circular platform in the center of the square, rising a few millimeters out of the ground. I couldn't make out the details from this distance, but I immediately realized what it was.

"An open-access ritual platform..." I whispered in a daze.

With a mischievous grin, Berla leaned on my shoulder and motioned me forward. "Surprise."

CHAPTER 40
UPS AND DOWNS

I was stunned.

All these weeks, I had been brooding over how I would figure out how ritual platforms worked without examining one. Maybe I could have figured something out by researching Omega more. Maybe the black stone would've given me a hint. Ultimately, it was all a shot in the dark. Gaining access to the script was the best-case scenario. Even if it didn't provide all the answers, it would still be an enormous leap forward.

I stared at the platform from afar until I felt Berla squeeze my hand. "Go on," she said, nodding toward the platform.

I swallowed my nervousness and gave her a nod in return. Down at my other side, Riala bounced around, anticipation blazing in her eyes. "Let's go. This is going to be very interesting," I said, taking her by the hand.

Riala and I scurried to the platform, with Berla in tow. We stopped in front of it, and Riala immediately knelt down to look it over. Since I had just arrived in this world the last time I was near one, this was my first good look at the peculiar device.

With a diameter of about two meters, it was significantly larger than I had imagined, and it was filled with intricate scripts written in what appeared to be the same blue paint that was used on the water sources. The only areas that didn't have scripts on them were a small circle in the center, which was presumably where you were supposed to stand, and an even smaller circle for a white stone.

After squatting, I slowly looked over the scripts closest to me. Just like the water source script before, I didn't understand all the functions that were in use, but I could make out certain details. For instance, the "signs" people saw weren't godly effects; they were mana taking on a shape determined by the stones.

This means that different stones can hold various bits of information... Magical flash drives? Works for me.

I kept reading, and my eyes went wide when they fell on the initialization script. The ritual platform wasn't activated by the stone, nor was it running indefinitely. It was activated by pressure!

How did I not realize that? Tomar told me the stone had been placed on the platform before he stepped on it!

Barely a minute had passed, and I had already gleaned extremely valuable information. "This is amazing... Thank you," I said, looking up at Berla.

If we hadn't saved her, we might've never found this place. The town was relatively small in comparison to Alarna, but this square was tucked away in a remote spot, making it highly unlikely that we'd have stumbled upon it.

"I don't understand most of these," Riala said, pouting.

"Don't worry, Ria. We'll go through them bit by bit."

As I went back to reading the scripts, Berla sat on the floor, watching us with a warm smile.

Evidently, chaining scripts was not the only new feature in this version of Omega, seeing how these scripts utilized several more I wasn't familiar with. As part of its design, the language was supposed to only support jumps, but there were actual sub-functions present in this setup.

I was ecstatic about each new thing I was learning. With further examination, my eyes finally fell on the part I had been looking for; the one at the core, responsible for actually *applying* the Calling.

"Here it is. The answer to how..." I froze and stared at the platform in silence. A single abbreviated instruction had crushed my hopes. I plopped down on my butt and buried my face in my hands. "EXTR..."

This was it. Reversing the ritual script wouldn't accomplish anything unless I wanted to become a white stone.

"What's wrong?" Berla asked.

I answered her in a low voice without raising my head. "It *extracts* the knowledge from the white stones. I wasn't just pulled from my world and tossed inside Tomar... I was inside a white stone first. I... I won't... Damn it!"

What did I expect? Find the right button and be back on Earth in the blink of an eye? Of course not. This entire idea was stupid. How was that even supposed to work? Where is this world even? And how would some simple script do something as complex as sending spirits across time and space? Why would that function even exist?

There had always been a sliver of hope, but at that moment, all I could think about was the end. That I wouldn't be able to return to my world via this path, and maybe there was no path at all, seeing how I must've been inside a white stone for some reason.

I sat there feeling sorry for myself when Berla spoke up again. "Hey, Miles. If the knowledge is inside the stones, why aren't the Callings random?" she asked.

"What do you mean?"

"Children usually get the same Calling as their parents. If the knowledge comes from inside the stones, shouldn't it be random?"

My eyes widened. "It's *not* random?" I shuffled to my knees to look at the script again.

It was most definitely extracting something from the stone and putting it inside the person on the platform. It only made sense that this "something" was all the ritual was supposed to give you, because as far as I could see, there was nothing else around that would do it. However, if it wasn't random, there had to be more to it.

A small spark of hope lit up inside me again.

"I need to know more."

Before I could do anything else, I noticed Berla's head snapping in the direction whence we had come. A man emerged from the shadow of a house and into the moonlight, where his face became visible.

Captain Lera.

I got up immediately, but more shadows were approaching from multiple directions. Ten soldiers of Alarna, all of them with spears at the ready, were focused on us.

"Somehow you're never where you're supposed to be, Mr. Remor. That makes my job... tedious," he said, coming to a stop about twenty meters away. "I would appreciate it if you didn't resist. I want to leave here before the sun rises. Know that four platoons are waiting outside town, so you're not getting away this time."

Intimidation? That's your tactic? I thought. Even if what he said was true, as long as we could make it past these guys, I was sure we could find *some* way out of here. Either he underestimated us, or he was in a real hurry. Maybe a bit of both.

I waved Riala over and stepped toward Berla to help her up. Retrieving a blue stone from my pocket, I held it up for the captain to see, prompting the aggressive soldier to halt.

"What happened between us last time was more of a warning shot, Captain. If you force my hand, you won't get off that easily again. Let us go in peace."

The captain furrowed his brows. "That won't be possible. I see it as my personal failing that a dangerous criminal like you managed to escape," he said before glancing at Berla. "Of course *you* will have to come with us as well. Your mother is worried sick. Although, I imagine she will be quite disappointed with your behavior. If you're looking for a chance to show your loyalty, this would be it."

I eyed Berla, but she simply hung her head, a sorrowful expression clouding her features. I didn't know anything about her family, but it seemed complicated.

"How do you picture this going, Captain? We could kill half of you before you even have a chance to react. Like that guy," I said, suddenly raising my arm at a soldier.

Visibly flustered by my threat, the man stumbled backward.

Good. They're scared of us. I lowered my arm again.

I doubted they would let us go, but I had to try. I wanted to avoid killing a bunch of people while controlling Tomar's body. I had also considered Riala's presence, though she already had two blue stones in her hands as well.

The non-lethal scripts would buy us a few seconds, but we wouldn't be able to knock all of them out before a few of them reached us. Even with Berla's aid, we would probably be done for, if that happened.

Though, it seemed like they weren't sure about it. Seeing how they hadn't immediately jumped us, I guessed the original plan had been to capture us while we were asleep. For the moment, our best chance was to create an opening and flee.

The captain looked admonishingly at the flustered soldier scrambling back into position. Captain Lera then locked onto me once more. "Believe me—they will do their job. Last chance, Mr. Remor."

"Likewise," I said. Taking up my fighting stance, I whispered to Riala and Berla, "We'll go through the captain. Defense on the right when I give the signal."

They nodded in understanding, and we stood like that for a few seconds, unmoving, while the captain looked us up and down.

"Get them!" he barked.

"Go!" I instructed.

In quick succession, I shot three water blasts at the captain and two soldiers on his left, and Riala took out two on his right. We immediately started running straight past him, while the others chased after us.

A few of the assaulted soldiers seemed to be out of it, but Lera was already recovering when we reached him. I shot another blast at his face, throwing him back to the ground with a heavy thud. We made it past him, and while Riala and Berla ran as fast as they could, I did my best to hold off the other soldiers, following my teammates shortly after.

Unfortunately, this had been the plan in its entirety at that moment. We were trapped in a walled town, pursuers hot on our tail. More danger awaited us on the outside, and we didn't know where else to go.

How are we in the exact same situation as last week again already?!

CHAPTER 41

NEW PLAN

As we fled, I did my best to keep our enemies on the ground. Some of them were easily knocked out by one or two water blasts, but half of them proved quite resilient, including the captain.

Berla was very mobile for the condition she was in, but sprinting faster than the soldiers was beyond her, and Riala was still tired from our journey. After several repeated attacks, I was reaching our pain threshold and decided that I didn't have another choice. They wouldn't stop, and we couldn't escape, leaving one option—make them stop.

I took out another blue stone, aimed at the closest soldier, and activated a different script than the ones I had used thus far. A stream of water shot out and hit his right leg, leaving a hole one could comfortably see through. He tried to get up again but failed and ungracefully fell back onto the ground.

One down, four to go.

Aside from stopping one of them, this attack had also flustered the others, realizing that we were ready to do more than just push them around.

It would be easier if I could just kill them, but Tomar would hate me for it, I thought in frustration.

Not knowing where to go was our biggest problem right now. Riala and I didn't know Cerus, and Berla hadn't been here frequently. If we went down side paths, they might catch us off guard from another direction, so we ran down the road leading south toward the main square instead. Glancing behind us, I saw Captain Lera closing the gap. I fired another stream, but he managed to jump to the side, roll on the ground, and was immediately up and moving again.

Tsk...

I didn't have enough time to grab another blue stone and was tackled and pinned to the ground by the captain. No matter how much I struggled, he wouldn't budge.

"It's over. Stop resisting!" Captain Lera scoffed.

Looking up, I saw Berla and Riala disappear between some stalls in the main square. Instead of going after them, the soldiers surrounded me, spears pointed at my vital organs.

"Captain, do we go after them?" a young soldier asked.

"The boy is more important. We'll secure him first and then we'll—"

"Miles!" I heard Riala yell from afar. I glanced up and saw her use a script, shooting a thin water stream toward my captors. I couldn't see who she had hit exactly, but I was suddenly free.

Taking advantage of the distraction, I jumped to my feet and made a mad dash toward her. Briefly glancing back, I saw that both the captain and another soldier were lying on the ground.

She must've hit them both at once.

I couldn't see their injuries, but they were at least still moving. While the one remaining soldier checked on them in a panic, I joined back up with the others. We kept moving, first south and then east, leaving the main square behind as we ran through small paths between houses. After a few minutes, we stopped in the shadow of a building to catch our breaths.

"Goddamnit!" I said. "Are you two okay?"

"We're fine! What about you?" Berla said.

"I'm fine. Flustered, but fine. They won't let us go," I said, anger heavy in my tone.

I certainly knew that we were valuable to them, but sending an army after us into the Wildlands seemed extreme. How many Fighters' lives were they risking with this stunt? Dozens? Hundreds? All for this ability?

"Is there any other way out of town?" I asked.

Berla shook her head. "Not that I know of."

I didn't know what to do. We didn't have a lot of blue stones left between us, our bag was at the inn, and we didn't have anywhere to hide. Even if we had our stones, we wouldn't get out of here in one piece, assuming the captain wasn't lying.

"Do you think there's really an army out there?"

"Most likely," Berla said, her gaze cast downward. "Captain Lera is not one to make empty threats. I don't see a way out, Miles."

I leaned against a wall and let myself slide down to the ground. It didn't matter if we could defeat the soldiers in town. If we couldn't leave, they could just keep sending in new groups. It seemed like they hadn't cooperated with the Cerus authorities; otherwise, I would've expected a larger force.

Wait...

"The authorities... They didn't tell the Cerusian authorities about us! But... why?" I tapped my temple, hoping to light the bulb in my brain, then it dawned on me. "Berla, how tight are Cerus and Alarna?"

"Uh, not at all, I'd say. I know the king hates the mayor of Cerus. And a little while ago, there were talks about seizing the town to make it part of Alarna again," she said. Her puzzled expression quickly gave way to one of shock. "Wait... Please tell me you don't want to go to the authorities!"

"Think about it. Nobody knows about us here, right? We can sell the story we originally tried in Alarna and offer them our knowledge in exchange for protection from the king."

It would be risky, but here we had a clean slate. Nobody suspected Tomar of being a Mad One, we didn't have our beastly auras anymore, we hadn't broken any laws, and nobody knew the extent of our abilities. We were just a boy and his two friends—maybe siblings? That would make more sense.

"That's assuming the mayor can stand up against the king," I said.

"Cerus *does* have a Fighter force, but it's incomparable to Alarna's," Berla said. "Not only that, the king hates the mayor. Apparently he's a ruthless businessman. He might try to capture and sell you back to the king."

"A businessman," I mused. "Even better. If we demonstrate that we're worth more than he could get from the king, he'll want to keep us here. We'll buy ourselves some time with that play."

"I suppose..." Berla said, unsure about my plan.

Granted, trying to make a deal with another leader, after two already tortured and tried to kill us, didn't seem like the best idea, but it was a chance.

The biggest risk was the mayor trusting the soldiers and handing us over, one way or the other. If he was indeed a shrewd businessman, he surely wouldn't give up someone who understands the scripture sigils and is able to produce water. He would be able to see the long-term value in this. And *if* he were to imprison us and try to get our knowledge that way, we would at least still be in Cerus—a much smaller town, with guards that weren't prepared for our abilities.

I conveyed my thoughts to Berla, and she fell into thought. "I'm not sure this is a good idea, but we need to do *something*. And I don't have a better one."

And just like that, we were off once more. Running toward the powers that be instead of fleeing from them for a change. A curious turn of events.

* * *

"Captain Lera! Are you okay?" a soldier asked, rushing to his side. He and the four others behind him had been the first to get knocked out, but unlike the captain, they were unscathed.

By the time these men had reached him, Lera had propped himself up against the wall. Though the hole in his left shoulder was bleeding profusely, he tried to tend to the injured soldier by his side. By the looks of it, the girl's attack had hit the soldier first, as his wound was much worse. The large puncture wound in his upper torso didn't look fixable, but the field medic patched him up the best he could.

Annoyed that the fugitives had escaped him once again, Captain Lera contemplated what actions he could take next as another soldier bandaged his wound. He knew that his targets only had a few options, but either way, he would need more men to assist in the search. This increase in military activity wouldn't go unnoticed by the Cerusians, so it was just a matter of time before they interfered.

"Jara, you're going outside. Get two more squads in here and systematically search the southern part of town. The others will come with me. We'll try to find a lead."

"Sir, you really should rest for—"

"Move out!" the captain instructed.

* * *

Mayor Cerus Balart III, a direct descendant of the founder of Cerus, was very proud of his lineage. Once upon a time, Cerus Balart I had declared independence from Alarna, and turned the former mining camp into a bustling merchant hub. He had worked in the camp for close to three decades when the workers discovered a ritual platform buried under a large pile of rocks. Its discovery changed everything. Not only were they no longer reliant on Alarna and the temple for their Callings, they were also right at the source for blue and white stones. Alarna relied on the mining camp for stones, but the town of Cerus didn't need to rely on Alarna any longer.

Well-liked among his colleagues, Cerus convinced dozens of workers and guards stationed at the camp that splitting off from Alarna would be to their advantage. Freed from the rules and regulations, they would be able to make deals with other towns, they could expand their operations, and strong-arm the king of Alarna into a deal.

In these early years, a war wouldn't have been a viable endeavor, and an agreement was formed that essentially formalized what the camp-turned-town had already done for decades. They supplied Alarna with stones and other products, while Alarna delivered clothes and other commodities that were more difficult to source in Cerus.

While Mayor Cerus III was proud of what his family had accomplished, he was also ambitious. He had done a remarkable job at leading the town and optimizing their businesses, yet he had done nothing that would put him in the history books.

He was dreaming of that fateful day when loud knocking woke him from his slumber. He pulled his blanket over his head, trying to ignore the noise, but when the relentless banging continued, his wife not-so-gently pushed him out of bed.

"Make it stop, Cerus!"

"Ugh..."

Drowsy and disoriented, he staggered out of their bedroom and made his way downstairs, lighting a candle on the way. Upon opening the front door, his bleary vision met an unexpected trio: a child with wide, innocent eyes, flanked by two young adults. The young girl's face was quickly covered by a hand, while the older pair averted their gaze politely.

"Um... Mayor Cerus?" the young man asked.

"Mm-hmm," the mayor confirmed, a disgruntled yawn escaping him. "What do you want?"

"I'm sorry for disturbing you, but it's an emergency."

"At this hour? I'd certainly hope it would be."

"Well, it's more of a... business opportunity."

With a bit of curiosity as to the nature of their offer, the mayor properly opened his eyes, prompting the youth to continue.

"But before we get started, could you maybe put some clothes on?"

"Ugh..." the naked mayor grunted.

CHAPTER 42

INTERVIEW

Upon my request that he put something on, if only for Riala's sake, the mayor briefly disappeared into another room. He looked to be in his early forties and his bare body looked fit for his age, though he didn't leave a great first impression otherwise. But really, who would in the middle of night? He returned moments later, wearing a simple gray robe.

"Thank you," I said.

"This had better be good," he said.

Still standing in front of his house, I started explaining our situation. "Sir, three weeks ago I received an unknown Calling that gave me certain abilities." The mayor's ears perked up. "The leaders of Alarna tried to torture everything I know out of me and even threatened to kill me. As you can see, I managed to escape, but soldiers have followed me and my sisters all the way here. We're asking you to give us asylum in this town. In return, I will share my knowledge with you."

Mayor Cerus looked once over. "An unknown Calling? And what would that be?"

He seemed curious, but doubtful. Luckily, our ability was possibly the easiest "Calling" to demonstrate. I took a blue stone out of my pocket and presented it to him, garnering me a questioning look. I then placed it on my other hand where I had tried my new script earlier, and a ball of water gathered in the air above it. The mayor was slack-jawed even before I gracefully let the water fly at a bush in the garden next to us.

While the mayor stared at the freshly watered shrub in a daze, I continued. "I'm able to produce water and I understand the scripture sigils. I have no doubt that you understand how valuable this knowledge is, and Alarna is desperate to get it for themselves."

At my mentioning of Alarna, his eyes locked onto me. Taking a step to the side, Cerus motioned us to enter his home.

He led us to a large living room, where he let himself fall into an armchair, and we sat down on a comfy couch across from him. Berla seemed on edge, still not sure whether this was a good idea, while Riala was in awe at the interior. In particular, she seemed to take a liking to the couch, which she bounced up and down on lightly.

After we were situated, the mayor looked at me with a sharp glint in his eyes. "You're saying this is your Calling? That would be the first unknown Calling in hundreds of years."

"I know how unlikely it sounds, but that's what it is. The priest at the temple didn't recognize the sign, and when they figured out what I could do, they branded me a criminal and imprisoned me. They even threatened my family, trying to force me to tell them things I didn't know," I said.

"Hmm... When you say you understand the scripture sigils, what exactly does that mean?" the mayor asked.

We couldn't make the same mistakes as before. When we were interrogated by the captain and the priest, we essentially told them the truth, leaving out only that Tomar had a voice in his head. Luckily, we wouldn't be under the same restrictions here because nobody knew anything about us.

"Don't get me wrong—I don't know everything, but I can read and write them. My main ability is being able to produce water without a water source, and..." I paused, adjusting my posture. "Beasts fear me."

The mayor furrowed his brows. "They *fear* you? Explain."

I was trying to pose as something akin to a magician. Fighters would get superhuman strength and agility in combination with knowledge that would help them during combat. However, they didn't suddenly have a doctor's understanding of the human body, nor knowledge about every fighting style in existence. There were limits. *I'm not a sigil Researcher, I'm just a magical Fighter.*

"Maybe you've noticed the aura around me. Unlike other people, who can only feel it, I can see it. And beasts have it as well. It just feels different. They avoid someone with my Calling like they would avoid other beasts. That's how we three made it here in one piece."

"Is that right?" he said, looking at Berla's missing leg.

"To be fair, we were caught completely off guard when that happened," I said with a sad chuckle. "My sister got separated from us at one point during our journey and was attacked by a beast. Fortunately, I found her just in time and it retreated."

The mayor leaned back in his chair, presumably contemplating my story. It sounded plausible to me, and he seemed intrigued.

"I'll admit, that *is* a fascinating story," he said. "That Calling sounds valuable, but what is it that you have to offer to me? You want asylum. From Alarna, no less. You're a fugitive, and your sister looks like an agent, so I assume she's a deserter. You're asking me to accommodate two criminals. Or is it three? What's with you, little one? Have you killed anyone recently?"

Riala was still distracted and only briefly glanced at the mayor to shake her head. "Nope," she said, looking around the room again.

For our story to work, she would have to hide her abilities for the time being, and she would have to stay close to me and Tomar so nobody would realize she had mana before receiving a Calling. Nevertheless, that was a small price to pay to finally be safe for a little while.

I spoke up again, detailing my proposition. "What I want to offer you is not the knowledge I have now, but what I will learn in the future. I'd like you to invest in me. What I showed you just now was the result of researching the scripture for just over a week, all while traveling through the Wildlands with a young girl and an injured woman. I want to know more, and I want to share it with someone who doesn't plan to torture or kill me." I paused for a moment. "Now you might be thinking 'What good do these water tricks do me?', but I ask you to look beyond that. For example, I was delighted to see your ritual platform freely accessible to anyone."

Once more, the mayor's ears perked up. "You truly understand what's written on there?"

"I do. And if you give me a little time to do some tests, I guarantee that I will make it worth your while."

It wasn't exactly an empty promise. There was no way that understanding the ritual platform script wasn't going to be useful. It might be possible to determine what Calling someone would get, or make it so they would get a specific one. It might be possible to extract entirely new functions from the platform, allowing new applications for scripts. Hell, just having me accompany their workers into the woods to ward off beasts would be worth the tradeoff. Beasts would stay away and I could hand out refreshments. While trying to not appear *too* desperate, I told the mayor why I thought it would be a good idea to help us. *Feels like a job interview...*

After several seconds, the mayor stood up and walked over, coming to a stop in front of me. "I'll give you a chance to prove that you can do what you claim. Until then, you may stay here," he said, extending his arm to shake my hand. "Mayor Cerus Balart III," he said, introducing himself.

"Tomar Remor," I responded in kind, shaking his hand.

"Don't let me regret this, Tomar."

"I'll certainly try not to."

"By the way, what have you named this Calling?"

I hadn't even thought about that part, and there was only one thing I could think of at that moment: Sourcerer—in honor of Phiona.

* * *

Captain Lera had found evidence that suggested their targets were somewhere in the southeastern part of town, and he did his best to follow them. He was hoping that reinforcements would arrive soon so they could finish this without attracting unwanted attention. If they hadn't known about a secret passageway into town, and had tried to get in through the gate, the guards would've alerted the mayor.

The captain hurried through the streets with light steps, the remains of his squad right behind him. Even though he was generally an optimistic person, he was starting to wonder if they would ever get the boy, who somehow managed to escape time and time again.

After taking a turn, the group saw five people standing in the center of the street a few meters from them. Captain Lera immediately recognized Mayor Cerus, and he and his men stopped abruptly. Even without a Ruler calling, he seemed to have a regal air about him, dressed in a neat suit and backed by Fighters.

"Good evening, gentleman. May I inquire what brings Alarnian soldiers to our town tonight?" the mayor inquired.

The captain grimaced. This had been the last man they wanted to encounter. Lacking a good explanation for their visit, Lera had no choice but to tell the truth.

"My apologies, Mayor Cerus. We're searching for criminals who fled from our town a few days ago, and we tracked them to this part of your humble town. We didn't want to burden you with our problems."

"That is very considerate of you, but you still entered my town without permission and you're running through its streets in the middle of the night, heavily armed. I must ask you to leave immediately."

"Please, we ask for your support in this matter. These fugitives are quite dangerous, and I promise you that you don't want them in this town."

"You may leave a description of them at a guard station. Should we find them, we will capture and return them to you. Now as I said, it's time for you and your men to leave," the mayor said definitively.

The captain gritted his teeth. The time and place where they had met the mayor was highly suspicious. There was a decent chance that he had already apprehended the three criminals. However, the captain couldn't risk a diplomatic incident without permission from the king. For the moment, he was forced to retreat.

"I apologize for our intrusion. We will be on our way," Lera said.

He instructed his men to follow him towards the gate. The mayor's guards followed them to make sure they actually left, leaving the mayor to walk back home alone.

An exaggerated yawn escaped his lips, while his confident appearance morphed into a tired frown. "What a bother. Couldn't they have done this in the morning?" he complained as he turned on his heel and disappeared into the darkness.

CHAPTER 43

NEW BEGINNING

Warm rays of sunlight caressed my face, bringing me out of a long, well-needed sleep. I had been truly exhausted when I had gone to bed yesterday evening, so it was no wonder that I had slept longer than normal. Enjoying the sensation of slowly waking up, I rolled over, planning to stay in bed for a few more minutes. However, I realized that waking up in bed was unusual. Miles always took control at night, and he probably wouldn't have stayed in bed.

I opened my eyes, and an entirely unfamiliar room came into view. It was easily four times the size of our room at the inn, with an abundance of light streaming in through three large windows. With a jolt, I sat up in bed, heart pounding.

"Miles, where are we?!" I squawked out in a panic.

«Shhh! Berla and Riala are still asleep. A lot happened last night.»

As he gave me a recount of their adventures, I took in my surroundings in awe. I was reminded of that night in the shed when he had first told me about being able to control my body, but this time, the situation was different. He had acted to protect all of us, and even though it was weird to not have been mentally present for it, I couldn't shake the feeling that it was rather nice to wake up on the other side of it. After all that, even Miles had wanted to lie down and relax for a few hours.

"So they made it here before us after all... We must've missed each other by a few hours," I concluded.

«Yeah. Berla thinks they must've gone back to Alarna right after being attacked by the beasts, and then set out for Cerus almost immediately. We lost some time due to her disability, so that's probably when they eased by.»

"And she didn't side with them..." I whispered, glancing at her sleeping soundly next to Riala.

«Huh,» Miles said, sounding confused.

"What is it?"

«I didn't even think about that last night. Not for one second.»

"Interesting."

The chances were high that Miles had some kind of influence on me. From time to time, I had thoughts that didn't quite feel like my own, and one possible explanation was my "Calling," which was still affecting me. However, Miles seemed to be changing ever so slightly as well.

"What's the mayor like? Will he keep up his side of the deal?"

«I'm cautiously optimistic. He seemed intrigued, and it was enough to kick the soldiers out of town, but we'll have to actually give him something. He most definitely won't help us out of the kindness of his heart.»

We talked for a few more minutes before someone knocked on the door and immediately opened it without an answer. An older gentleman in a suit stepped into the room.

"Morning, Tomar," the man said.

«That's him. Be casual, but polite. And call him Mayor.»

"Good morning, Mayor."

"I see not everyone is awake yet," he said in a quiet voice. "Should we go somewhere else and talk alone?"

«Not good. Wake them.»

"I'm sure my sisters would rather accompany us. We'll be right out," I said, per Miles puppetry.

"Alright. See you in a minute," he said.

When he left, I heard him walk down the hallway and down a flight of stairs.

"Sisters?"

«Right. I hadn't mentioned that yet,» Miles said with a sigh.

He quickly summarized the most important points I had to remember, while I shook Berla and Riala awake. *Apparently I have two sisters now.* Not that I minded, but it sounded a little weird.

Riala, bright-eyed and full of energy just seconds after waking up, jumped out of bed and hugged me. "Good morning, Tomar!"

"Morning, Riala," I said with a smile.

"Did Miles tell you everything already?"

"He did, but we can talk about that later. Right now, we need to get up. The mayor wants to talk to me."

"Ah, I see. Let's go."

When we stepped out of the room, I was startled by two guards standing on either side of the door, but it wasn't surprising that the mayor of Cerus wouldn't have us looked after.

The guards and us briefly greeted each other, and they escorted us into the living room to speak with the mayor. I tried not to look around too much, since I was supposed to have seen this room already.

"Alright!" Cerus said, clapping his hands together as soon as we sat down. "Now that we're all awake and able to formulate clear thoughts, let's make a proper deal. You promised me a lot of exciting things last night, but you have very little to show for it at this time. It's not clear what your actual worth will be yet, nor what your job would look like should you plan to stay here permanently. I'm willing to offer you six days for the start. If you can show me results by then, we'll talk more. How does that sound?"

Six days? Miles was right. The mayor wouldn't help us for nothing. Six days was the amount of time it would take the soldiers to reach Alarna and return. *We have to prove ourselves useful before they come back.*

Miles and I had briefly broached the subject in the bedroom. If we couldn't satisfy the mayor, we'd have to flee. Assuming there wasn't an army in front of the gates anymore, we would have a decent chance of getting away.

Almost as planned, we're in Cerus and we're thinking about where to go from here.

"'Six days sounds fair. We'll have something for you by then.'"

"My expectations are high. Inviting you to stay here in the middle of the night already brought on a stern talking to from the missus, after all," he said with a chuckle. "Now, I have business to attend to, but you're free to move around with your escort. They will also supply you with what you need for your research. Within reason, of course. You'll find a modest breakfast in the kitchen, but I expect you to supply your own water. That won't be a problem, will it?"

"Not at all. Thank you, Mayor Cerus."

He rose from his armchair and straightened his suit jacket. "We'll see each other tonight."

With that, he left the house, leaving the two guards almost out of sight, but definitely not out of hearing range.

"Breakfast!" Riala exclaimed happily after the mayor had left.

Miles informed me she had been instructed to say nothing in the mayor's presence, to reduce the risk of any slip-ups. Just in case, I signaled to her that we still needed to be careful in front of the guards.

To the delight of all of us, the "modest breakfast" was enough to satisfy our hunger twice over. After we were done, I prepared a bucket and used a script to fill it with water, at which point one of the guards curiously glanced over. He then motioned for the other guard to take a look as well. While the first guard watched in fascination, the second threw one curious glance our way before turning around again. The mayor had presumably prepared them for what they would be seeing.

With them around, I couldn't freely talk with Miles, which was a minor issue, but I was sure that we would manage. It wouldn't be the first time that we'd be working this way, after all.

Excitement suddenly washed over me. A new day in a new town, and a new, temporary job—I couldn't wait to start this new chapter in our story.

* * *

Aelene looked deeply fascinated at a large log that had been reduced to splinters by the scripture she had used at Oryn's instruction.

In an attempt to enjoy normality for just a bit longer, she had been evasive and put off any experiments for as long as she could, but eventually she had to give in. She and Oryn had gone to the garden behind the temple. Here, the excess water and experiments wouldn't bother the other clergy members. Even the first test of a normal water source scripture had been enthralling to Aelene, but shooting things to smithereens was an experience unlike anything else. Her face was flush with anticipation as she waited to continue.

"That was great!" Oryn said, his spirits high. "Wait a second. I'll adjust the scripture. There's so much more we can test!"

Eyes still fixed on the destroyed log, Aelene silently held out her hand for him to wash away part of the previous scripture sigils and make modifications. Once he was done, she aimed at the next log. After placing a blue stone on the back of her hand, a stream of water shot out. Instead of blasting the log apart, the water gave it a push, sending it through the air for a few meters before falling to the ground.

Aelene looked at her hands with curiosity. She opened and closed them, as if trying to determine something. "Oryn, what is the purpose of the stones?"

"I don't know yet. That is something we have to research as well! Oh, I can't wait until the caravan gets back from Cerus with white and black stones!"

Ever since he had accidentally destroyed the water source, he hadn't been able to test any of the new ideas he came up with, and now that Aelene had finally agreed to test scripture sigils on herself, there were dozens of tests Oryn wanted to run. He had been worried she would be unwilling the entire time, but now she seemed at least somewhat interested in what was going to happen next.

Oryn finished his next modification and Aelene aimed at yet another log. This time, nothing happened as she watched the blue stone dissolve.

"A dud. No worries, I've got more."

"Let's go back to one that works," Aelene instructed him.

"I understand that you're eager," he said with a chortle, "but we should continue with the tests."

"Oryn, please." She stood firm with her request.

He didn't understand what this was about, but it seemed like she wanted to test something, so he revised the scripture once more.

Aelene raised her arm but opted out of using a stone. She concentrated hard, as if she was searching for something within herself. A moment passed, then several, but nothing happened, and eventually she gave up.

"What did you try to do?" Oryn asked.

"Oh, nothing. I just had such a hunch," she said.

With a devious grin, Aelene swiped up another blue stone and proceeded to blow apart another log.

AFTERWORD

Hey everyone!

It's been a long road from posting the first couple chapters on RoyalRoad on a whim, to finally turning this into a real book. But you reading this is proof that it's been done, through troubles, tribulations, and tears, and I couldn't be happier for it to finally be here.

The First Mage is the result of me binge-reading multiple novels focused on the art of magic in late 2021. At some point, I began to wonder what these worlds were like before magic was discovered. How would this happen? How would the magic develop? And how would it shape the world over time? It's a topic rarely covered, and as a programmer who has a tendency to just go and create what I'd like to have, I did just that. I sat down and began writing for the first time in my life, until I sent the first three chapters to my first beta reader, with the words "I did something weird..." From there, I couldn't stop and have written hundreds of chapters since then, spurred on by all the interest shown in this story.

I want to thank all of you for reading my work, and I hope you've enjoyed the adventures of Tomar, Miles, and the others so far. I also want to thank all the readers of the web version for their plentiful feedback, as well as my editors, Terri and Bao from MoonQuill, for their patience with this stubborn first-time author, and their help with turning volume one into what you have before you now. Finally, I want to thank my sister for acting as my foremost guinea pig and for always encouraging me to keep going.

The First Mage is far from over, and whether it be in physical or digital form, published or web version, I'm looking forward to you experiencing more of it.

Until we see each other again!

—Exec

DOCUMENTATION

DATES AND TIMES

In this alternate world, time operates differently compared to Earth. While a minute remains roughly the same, the time units deviate significantly. An hour consists of sixty-four minutes, a day of sixteen hours, a week of eight days, a month spans thirty-two days, and a year encompasses eight months. Notably, all of these numbers are multiples of two, as commonly found in computing and programming.

Considering these time intervals, a year in this world is shorter than a year on Earth, amounting to roughly half the duration. For example, a fifteen-year-old individual, like Tomar, would be approximately seven years old by Earth's standards. However, to compensate for this, the inhabitants of this world seem to age faster, physically reaching the same level of maturity within the same number of years. This accelerated growth leaves them lacking in life experience that would accompany those years, which is mitigated by help of the Calling ritual.

The citizens of Alarna typically work seven out of eight days a week, reserving the eighth day for rest and leisure. While they may work more days than people on Earth, each workday is shorter in terms of actual time, leading to a 32-hour workweek in Earth time. Furthermore, their daily routines closely parallel those on Earth, with an average of seven to eight working hours and four hours dedicated to sleep, allowing for approximately four to five hours of free time.

OCTAL

Octal is a base-8 numeral system, as opposed to the more commonly used base-10 "decimal" system we are all familiar with. Rather than using the full roster of ten numerical characters, ranging from 0 through 9, octal uses a set of eight, spanning from 0 to 7. Once you surpass 7, you hit the number 10 in octal, a representation of what we typically consider as eight.

Decimal:	0 1 2 3 4 5 6 7 8 9 10 11 12 13 14 15 16
Octal:	0 1 2 3 4 5 6 7 10 11 12 13 14 15 16 17 20

While octal once held historical significance for select cultures and found utility in computing, it has largely faded into obscurity today, having been replaced by numeral systems that better suit the needs of the modern world.

For the sake of clarity, all numbers in this story are presented in the decimal system unless stated otherwise.

CALLINGS

CHARMER

Whether it's enticing customers to purchase their products, convincing others to part with their most cherished possessions, or even luring people into their inner sanctums, Charmers possess the unique gift of persuasion. Those who engage in the art of bargaining are considered part of this vocation. Likewise, entertainers employ their charismatic talents to captivate and distract people from their often-monotonous daily routines.

Given the inherent nature of their Calling, Charmers occasionally face allegations of deceitful behavior. These accusations are unfounded in most cases, as strict laws ensure those with this Calling adhere to ethical standards.

FIGHTER (GUARDS)

Typically more brawn than brain, Fighters are distinguished by their extraordinary strength and agility, enabling them to confront even mid-tier beasts. Moreover, they possess enhanced recovery capabilities and an impressive tolerance for pain, allowing them to persist in battle until the bitter end. The majority of Fighters find employment as hunters, guards, or agents, depending on their unique areas of expertise.

The laws of Alarna mandate that Fighters commit their lives to the town, all in the interest of the broader population. Without them, the citizens' way of life would simply not be sustainable. In recognition of their commitment, they receive generous compensation and enjoy privileges not available to other common folk.

FIGHTER (AGENTS)

When people think of Fighters, the common imagery that springs to mind is that of guards. Agents, on the other hand, exist as a clandestine entity, and are more of an open secret to the public, with the official designation being "private guard." The occupation was born from the necessity of those in power to discreetly observe their rivals, potential suspects, or neighboring settlements. Set apart from the traditional hierarchy of guards and soldiers, agents operate under the direct authority of a single leader.

WORSHIPPER

Little is known about the lives of Worshippers beyond the temple's walls. These devout individuals usually hail from Worshipper families and dedicate their lives to the gods from a tender age, with their fervor only intensifying after they receive their ritual. Some among them also oversee services in the temple's educational and medical facilities.

SOURCERER

The term "Sourcerer" was coined to explain the ability of certain people to understand scripture sigils. Those who receive this made-up Calling are supposedly able to use sigils on their bodies, emit an aura similar to that of beasts, and possess uncommon amounts of knowledge about Omega. However, their primary gift is the ability to produce water, much like a water source. The application of Omega for other purposes requires dedicated learning, aligning them more with the role of magic Fighters rather than magic Researchers.

The word combines *source,* as in water source, with the common suffix, *–er,* found in all Calling titles. The term was conceived by Tomar's mother, Phiona, as a jest when she predicted that her son would one day become someone working with water sources—a "Sourcerer." Any resemblances to other magical terms are purely coincidental.

Thank you for reading a MoonQuill original novel. More exciting stories can be found on our website, www.moonquill.com.

We would greatly appreciate it if you would take a moment to leave a review. Every review helps the author and supports their ability to continue writing fantastic books for everyone to enjoy!

Additionally, we're looking for dedicated ARC reviewers and experienced readers to join our beta reader team. To learn more, drop us an email at info@moonquill.com or stop by our Discord.